UNTIL
You

NEW YORK TIMES BESTSELLING AUTHOR

K. BROMBERG

PRAISE FOR K. BROMBERG

"K. Bromberg always delivers intelligently written, emotionally intense, sensual romance . . ."

—USA Today

"K. Bromberg makes you believe in the power of true love."

—#1 New York Times bestselling author Audrey Carlan

"A poignant and hauntingly beautiful story of survival, second chances, and the healing power of love. An absolute must-read."

—New York Times bestselling author Helena Hunting

"An irresistibly hot romance that stays with you long after you finish the book."

—#1 New York Times bestselling author Jennifer L. Armentrout

"Bromberg is a master at turning up the heat!"

—New York Times bestselling author Katy Evans

"Supercharged heat and full of heart. Bromberg aces it from the first page to the last."

—New York Times bestselling author Kylie Scott

ALSO WRITTEN BY K. BROMBERG

Driven Series
Driven
Fueled
Crashed
Raced
Aced

Driven Novels
Slow Burn
Sweet Ache
Hard Beat
Down Shift

The Player Duet
The Player
The Catch

Everyday Heroes
Cuffed
Combust
Cockpit
Control (Novella)

Wicked Ways
Resist
Reveal

ISBN: 978-1-942832-61-4

Cover design by Indie Sage, LLC
Editing by Marion Making Manuscripts
Formatting by Champagne Book Design
Printed in the United States of America

UNTIL
You

Chapter One

Crew

EXHAUSTION MIXES WITH EXHILARATION AS I PULL UP TO THE OLD Victorian house and shift the truck into park. Dust from the unpaved driveway catches up to us, and exaggerated coughing comes from the back seat as its cloud filters in through the open windows.

"If this is the fresh country air you've been talking about," Addy says sarcastically as Paige fakes another dramatic cough while waving the dust out of her face, "then, *no thank you.*"

I chuckle. My city slickers are in for a rude awakening. All they've ever known is the hustle and bustle of Chicago. "It's just dirt, ladies."

"Next, you're going to tell us that dirt *builds character*," Paige says with a roll of her eyes.

"Of course, it does."

I watch through the rearview mirror as they exchange a look that could mean either trouble or acceptance. Who knows with the two of them. But before I have time to think much more, both girls open their respective doors and bound out of the truck. Their whoops of excitement intermingling with their laughter echo through the air as they run to the porch, hands cupped on the windows looking in, and then down the steps and through the grass leading to the unfenced backyard.

I remain in the truck, my hands on the steering wheel, a relieved smile on my lips, the tension of what feels like the last eighteen months slowly draining from my body. Or at least starting to because it's going to take a lot more than a few minutes to right all the wrongs that have led us to this moment.

The house and the property around it don't disappoint from my childhood memories. It has gray siding with dark blue shutters and, while its physically small compared to the parcel of land it sits on, its presence is undeniable amidst the field of wildflowers at its right, the outbuildings to the left, and the huge wraparound porch complete with a swing just in front of me.

Home.

Away from the city lights, the traffic, the chaos, and the danger.

That's what this will be for the next few months—with its creaks and cracks, its solitude, and everything in between—a place to relax and recover and *just be* without the havoc of the outside world. And I couldn't be more grateful.

The moment I give myself is fleeting. A deep breath to absorb the fact that I really did just do this. That I pulled it off. That this place of solace I had as a kid has now come full circle to be one for me as an adult. One that feels so very different than Chicago with the constant chatter on the scanner and the underlying fear mixed with adrenaline that came with every call I received.

Of the continual reminder of what happened everywhere I turned.

The girls aren't the only ones who will have to get used to the country.

"Dad! *Dad!* Come look," Paige shouts, waving her hand for me to come see what they've found.

Her eyes are alive with excitement, and I'm staggered momentarily as I stare at her, the spitting image of her mother.

How could *she* walk away from them? Walking away from me is one thing—I definitely have my faults—but them? The two incredible humans we created? How is the idea of a foreign country, a fleeting affair, and being content with rushed phone calls satisfactory to any parent, let alone their mother?

I just don't get it.

"Dad." A huffed word by my impatient tween.

"Yes. Coming." I shake my head, trying to rid the sudden pang that I get every once in a while—that I failed my girls by not being able to make their mom see the importance of being present and in their lives. That's on you, Britt. My smile widens, however, as I slide out from behind the wheel, stretching my legs on the dirt that has been in the Madden family for longer than I've been alive.

Family. Roots. Peace.

Isn't this what I wanted for them? Some fresh air? A chance to roam? New experiences? Away from the constant reminders of . . . loss, and the job that almost took me from them?

"What did you find?" I reach Paige and run a hand down her back as she points to the backyard, her whole body vibrating with disbelief over the one thing I neglected to tell them. I needed some kind of surprise in case they were silently freaking out about leaving their lives behind for a while.

"A pool?" Addy shrieks, her gray eyes wide as saucers, her cheeks flush. "*We have a pool?*"

"What do you mean we have a pool?" I ask nonchalantly and walk to where I can see it. "Huh. What do you know? How'd that happen?"

Their shrill screams fill the air as two identical eleven-year-olds launch themselves at me and smother me in the best kind of hugs. *Thank yous* and *oh my Gods* fall from their lips over and over as they run to its edge to stick their hands in and test the water.

That tightness in my chest eases even more.

This was the right decision, Crew. It may not have been an easy one, taking them from everything that was familiar to them, but it was the right one.

"Should we go check out the inside? Fight over rooms and—"

"Yes," is yelled in unison as they scramble around me and run to the front door. I follow, my step lighter and my heart fuller.

The next twenty minutes is a chaotic exploration. We move from room to room around cloth-covered furniture that, when I peek beneath, looks brand new. For a house he's virtually moved out of, I'm grateful that he didn't sell the furniture yet.

Bedrooms are picked—Paige decides on the yellow one and Addy on the tan one—even though I know they'll most likely be sleeping in the same one seeing as they rarely leave each other's sides. But I cautiously accept their decisions. They came way too easy for this dad, who is used to them bickering over more things than not despite being each other's best friend.

I peek into the primary bedroom that has more space than I'll ever need. The bed against the wall has a brand-new mattress wrapped in plastic. Large windows framed by a seat face the west. The en suite bath has a walk-in shower and a free-standing tub.

Everything is absolutely gorgeous.

I knew my great Uncle Ian had had the place remodeled a few years back, but this is most definitely not what I expected. He's more the half-finished projects and overstated décor type of guy if my memory serves me right.

That's why I agreed to take him up on his offer: come to Redemption Falls and fix up a few things on his house that needed to be repaired before he puts it on the market in late September.

Some handyman work and a bit of manual labor in exchange for a place to stay for the next four months.

Not a bad deal for me.

But this is anything but the half-finished projects I expected.

"Awesome."

"So cool."

The girls' repeated comments follow me through the house as I check out every room. Habit has me noting where doors and windows are for the state-of-the-art alarm system I agreed to facilitate the installation of over the coming days.

Even when I'm on mandatory leave from the force, it's still in my blood.

It's a hard thing to get used to. Being a cop but not allowed to be one. I run a hand over my right flank, the hardened scar tissue beneath my shirt a stark reminder of another reason I'm standing here. Why I stepped away from Chicago for the two girls giggling as they tromp down the stairs one after the other.

"We've decided the extra room up there will become our influencer room," Paige says, matter of fact.

"*Influencer room?*" I ask, inwardly groaning as I set down the few bags of groceries we picked up on our way through town.

"Yep. People love twins. We'll put up a backdrop—"

"Sequins or plain on the backdrop?" Addy interjects.

"We'll have one of each. Variety is important. And then we'll get that ring light Dad said we could have and—"

"A tripod to hold the phone."

"This is gonna be *so* awesome," Paige finishes for both of them. And as if practiced, they both angle their heads and look at me expectantly. "Right, Dad?"

My sigh is an audible resignation to the fact that watching a million more hair and makeup tutorials are on my horizon. There's only so much a man can handle, and honestly, I'm about there. "Yeah, sure. So awesome.

But I'm not exactly thrilled with you putting your faces out there on the Internet. I will be the one in control of what gets posted. No real names. No indication of where you are. There are a lot of—"

"Bad people out there who want to do bad things." Addy rolls her eyes and huffs while Paige mouths the refrain they've heard about as many times as I've watched beauty tutorials.

"Aren't you the one who says every situation can have a compromise?" Paige asks with a bat of her lashes and a nudge to her sister she thinks I don't see.

I know when I'm being tag-teamed, and right now, no doubt, I am.

"I am," I say with a nod as I start pulling the food out of the bags and setting each item on the counter beside me.

"Why do you do that?" Paige asks.

"Do what?" *Are we still talking about Internet safety? Being an influencer? What?*

"Take all the food out of the bag and put it on the counter? Why don't you just take it from the bag straight to the cupboard?"

My hand stills as I'm about to set a jar of pasta sauce on the kitchen counter. She has a point. "It's something . . ." *your mother used to do.* The words die on my lips, and I force a smile to hide it. "Never mind. You know what? You're right." I walk over to the pantry with the grocery bag in hand and start placing its contents on the shelves without rhyme or reason. I know I'll stock it fully later this week and will be reorganizing it, but for now, it'll do.

The few items look measly on the bare pantry shelves, but we have a pantry, and that's more than we had at our old place where we used a coat closet to store our food.

Now to find the plates in the mess of boxes I brought in from the back of the truck. With my hands on my hips, I contemplate the ten boxes stacked in the kitchen, cursing myself for not labeling any of them.

"There's a letter here from your whoever he is," Addy says, pointing to a stack of papers on the end of the counter.

"He's my great uncle, which means he's your great, great uncle," I say and set the last of the groceries down.

"Wow. This person is *really* pissed at you."

"*Language,*" I warn as I turn around to see her shuffling through said stack of papers. "One, quit being so nosy. And two, who's mad at me?"

"The person who wrote these." She holds up the haphazard pile. "And they were just here for me to look at them. Aren't you the one who says whatever is left out is fair game?"

It's amazing the things kids remember when it suits their case.

I walk over, take the stack of papers from her, and playfully whack them on her head. "Someone brought her sass with her all the way from Chicago."

"Did you think I left the best part of me behind?" She flashes a grin that tells me I'm most definitely in trouble in the coming years.

Who am I kidding? *I'm already in trouble.*

"Lucky me," I tease.

"Are they from the lady who lives over there?" Paige asks, pointing in the direction of the cottage.

"I believe so," I say.

Wasn't this the one and only drawback to accepting Uncle Ian's offer? That I was now a landlord to the tenant in that little cottage off to the right of the driveway? I've been a landlord before, and it was nothing less than a nightmare.

"Can we go say hi to her? See what she's like and if she has kids?" Addy asks.

"No. Leave her be. If she lives out here, she probably likes her privacy. The last thing she's expecting is you two overwhelming her. Besides . . ."

"Besides, what?"

Besides, I haven't had a chance to run a background check on one Miss Tennyson West yet.

"Nothing. Never mind." I smile at the girls and then look down at the notes as I flip through them.

They are complaints about her cottage.

A renter complaining? *Go figure.*

The water pressure isn't consistent.

The air conditioner works intermittently.

The hot water heater seems to be on the fritz, only working sporadically.

The notes are polite at first. Then a little more forceful as I flip through them.

Some are handwritten, others typed or in black felt pen. They range from sticky notes to formal stationery. And each one is signed with the name *Tenny*.

They're all legitimate complaints from a tenant. Can't say that I wouldn't have written similar notes if it were me.

But complaints are the last thing I want to deal with. I came here for simplicity for the girls and me. Not to have to take care of one more person, one more complication, one more headache.

And having a tenant, regardless of the fact that she likes to keep to herself, is in fact a complication.

I'm not a big fan of complications. Especially because when there is one issue, there's usually bound to be more.

And that is what worries me.

I glance out the bay window of the kitchen nook in the direction of the cottage. It's about one hundred yards away, and the old oak trees scattered around the property almost obscure it from my line of sight. That doesn't mean on the way past it up to the house that I didn't already look and assess who I'd be sharing this property with.

Colorful flowers spilled over eclectic pots on the front porch, and a pair of pink flip-flops had been placed at the top of its steps. An older but clean and clearly well-cared for Jeep was parked in the driveway. The front yard landscape was trimmed and grass neatly mowed. There was a security screen on the front door, which seems a little out of place considering the worst crime that has happened in Redemption Falls in the last year is a bunch of teens playing mailbox baseball. But then again, I plan on installing an alarm system here, so who am I to judge?

She takes care of the place. I'll give her that.

Let's just hope she's more of the nice, clean, keep to herself type of neighbor than the demanding and pestering kind that these letters could depict.

"Dad? Earth to Dad?"

Paige's waving hands in front of my face bring me back to the mirror images standing before me. Grins blanket their faces.

"Yes. What? I'm here. Just thinking."

"Pick a number between one and three," Addy says with a mischievous grin.

I look from one to the other. "Two."

My girls whoop as they jump up and down and start running to the back door. "Wait. What does number two mean?"

"One was unpack. Three was eat dinner. Two was swim," Paige yells over her shoulder.

"And you picked two," Addy says as she shucks her shirt off so she's in her sports bra and shorts.

Before I can respond, I hear a splash, then another, followed by sputtered laughter through the back door they left wide open.

I've been had. No matter what number I picked, it would have corresponded with swimming first.

I know my girls well enough.

And despite the million things I should do while they're occupied, I move to that open door, not wanting to look at anything other than them. My smile is automatic, my heart a little more settled, seeing them acting like the kids they are after everything they've endured this past year.

This was the right move, Crew. The right place. The right time.

No looking back. Isn't that what I told myself when we left the city limits of Chicago a few days ago? My new motto going forward? That I need to take things as they come, not sweat the small stuff, and don't look back.

You've got to stick to it, Crew.

The laughter outside only serves to reinforce that.

"Cannonball," Addy yells seconds before a huge splash has water flying every which way.

Now, to find the towels in this mess of boxes and then to figure out how we're going to eat the spaghetti I bought to make for dinner when I neglected to realize that my Uncle Ian took all the pots and pans with him when he packed up and headed for Florida.

Chapter Two

Tennyson

IS IT HOT IN HERE OR WHAT? *Whew.*

I shift in my chair and reread the scene that's playing out on my computer screen. One deliciously, sexy Delta Force agent, the defiant woman he's supposed to be rescuing but who is fighting him at every turn, and the electric chemistry between them that just snapped, turning into an all-out greed fest of hands and lips and naked bodies.

My editor's mind has gone to the wayside in the midst of this seriously hot sex scene. I'm supposed to be thinking about how it's not feasible for him to have one hand on the wall and one hand on her neck while simultaneously holding her up against said wall with an additional hand . . . but I'm not.

I've gotten lost in the story. In their chemistry. In the damn good scene.

"You're losing your mind, Tennyson," I mutter as I rub my eyes and push back from the manuscript, clearly needing a break since I'm imagining myself as the heroine pinned against said wall.

While my daydreaming is a complement to the author's abilities, it's not exactly a positive when it comes to turning this copy edit around by my deadline.

But as I rise from my desk and move the few feet into the kitchen, the sweet ache in my lower belly is still there, a very present reminder of how long it's been since I've had sex with someone, or rather *something*, other than my battery-operated boyfriend.

"And it's going to be a long time yet," I mutter still uncertain exactly how to navigate the relationship minefield after recovering from the chaos that used to be my life.

A life I loved until . . . *I didn't.*

This life is better, Tenny. It's one you built yourself. One you are in control of. One you don't have to hide from.

Staying single is my . . . choice. And for now, I'll just live vicariously through the stories I edit to satisfy those needs. Or at least I'll convince myself that it'll do the trick.

I turn on the kitchen sink to wash my hands and it shudders loudly, vibrating the entire counter and the stainless-steel sink with it.

And here we go again.

Nothing like shoddy plumbing to pull you out of a sexy, little daydream.

My groan floats through the kitchen and out the window. And maybe I make it even louder and more dramatic than necessary in the hopes that whoever Ian had move in and take over his landlord duties might hear it from his house. That the sound would have him rushing down here to fix this compiling list of issues I was promised he'd fix on day one of his arrival here.

Sounds like a romance novel that needs to be written. Nothing is sexier to a woman than a man who can use his hands and fix things.

Especially when those things are hot water and cool air and not worrying that a pipe is going to burst through your wall and flood your house.

But my dramatics go unanswered, seeing as the person I'm trying to summon is at least a football field length away.

That doesn't stop me from pursing my lips and shooting undeserved daggers toward his house. Edit some more of my manuscript or finally confront the new guy I'm hoping will be way more responsive?

Besides, Ian's parting comments were that his nephew had promised to fix all my issues within his first week of being here. That it was part of their agreement—whatever that meant.

And it's been more than a week for sure. A few service type trucks have come and gone—pool service, appliance repair, and the like. The new resident himself has driven by numerous times without ever pulling down my little driveway and stopping to introduce himself.

I'm sensing the new guy has more of the same style as his uncle—avoid me until I take care of it myself just so I can get it done.

It's not that I'm unsympathetic to the fact that Ian has had a clear decline in his mental health, but at the same time, I still have to live here.

I'm not a plumber or an HVAC expert. Those items are technical and a lot different than simply replacing a torn screen or dealing with a broken shutter.

I glance at my computer with the cursor still blinking and then back toward the house.

Work? Meeting the landlord and feeling out how I should approach him over my outstanding issues? Or heading into town to have a glass of wine at the Redemption Pub, where I'd get some socializing in, but no doubt, would cause gossip by simply being there?

When you're called the "new girl in town" two years after you move there, you start rumors with everything you do outside of the normal routine.

And drawing attention to myself is the last thing I want to do.

I try the faucet again and am greeted with a moaning noise from the pipe this time.

The new landlord, it is.

"Wish me luck, Hani," I say to my cat, curled up on the couch, flicking his tail in indifference, as I head out the front door and up the dirt drive.

I've caught glimpses of my summertime landlord. At least the male one I'm assuming is Ian's great nephew. A tattooed arm angled outside of his open truck window, and a baseball cap pulled down low over his eyes. But glimpses are all there are because once the cloud of dust plumes up behind the truck, I haven't been able to see much more.

And despite not physically seeing his wife or children, I know there's a family that comes with him. At least that's my assumption, considering the shrieks and yelps and belly giggles that I catch a hint of every now and again when the breeze carries them my way.

That house deserves a family. Kids playing and dogs barking and memories being made. Maybe Ian recognizes it too and that's why he's putting it on the market come fall.

Kids playing.

A family making its milestones.

The pang hits a little harder than expected. Aren't those the things I used to want? That I thought I was going to have? And now wonder how any of that will ever be possible . . . given what *I* let occur.

I give a quick shake of my head as if the action will clear the sudden melancholy that I refuse to give space in my mind.

What-ifs aren't something I allow myself to live in.

Besides, there's sunshine overhead, wildflowers growing all around me, and I'm living my life on my own terms. How could I be disappointed with that?

Now if I could just get the issues with the cottage fixed, then I'd be set.

The question is, do I kill him with kindness, or do I come in assertive and demanding so he doesn't think I'm a pushover?

And what would either of those do to our longstanding relationship? Does he want me seen and not heard? If that's the case, then taking care of my issues quickly would behoove him.

Who knows? Maybe his wife is nice in that non-invasive, *I want to be your friend but not ask a million questions about you* kind of way.

Having a friend to share a glass of wine with every now and then would be welcome.

This might not be so bad after all.

And maybe I should learn to stop overthinking everything.

Wouldn't that be nice for a change?

I laugh at myself as I reach the bend in the long, dirt driveway, just past the huge oak tree, when the house comes into view. In the short time since they've moved in, the place looks more lived in than it ever did in the years prior. A turquoise hoodie is thrown on the porch swing. A black scooter is on its side on the front lawn. The trash cans near the garage are overflowing with broken-down moving boxes.

Signs of life. For some reason, they make me smile.

My knock on the front door goes unanswered despite the pickup truck parked in the driveway. I stand there for a few minutes, just in case, but no one comes. Resigned to another night of my daily roulette game of "Will there be hot water?", I turn to head back home.

It's then that I hear someone talking on the far side of the house. I know it's a little forward, but I traverse across the yard, hoping to have a few seconds with whoever is home, even if it's a friendly greeting.

I'm just about to announce my presence, the *hello* on my lips, when I turn the corner and falter from the sight that greets me.

The man I've seen driving the truck? The one with the tattooed sleeve I've only ever gotten glimpses of. He's standing about fifty feet from me, and that tattooed arm is attached to a very attractive, shirtless and sweat-misted man. All six foot plus of him.

That's the landlord I'm supposed to be pissed at? Him?

Jesus.

He wouldn't happen to be a Delta Force agent, per chance, would he? I guarantee I wouldn't be worried about where he put his hands and if it were feasible so long as they were on me.

He grunts as he bends over and picks up what looks like a railroad tie. The action causes a chain reaction of muscles to contract in his shoulders and back that I never even knew existed. He takes a few, laboring steps to a wheelbarrow and dumps the tie in it with another grunt followed by a loud clang.

When he turns, I'm granted a fleeting glimpse of his profile—a straight nose, a dusting of stubble, his dark hair falling over his forehead—before he moves the few feet back over to the old barn which, by the pile of junk, looks like he's trying to clean out.

"Christ," he mutters. A sigh follows soon after before he hefts up another large beam of wood and moves it to the wheelbarrow.

"Dad," a girl's voice calls out from the other side of the yard. I shrink back while both of our attention is drawn to her.

A girl about eleven or twelve stands at the edge of the yard, a hand on her hip and her head angled to the side. She's tall and gangly with a heart-shaped face and a head full of thick brown hair.

"What did Mom have to say?" he asks, wiping his brow on his forearm.

"The usual," the girl says. A shrug. A shuffle of her feet. A sniffle. "You know."

His shoulders sag momentarily, and his sigh's audible before he moves toward her. Clearly, she didn't get the answer she wanted in regards to whatever she asked her mom.

"Sorry," he murmurs and squats down in front of her so he's eye level with her. "You okay?" She nods, but her expression—bottom lip worrying between her teeth and rapid blinking of her eyes as if to push back tears—clearly reflects that she isn't. "It'll get better. I promise." He cups the side of her face with his hand. "Trust fall?"

She gives him a ghost of a smile, the subtlest of nods, and whispers, "Trust fall."

"That's my girl."

Despite the scrunch of her nose when she notices how sweaty he is, the adorable girl lets him pull her into him for a hug.

They make quite the sight. A big, strapping man comforting his tween daughter. If I didn't already feel like a voyeur, then I most definitely do now as I witness this tender moment between the two.

It's definitely not the time or place to make my presence known. Without a word, I step back behind the cover of the house and retrace my footsteps home.

Just as I hit my doorstep, I cringe. *Crap.* The truck with Redemption Falls Security on the side that drove up to the main house the other day . . . what if they installed security cameras on the house already?

If they have, then my new landlord will have recorded footage of me spying on him and his daughter.

Hell of a way to make a first impression, Tenny.

Or get yourself evicted.

No eviction. *Please.* Anything but that. Credit and background checks still give me pins and needles. And might always.

And I love it here. And not just meaning the town of Redemption Falls, but here, at the cottage. The peace and quiet allows me to work without interruption. It has meandering trails where I can take long walks when I need to clear my head. And I feel safe here when I never knew if I'd ever really feel that again.

So yes, the last thing I need to do is piss off my new landlord with my lease expiring in a few months. Finding a new place to live isn't on my agenda for some time. *It should be fine, Tenny.*

I glance back toward the main house when I hear another clang from wood being dropped into the wheelbarrow. The visual of him working stays front and center.

He's just a man, Tenny. Quit acting like you've never seen one before.

Two words: *dry spell.*

That's it. That's why I give one more glance over my shoulder, even though I know I can no longer see him.

Besides, he's a dad, a husband—*taken.*

But as I open my front door and am greeted with a lift of Hani's head in greeting, I know focusing on my thirst trap new landlord is way easier than falling back into the vortex of what-ifs that have been plaguing me recently.

What if Kaleo had turned out to be the man I thought he really was?

What if I had listened that night? Would I still be ignorantly blissful in our house on the rocky coast of Kapalua Bay? Would I still love the life I was living, not knowing the lie that it was?

My sigh mixes with Hani's purring as he jumps up on my workspace and demands attention.

Those are a lot of what-ifs.

And I don't deal in what-ifs anymore.

I can't afford to.

My darkened computer screen calls to me. The story I'm editing even more so.

It's no wonder I prefer dealing with fiction these days.

Chapter Three

Tennyson

MY HANDS TREMBLE AS I STARE AT THE LETTER. MY NAME AND address in scribbled handwriting. The lack of a return address. The postage meter showing it was sent locally.

A personal letter.

But there's no one who knows where I am to send one. No one who knows I'm even alive, unless . . .

Panic has me dropping the rest of the bills on the table and tearing into the envelope, my heart in my throat, and the acrid taste of fear on my tongue.

The chuckle I emit is part hysteria, part relief, when I pull the letter out, only to find it's an invitation to help organize Redemption Falls Founder's Day from Bobbi Jo Simmons, the town's self-proclaimed socialite.

Founder's Day.

That's it?

"Jesus," I mutter with a shake of my head. Talk about overreacting.

I've learned to live with the paranoia. To place it on the back burner of my mind only to resurface when someone I don't know looks at me a little too long or when the phone rings and there's that slight delay before the salesperson on the other end speaks. And as I learned just now, when I receive handwritten letters.

But the fact that the letter is harmless doesn't do anything to abate the panic attack still rioting through my body—hands shaking, heart racing, head dizzying. I walk unsteadily over to an apothecary cabinet I have in the family room and open the top drawers, looking for my prescription to help settle me.

The first one is empty.

I rifle through the second drawer with one hand while opening the third—and the picture I forgot I'd placed in there months ago stops me dead in my tracks. It's of a different time. A different place. *A different me.*

My hair is light, blonde, and it's weird how I suddenly remember how much time it used to take at the salon to get it that color.

But it's not me I stare at.

It's the man standing at my side. His dark hair, a little long, curls over his expensive suit jacket's collar. His olive skin only serves to deepen his brown eyes and make the brilliance of his smile that much brighter.

Kaleo.

The man I thought walked on water.

Until I found out it was just the opposite.

I remember that night like it was yesterday. The party and its extravagance. The company—A-list movie stars, Fortune 500 businessmen, magnates of industry. The way everyone looked at us.

Memories I'd prefer I didn't have. Memories I'm supposed to pretend never happened.

I flip the picture over and shove it back in the drawer.

My breath is steadier now, my head clearer, but my pulse still thunders out of control.

Screw the prescription and bring on the wine.

That's what I need.

A nice rosé to sip and enjoy while I figure out what to make for dinner—if I make anything—because I'm not against a bowl of ice cream for dinner every now and then.

And tonight might just be one of those nights because I've been so busy with work, I've put off going to the grocery store for far too long. If there was a contest on what is the oldest thing in your refrigerator, I could probably win at this point.

The problem? When I open my freezer and pull out the container of ice cream, there's only a spoonful left.

That pat on the back I gave myself for having restraint and not finishing off the carton the last time I had some just came around to bite me in the ass.

Figures.

Doesn't that feel like the story of my life as of late?

Wine it is then.

I pick up the letter that started this just as the first sip of wine hits my tongue. When she's seen me in town, Bobbi Jo has asked me a few times to help with town events.

I've always avoided her. Played off her requests. I've forever said no.

Why?

Because I'm afraid someone will recognize me? Because I'm scared to get too attached to this place and these people in case I'm forced to move on? Because all the above terrify me?

My sigh weighs down the room as I toy with the edges of the letter and question myself.

Clearly that damn letter has affected me more than I'd like to admit.

Someone knocks on my front door, and I jump at the sound, nearly dropping my glass of wine.

It takes me a beat to gain my wits and settle my pulse before it hits me. *The landlord. Hottie McTotty.*

That's the only person I can think of who would be knocking at my door. But when I swing it open, the man I saw the other day isn't there.

His daughter is, though. But this time, there are two of them, identical in every way except for their clothing. And the one on the right with the jean shorts and yellow tank top is holding Hani against her chest.

"Hi," they say in unison, mischievous smiles on their lips. Hani greets me by purring contently and eyeing me up and down as if he's letting me know I wasn't paying enough attention to him so he escaped to find it elsewhere.

Traitor.

Then again, the fact that I didn't notice he'd slipped out when I went to the mailbox is on me, not him.

"Well, hello there," I say, looking from one to the other, the smile coming easily to my lips.

"We're Paige—"

"And Addy," the one with the yellow top says. "We live in the big gray house." She points over her shoulder as if I don't know which one she's talking about. "Is this your cat?"

"So nice to meet you girls. I'm Tenny, and yes, that's my cat. His name is Hani."

"He was in the barn," Paige says.

"Dad says we're not supposed to go in there until he finishes cleaning it up and making sure it's safe, one of the things on the list of things Uncle Ian left him to do, but—"

"But we heard meows and decided to investigate . . . and there he was."

I laugh. These two girls are adorable, not only in looks, but in how they operate on the same twin wavelength finishing each other's sentences.

"Well, I thank you for bringing him back home. He's not usually an outside cat, so I'm surprised he took off."

"He wanted to meet us," Paige says. "That's probably why."

"Probably," I say as Addy rubs between his ears, sending him into a state of bliss. I take the two of them in. Addy has freckles dusting the top of her nose while Paige doesn't.

At least there's a way to tell them apart.

"You left a lot of notes for Uncle Ian," Paige says and then snickers. "Dad said it's a prime example of why tenants are a pain in the you-know-what."

"Did he now?" I ask, biting back a laugh. Nothing like a kid to spill your secrets when you don't want them to.

"Yep. He did, but that was before we met you," Addy says.

"And you're cool. You have a cat," Paige adds.

"I'll let you in on a little secret," I whisper. "I promise I'm not a pain-in-the-you-know-what."

"We know," they say in unison as one rocks on their heels and the other cranes their neck to look inside the house.

Either their dad sent them to check me out or they're really curious.

Hani jumps out of Addy's arms and moves gracefully toward his bowl and meows. "It's his dinnertime. Can you tell he's never missed a meal?"

Addy quirks her head to the side and twists her lips in contemplation. "Now that you mention it, he is kind of fat."

"Shh," I whisper. "You'll hurt his feelings." That earns me the giggles I was working for. "Thank you for bringing him—"

"Can we help feed him?" Paige asks and, before I can answer, she walks through the open doorway and makes herself at home.

"Yeah, can we?" Addy follows suit. "This place is cool. Cute." She walks around the open space that serves as a family room, a dining room, and an office space all in one, her fingers trailing over the table and then the back of the couch before she turns to face me. "We've always wanted a pet—a dog—but we couldn't because—"

"We live in Chicago and Dad says it's not fair to have a dog when there isn't a yard."

"But there is a lot of yard here, so we're going to work on him to foster a dog while we're here. Then we'll fall in love with it, and he won't have a choice but to take it home with us when we go back."

"Oh. You're not moving here permanently?" That's news to me.

"Nope," Addy says as she picks up a photo of my "family" and examines it. "Just for the summer. Dad told his uncle that he'd help him with the house, so we came out here."

"At least that's the reason he told us—fresh air and sunshine and less screen time—but we know it's more for him," Paige says with a roll of her eyes. "But it's cool because this house has more rooms, so we have an extra one to make an influencer studio for us."

"An influencer studio?"

"Yep. Dad likes to focus on one project at a time. Uncle Ian's stuff, first. Then something he calls a pipe dream that makes no sense to us. We know better than to ask for too many things at once," Paige adds, "but it's on our list."

"You have a list?" I ask as I move to the kitchen and pull out the container that holds Hani's food. By the way he rubs himself against my legs, I've now regained the favorite person in the room status.

"Yes. We do. Dad says lists are important," Paige says, picking up Hani's bowl without me asking her to and bringing it over to me. "Why would you name a cat Hani?"

Images flash in my head that feel like forever ago. Turquoise water. Black sand beaches. My friends I miss dearly. So much left behind in a life that it took me quite a while to remember what it felt like to live it.

"It sounds . . ."

"Hawaiian," I finish for a struggling Addy. "It means lucky."

"Lucky?" Paige asks. "Why not just name him Lucky, then?"

Because that's what I am.

"Because everybody needs a little bit of luck in their life," I say.

"Are you Hawaiian?" Addy asks, scrunching up her nose to study me.

"Nope. Just liked the name is all."

I wait for more questions that I'll have to fake my way out of, but before they come, Hani's purrs grow louder.

"Here," Paige says, noticing him, and takes the container of food from me.

"He only gets one cup for dinner," I instruct as Addy sits cross-legged on the ground beside the bowl and both of them run their hands down his back while he begins to eat.

They really are adorable, even though my head dizzies trying to keep up with their energy.

I have a feeling Hani is going to be running away often now in search of this type of adoration.

"Chicago?" I ask. "That's where you guys moved from?"

"Yep." Paige laughs when Hani flicks his tail. "After everything that happened, Dad said he wanted fresh air and firmer ground under our feet."

"Whatever that means," Addy says with a roll of her eyes.

"I take it that means neither of you wanted to spend the summer here? That has to be hard leaving your friends and home for that long."

Dual shrugs. "Yeah, but it's okay. She's my best friend so it's not like I don't have her." Paige gives her sister a glance and her expression softens. "The only reason we didn't want to move was because she was at the top of the waiting list to get into the Bolinger Studio. And now . . . we're here."

I expected my question to be met with grumbling. Leaving friends. Leaving familiarity. But hoping to attend one of the most prestigious dance studios in the country was definitely not it. And Paige's admission is like a knife to my gut.

I knew that love once. I had that passion. And I know exactly what it feels like to have to leave it all behind.

"I had a friend who danced with their troupe a few times," I say softly before I can catch myself. Hints of my past aren't allowed, but the slip has Addy snapping her eyes up to mine and her smile widening.

"You did?"

From pointe shoes, damaged toes, and endless hours of rehearsal to ridiculous screen time, neck cramps, and reading for a job.

My, how my life has changed.

"I did. It was a long time ago. She loved the experience. Said it was one of the best of her life." The lie comes easily, as they all do these days, but the memories are crystal clear in my mind of the short time I spent with the dance troupe. "I bet you anything that spot won't open back up until school starts again. You're probably safe."

"You think?"

"I think," I say with a reassuring smile.

"Did you dance?" she asks as if she sees right through my mistruth.

"I did." I nod. "A long time ago."

"That's so cool," Addy says, standing.

"Just because you're here in Redemption Falls doesn't mean you have to give up your training. It doesn't mean you won't achieve your dream." She nods, but the sadness in her eyes remains.

"She will," Paige says with an unwavering confidence in her sister that melts my heart. "I know she will. Besides, the best thing about being here for the summer is getting a break from Ginny's breath."

My laugh is probably uncalled for considering I'm the adult here, but Paige's comment is so out of the blue, I can't help myself. "I'm afraid to even ask what that means."

"Our babysitter." A mock gagging from Addy. "She's nice and all that. She does stuff with us after school, but if she gets too close to you and breathes out, man, her breath is enough to knock you out."

Another inappropriate laugh from me as Paige mock puts her hands on her neck and sticks her tongue out like she's been poisoned.

"I'm sure it isn't *that* bad."

"No." A definitive nod. "It is. We promise. Even Dad said it's so bad it can curl the hair on your chest."

My cheeks hurt from smiling at these two. "Speaking of your parents," I say, taking a quick glance out the kitchen window toward their house, "they're probably getting worried, wondering where you two are."

"Oh, right. We forgot." They exchange a look I can't quite read, and then I'm greeted with grins that spread from ear to ear. "Dad wanted us to come down here and invite you over for dinner."

"He did?" I ask, taken back by the invitation from a man who hasn't stopped once to meet the person he shares his property with.

"Yep. He did." Addy nods.

"He said he's been super busy getting everything settled and feels bad that he hasn't taken the time to come down and meet you," Paige says, adding a sweet smile for good measure.

"I don't want to impose. I mean . . ." I don't exactly look the best in my yoga pants, tank top, and messy bun, but then again, I wasn't expecting an invitation to dinner. I'd like to make a better first impression.

"Please. Come on. You can't say no," Addy says, all but bouncing on her toes. "We already figured you were going to say yes, so we made enough for you."

"Oh." I glance back out the window, feeling more than obligated now.

"Plus, we're persistent," Paige states, batting her lashes and grabbing my hand and tugging on it.

"Clearly." I chuckle. *What would it hurt?* "Sure. Okay."

A set of cheers sounds off that has Hani walking down the hall, deciding my bedroom is quieter.

"What time?" I ask, trying to think of something I can bring from my depleted cupboards to contribute to the meal.

"Now," Addy says, sliding a glance over to Paige and then back to me. "By the time you guys meet and talk for a bit, it'll be ready."

"Oh. Okay. Um . . ." *I wasn't expecting that.* "I need to figure out something to bring. I don't want your mom to—"

"We don't have a mom," Paige says, and I'm pretty sure the surprised look on my face catches them off guard. "I mean, we have a mom, but—"

"She doesn't live with us," Addy says. "Or even in the United States for that matter."

Another roll of their eyes in unison as I mentally sputter over how to react.

"I'm sorry." It's the only response I can think to give.

They both shrug in a way that says they don't care, but the fleeting sadness in their eyes says otherwise. "It's okay. We deal," Addy says nonchalantly. "So? *Dinner?*"

There's no way I can back out of going now because the simple question has brought the fire back into her eyes.

"Sure. Yes. Okay."

The walk up the drive to their house is filled with their idle chit-chat, which helps to dissolve the sudden unease I have about being invited over to have dinner with the twins and their single (and very hot) father. The range of topics we cover in our rapid-fire conversation is wide and disjointed but definitely brings a smile to my face.

They're eleven years old. While Addy is the dancer, Paige is the soccer playing artist and is the rec soccer team any good? They'd prefer a dog over a cat (if they're honest), and they hope that doesn't hurt my feelings. They're trying to figure out a cool name for their influencer account and if I have any suggestions, could I let them know? Their dad makes them eat their vegetables, and it's *so* annoying that he does because dessert is the best part of the meal. They've already taught themselves to swim the length of their pool without taking a breath and wonder if I can too.

And why is my name Tennyson? It's strange and different, and they're not exactly sure if they like it but, in the end, decide that at least no one else has the same name so it must be cool.

Their bond is undeniable and enviable, especially coming from this only child, but holy hell are they full of the type of energy I'd kill to have.

Chapter Four

Crew

I'M GOING TO KILL THEM.

Correction. I'm going to hug them first and then I'm going to kill them for scaring the shit out of me.

Then I'll buy them cell phones first thing tomorrow morning—but doesn't that mean they win in their quest for the amount of screen time I'm trying to limit while we're here?

I'll figure that out later because first, I need to find them.

I've covered every square inch of this property. Slowly at first, assuming the girls were just outside playing. Then with fear tickling the nape of my neck. And now I'm in an all-out panic as I run back into the house from where I had just been searching the barn to go through the house once again.

"Addy?" Up the stairs, two at a time as the oven timer goes off. *BEEP. BEEP. BEEP.* "Paige?" Open one bedroom door. *BEEP. BEEP. BEEP.* Then the other. *BEEP. BEEP. BEEP.* My pulse races and fear ratchets up.

Back down the stairs to grab my phone. But who am I going to call here? The sheriff? It's not like we know anyone here yet I can call to ask if they know where the girls are.

BEEP. BEEP. BEEP.

Think, Crew.

BEEP. BEEP. BEEP.

Fucking think.

I slam my hand against the timer and turn the oven off without pulling the frozen—now cooked—lasagna from its rack.

Then I hear them. Footsteps on the front stairs. Footsteps I know by heart. There's a split second where all the horrible things that have been flashing through my mind are wiped away by one of their muted laughs. I'm reminded of the reason I chose to take this time here. I wanted the girls to be able to roam and explore without fearing their every move. I wanted people to know them and them to know people in a place where the sense of community was valued.

I *didn't* want to have to worry every single time they were out of my sight.

I guess I blew that theory out of the water with my panic, huh?

Then again, I've been around the block more times than I care to count and know the places that seem safer have their own issues.

They open the door before I can get to them. "Where in the hell have you been?" I scold while at the same time wanting to pull them near and hold them tight. "You disappeared without a word and—"

"I'm sorry. That was my fault."

I startle at the unfamiliar voice and then stop in my tracks when the girls step apart, and I'm left face to face with a stranger standing in my doorway.

An absolutely gorgeous stranger at that.

While she's not much taller than my girls, she's most definitely all woman. Her leggings and tank top, while seemingly casual, are anything but in the way they cling to the curves of her slender but toned body.

She doesn't have a stitch of makeup on her face, and hell if she's even prettier for it. Her auburn hair is casually piled on top of her head and dark brown eyes meet mine that hold equal parts curiosity and warmth. Her full lips are a subtle pink that tug on parts of me that shouldn't be tugged on in all honesty, especially in the presence of my girls.

She's a stranger and yet seems familiar somehow.

She extends the bottle of wine she's holding, a tentative smile on her lips. "Hi. I'm Tennyson—Tenny, really. I come bearing house-warming gifts."

The quick shake of my head is to partly clear the sudden stupor I find myself in. *This is Uncle Ian's tenant?*

"Sorry. Yes. Where are my manners?" I take the bottle she's offered and extend my other hand. "Crew Madden. Nice to finally meet you. And thank you for the wine. That's kind of you."

The handshake is over, but my eyes are darting warnings to Paige and Addy, asking what the hell is going on here.

"It's the least I can do." She shifts on her feet, sensing something is off here. "My cat, Hani. He escaped. The girls found him in the barn and were nice enough to return him to me."

"The barn?" I ask with raised eyebrows, turning to them.

"We know," Addy says, ever the diplomat, "but we heard him meowing and thought maybe he was hurt on all the things you're afraid we'll get hurt on, so there was no other option than to rescue him." The pair of smiles flashed my way are so sugary sweet it's a wonder they don't get cavities from it.

I ignore their attempt at using Tenny's presence to mitigate any trouble they might be in for disobeying my orders. I'll address that later. But the knowing glances the girls keep exchanging tell me there's definitely more going on here than meets the eye.

"Please. Come in," I say to Tenny as I step back and make room. "We're still unpacking some of our stuff and packing up some of Ian's things to send to his new place in Florida, so please, excuse the mess."

And it *is* a mess.

"You haven't had much time to settle in," Tenny says, taking a timid step inside. "It looks way better than my place did—I mean your place that's my place—when I was at this point."

"And your place that's my place . . . everything is fine there?" I ask, the notes she left Ian suddenly forefront in my mind.

Her laughter fills the house, the sound making my stomach feel odd. "We'll get to that after dinner," she says.

"After *dinner?*"

"Yes," Paige says, stepping in front of me, her eyes pleading. "Dinner. Remember *you* invited Miss Tenny over for dinner tonight?"

My eyebrows narrow and shoulders tighten. "How could I forget?"

An awkward silence falls between the four of us momentarily, and it has Tenny taking a step back into the still open doorway.

"Thanks for your help with Hani, girls, but I just remembered . . . that I—uh—have something—"

"No!" Paige says, grabbing Tenny's hand and pulling on it. The reaction surprises me. "You can't go. You said you'd have dinner with us."

"Pretty please," Addy piles on, begging like they used to do when they were little and really wanted something.

The question is, what is it that they want here?

I meet Tenny's eyes and smile. "Please. Stay," I say, trying to convince myself I'm asking her out of obligation rather than because she's more than easy on the eyes. "Make yourself at home while I open the wine. Would you like a glass?"

She stands there for a beat as the girls stare at her with puppy-dog eyes. Her smile is soft, reticent as if she's uncertain she wants to be here. That makes two of us. "Yes. Sure. That would be lovely."

"Girls? Can you help me in the kitchen, please?" I ask without waiting to see if they follow.

The minute we clear the doorway, I tug both of their arms so they're forced into the small pantry space in the hopes that our location will prevent Tenny from hearing this conversation.

"Explain," I demand.

"We found her cat," Paige says.

"That's not what I mean," I say. "Since when is it okay to randomly go with strangers?"

"We're eleven, Dad."

"Exactly," I whisper yell.

"Chill," Addy chimes in, which only serves to irritate me more. "She didn't offer us candy. She didn't ask us to help her look for her lost cat. We're the ones who found it. We're the ones who returned him."

"And you're the *ones* who went into a stranger's house without anyone knowing where you were."

"And we're perfectly fine." Paige raises her eyebrows as if to ask what the problem is.

And there are a whole lot of problems, but ones to be discussed at another time when we don't have a guest within hearing distance.

"We'll discuss that later. But why did you lie and tell her I invited her over for dinner?"

Their devious grins have me groaning. "We thought you might need a friend, and she's super pretty."

"Why in the hell would you think that?" I ask, glancing out of the pantry to make sure we're still alone.

"*Language*," Addy says, which I answer with a glare.

"Because you have to be lonely with just us keeping you company," Paige explains.

I pinch the bridge of my nose and sigh as I read between their eleven-year-old lines, and then look back at them. "I can handle my own love life, girls." Fucking hell. Seriously? I look so desperate that my own kids are trying to set me up?

"We know, but we thought maybe if you were happier . . . it would help with—*everything*," Paige says softly as the knife twists in my heart.

I hang my head for a beat, the tightness in my chest returning. How dumb was I to think simply being here would be enough to make up for what they've gone through?

"Girls—"

"Besides, we'll be dating boys soon," Addy adds before I can apologize again for things I have no control over, "and the last thing we want is for you to be lonely when we're out with our boyfriends."

I choke over my laugh. "You do remember that you're only eleven, right? There will be no dating while we're here in Redemption Falls or *ever*."

"Dad," they say in unison.

"Or at least until you're . . . *thirty*."

My comment is met with groans punctuated by smiles. "And *that's* why you need a girlfriend," Paige says.

I can't help but laugh, so appreciative for their levity, for them. They've gotten good at trying to make me laugh, at being the parent when they should never have had to.

Guilt is a bitch sometimes. *Scratch that*. All the time.

"So?" Addy says, nudging me with her elbow. "Go pour her some wine. Be a nice host." She winks and owns every part of my heart. Oh, wait. They already do. "We'll get the lasagna out of the oven and serve you guys."

I eye her warily, not naïve to their sudden capability. It's amazing how they suddenly want to help when normally they're nowhere to be found around meal prep time.

"Fine," I say as all three of us step out of the pantry. I watch them move about the kitchen, knowing looks being shared between them as I uncork the wine. "Before I walk out there, can we agree that setting up Dad isn't going to be your hobby while we're here?"

They both snicker.

"Girls?" I repeat.

"If we had our ring light, we'd be busy filming videos instead of med-dling in your—"

"Okay. Okay." I chuckle as I pick up both wine glasses and hold them up as if in surrender. "You're cute for blackmailers."

"We know," Addy says, a hand on her hip and a grin on her lips. "So?"

"We'll talk later." And before they can respond to my lack of commit-ment, I head into the family room.

Tenny is standing at the window looking out at the slowly darkening sky when I approach. She turns to face me. "I promise I didn't know what they were up to," she says.

"You heard?" I wince. Now I know who the girls get their lack of sub-tlety from. "I'm sorry. That wasn't meant—"

"Don't be." She laughs and takes a sip of the wine I've handed her. "You can't blame them for trying. Besides, that determination will serve them well someday."

"One can hope." I sigh, *again*, more embarrassed than I prefer to be when around a beautiful woman. It's only fair that I give her an out. "You're welcome to stay for dinner, but don't feel obligated to. Besides, I've never claimed to be a good cook, so be warned that frozen lasagna is the best I have to offer."

Her smile lights up, but before she can answer, Paige clears her throat from the doorway. "Dinner is ready," she says.

"Last chance to bail," I joke.

Tenny doesn't leave. In fact, she's a great sport as the girls show us to our seats at the dinner table—across from each other. It's not lost on me that there is a lone candle burning behind us on the kitchen counter that wasn't there moments before. Silverware is set on folded napkins and squares of lasagna have been cut, plated, and sprinkled with parmesan cheese.

"Wow, ladies. You rescue cats, you're up-and-coming influencers, *and* you're chefs," Tenny says. "I'm more than impressed."

"It's frozen lasagna. You can't exactly mess that up," Addy says but the blush on their cheeks from the praise is cute.

"I'm the queen of messing up simple dinners," Tenny says and laughs as Paige takes the first bite.

"Oh my God," Paige groans around a mouthful of food, her face squishing up. "What is in this?" She looks from Tenny to me, her eyes wide before she brings a napkin to her mouth and spits her half-chewed food into it.

"Gross," Addy says.

I cringe. "Clearly our table manners need help."

Tenny laughs politely as we both take a bite of the meal. It tastes like noodles, ricotta, sauce and . . . then I chew something that has me pausing at the same time Addy says, "Disgusting," before running to the kitchen trash can and crassly spitting her mouthful into it.

I want to die.

A pretty woman. A decent evening. And . . . are those peas I'm tasting? No. It can't be.

Paige runs to the counter and picks up the box the lasagna came in. "Vegetarian?" she screeches. "You bought vegetarian lasagna? Who puts carrots and broccoli and peas in pasta?"

"Apparently a vegetarian," Addy says then rinses her mouth out with water and spits it into the sink.

I try to save face. To make it seem like one of us Maddens is capable of eating dinner without spitting their food out. "I think it's good." I force down the first swallow of it, darting a quick glance in Tenny's direction to catch a stoic expression. "Nothing is wrong with vegetables." I take another bite to try and prove a point, only to struggle when my teeth bite into a big spear of broccoli.

I catch myself from gagging, and this time when I look back to Tenny, she meets my eyes as she politely, but clearly struggling, swallows her bite of pasta.

And it's that look, those brown eyes that say *help*, that make me lose it.

"Screw it. I can't do it," I admit and grab my glass of wine and take a big gulp.

"Thank God," Tenny says, following suit with her own wine.

We look at each other over the rims of our glasses and then start laughing. It's the kind of laugh where snorts are involved and then the sound of the snorts sends you into another fit of laughter.

The tears in Tenny's eyes make me laugh even harder, my breath short, my cheeks hurting from smiling so hard.

The girls stare at us with dumbfounded looks on their faces.

"I tried," Tenny says when she can finally manage to talk through her laughter. "I really did. But radishes?"

"And peas?" I add as she wipes tears from the corners of her eyes. "I guess this is one way to guarantee you won't be coming back for dinner."

She holds a hand up as she tries to not start the giggles again. "I've had veggie lasagna before. Eggplant. Squash. It was good. But this? This was . . ."

"It was so good you don't even have words for it." Her smile softens, and she meets my eyes. "It's okay to say it was terrible. I won't get my feelings hurt."

"Let's just say, I won't be running out to buy that from the store anytime soon."

"Thank God," the twins say, and for the first time, I notice them standing there, hips against the counter, smug smiles on their lips, as they take us in.

They think their little plan worked.

I shoot a visual warning at them that has them scurrying toward us. "We'll do the dishes," Paige says.

"Of the dinner we didn't eat," I say and look around the kitchen to try and salvage whatever is left of this moment because God, did it feel good to laugh like that again.

I think maybe until now, I'd forgotten how.

Chapter Five

Tennyson

"CHEERS," CREW SAYS, TAPPING HIS OREO AGAINST MINE. "Thank you for being such a good sport about it. *About this.*" He motions to the open package of cookies sitting between our glasses of wine. "I'm sure this was the last way you thought you'd be spending your evening."

"Oreos and wine? You're a man after my own heart. I mean, who'd complain about this?" My smile comes easy as I lean my head back against the chair.

We're sitting on the verandah, enjoying the warm night air. The sound of crickets singing is accompanied by the muted laughter coming out of the open windows, where the girls are inside cleaning the kitchen from our non-dinner.

And yes, they are taking their sweet ol' time doing so.

Naïve me, didn't see the setup happening when they invited me for dinner. The shocked expression on Crew's face when I thanked him for inviting me to dinner did, though.

But it didn't hurt to stay. At first it was out of obligation and then . . . then that atrocious lasagna and the aftermath made it worth it. And God, had it been good to laugh like that—snorting in front of a stranger and all. I honestly can't remember the last time I've felt that carefree.

As if Crew can read my thoughts, he shifts in his chair and looks at me. "I'm sorry. They have . . . wild imaginations." His smile is disarming in a way that makes me want to shift farther away from him in my seat because Jesus, is he good-looking.

I take him in, much like I did that first day when I saw him lifting wood. But this time I do it with the knowledge of what his voice sounds like, what his laugh feels like, and the love that floods his eyes when he talks about his girls.

His dark brown hair is a mass of messiness, slight waves that look like his hand has permanently been running through it. His light gray eyes are observant, watching, and taking everything in, but even when he's smiling, there's a sense of something that I can't quite put my finger on. Sadness? Loneliness? Discord? I don't know, but it does nothing to lessen his attractiveness.

Because if I learned one thing tonight, it's that the appeal I thought he had that first day I saw him has only grown after getting to know him just this little bit.

"Wild imaginations aren't always a bad thing," I say. "They're sweethearts."

"At times. And others, they're more than a handful."

"I can imagine. Double trouble, no doubt. But the fact they are best friends had to have helped them accept you coming out here for the summer."

"Should I assume they complained to you then?" He chuckles.

"Not at all. There is a dance studio in town if that's something you want to look into for Addy."

"Thanks. I'll talk to her about it." He takes a bite of an Oreo. "Should I worry about what else they said to you while they were at your place? I know my girls, and they definitely don't have a filter." I twist my lips and chuckle. He winces in reaction. "Do I even want to know?"

"I believe there was a mention about your uncle's tenant being a *pain in the you-know-what*," I say playfully, loving that I can give it back to him.

"And the night gets even better." He sinks down in his chair and groans. "I promise it wasn't meant—"

"I don't care." I wave a hand his way. "Tenants usually *are* nightmares. I get it. But I promise, I'm not one." I put my hands under my chin and bat my lashes at him.

His laugh is full and rich. "I sense a *but* coming here."

"Maybe more of a *while*." I take an Oreo of my own and screw the top off. "Meaning, *while* I promise I'm not one, the cottage might have issues that are."

"He didn't fix anything on those requests you sent, did he?" Crew asks, and I assume the *he* he is referring to is his Uncle Ian.

"There were a lot of notes sent, so I'm not sure which ones you're referring to, but probably yes, to some of them."

"I apologize on his behalf. I was told everything was taken care of, but considering he's starting to struggle with his memory, I should have checked in sooner with you."

"It's okay."

"No, it isn't. My excuse is lame. I figured once the girls met whoever lived in your place, they'd never leave you alone. They're kind of in your face like that, in case you haven't noticed. That and, I figured if your issues weren't fixed, you'd seek me out."

I've never been more grateful for a darkened patio before as my cheeks flush from the images of him sweaty and shirtless flashing through my mind.

"I thought about it, but I figured I'd give you some time to settle before I became a *pain in the you-know-what*," I say in the girls' sing-song tone.

"I'm not going to live that down, am I?"

I lick the center of my Oreo. "Nope. I hold horrible grudges that include toilet-papering houses and forking lawns."

"Forking lawns?" he asks through a laugh.

"How do I know that and you don't?"

"We lived in Chicago. High-rises and no lawns, I guess?" He tops off both of our glasses. "What in the hell is forking lawns?"

"Well, you take plastic forks and stick them all over someone's lawn." I shrug. "Redemption Falls' rival football team did it to the high school principal's house before the big homecoming game last year. Something like five hundred forks. It was big news around here because it was a slow news day. Then again, all days around here are slow news days."

"I'm sure that was fun to pick up." He cringes. "Scratch that, because that makes me sound *really old*, doesn't it?"

We both laugh, and ours is echoed by the girls inside laughing at something. He pauses to listen to the sound of them. The way his expression softens and his smile curves is seriously adorable.

"They're welcome at my place anytime, Crew."

He eyes me warily as if I don't know what I'm committing to. "Be careful what you wish for."

"Hey, so long as they think I have better breath than Ginny, I'm good."

This time his laugh echoes around the covered patio. "Oh, God. They knew you a whole thirty minutes, and they actually went there?"

"Fifteen minutes, and yes, they did."

"Christ. She's not *that* bad. I mean, yeah, her breath can make my chest hairs curl, but—" He loses his battle against trying not to laugh. "God, that's horrible that I'm an adult, and I'm saying it. Right? That makes me an awful person."

"No judgment here." I hold my hands up—an Oreo in one, my wine glass in the other—to reinforce my words.

"In all honesty, in the upheaval of the last two years, Ginny has been a huge, steadying help. Yes, she's a fortune, and her breath is something else, but that doesn't take away from the fact that she treats the girls as if they were her own. She's great at math homework, when I'm not. She is a way better cook than I am—as demonstrated tonight. I don't know." His words fade off as he stares at the rising moon.

There's something more there. Something I don't have a right to ask about or dig deeper on, but by the tone of his voice and his sudden silence, there's definitely something there.

"So why here?" I ask. "Why now?"

He purses his lips as he finishes contemplating whatever seemed to be weighing his thoughts down. When he turns to look at me, he tries his best to clear it—whatever *it* is—from his eyes and is *almost* successful.

"Why now? A change of scenery. For the girls. For me." His sigh falls heavy. "The last year or two has been brutal. I was hurt, and if I'm honest, it not only scared them, but it scared me too. With mandatory time off, I figured why not take that much-needed break." His smile doesn't quite meet his eyes.

"You are . . . *were* hurt?" I ask, thinking of him the other day flexing his strength by moving the railroad ties.

He gives a measured nod. "Yes, to both."

I slide a glance his way. *How am I supposed to decipher that answer?*

"I was hurt in the line of duty," he says. "I'm a cop." I think I cover my staggered surprise well enough, but his narrowed eyes and quick chuckle tells me otherwise. "*What?*"

"I don't know. You don't exactly scream *cop* to me."

"Why's that?"

"You're too relaxed?" I shrug. "I don't know. Every cop I've ever known is Type A, high-strung."

"Give me a bit. I'm sure that will shine through the more you know me." He runs a hand through his hair, his exhale unsteady. "To say we haven't been tested in the past two years would be a lie. Everything has changed for us, first with their mom, then with my work."

Their mom. Not my ex-wife. Huh.

"I'm sorry," I say softly.

"Don't be. We survived on all fronts, right?" He leans forward and taps his wine glass to mine. "We were blindsided by both, but maybe quick and shocking is better than dying a slow death? Jesus. Sorry." He shakes his head. "I seem to be saying that word—sorry—a lot tonight. I promise I didn't mean for that conversation to get so heavy so quickly. Can we shift gears? What about you? Where are you from?"

I smile. "Not much to tell, really. I'm an only child. Book editor."

"No shit?"

"Yep. I make a living cleaning up the beautiful words that writers string together while turning a blind eye to punctuation, grammar, and the ever-elusive run-on sentence in everyone else's writing but my clients' work."

"Remind me to never send you anything in writing. I'm sure you'd be appalled at my grammar."

I roll my eyes and wave a hand his way. "That's what everyone says. Don't worry. I never notice," I lie.

"Noted." He pauses, and for a brief moment we stare at each other through the moonlit darkness. Crickets chirp and the porch swing creaks as it sways just slightly under the force of the gentle breeze. "Why Redemption Falls, Tenny, or have you lived here your whole life?"

The events that led me here flash through my mind, and I shake them away just as quickly as the question makes them come. "I settled on here a couple years ago. I've done the big city thing, never thought I'd like the country, small-town stuff . . . but now that I've been here, experienced it, I don't think I'll ever go back to it."

"No?"

"Nah. It's not me anymore. I moved around most of my life, and this is the first time I can see myself staying somewhere."

"Really?"

"Yep."

"Why did you move around so much?"

"Army brat."

"Mom or Dad?" he asks.

"Dad," I say, the lie so rehearsed that no one would ever think differently.

"Me too. I get it. I do." He pauses for a beat before asking. "What made you choose Redemption Falls?"

"Probably the same reason you're here. Simplicity. Safety. A slower pace."

"Pretty much. Shit, I haven't been back here to my Uncle Ian's place for at least twenty years. With everything that was going on, he reached out and told me what I needed was the fresh country air. Distance. That I could stay here during the summer and in turn, do some handyman work on the place. I thought he was crazy for a while, but the more I thought about it, the more I knew it was what I needed. So I came here thinking Redemption would have changed with all the time that has passed. It has, but at the same time, it's completely the same, if that makes sense."

"It does. I get it. Same feel but the town has grown up some. Right?"

"Exactly."

There's a noise behind us, and we both turn and get a glimpse of the curtain swaying and a nose print against the glass.

"Scheming again," he says.

I stand as he does. "Scheming and adorable. That should be an illegal combination."

"More like it's going to be the death of me combination."

"You'd still enjoy every minute of it."

"True." Giggling is heard behind the curtain, and Crew just shakes his head. "How about you go upstairs and get your pjs on."

His words are met with exaggerated and unmistakable groans.

I smile. "It's been an unexpected evening, but I should let you get back to your original plans. Besides, I have a looming deadline," I say, wondering why I feel the need to have a reason to leave.

"Pesky deadlines."

"Something like that," I murmur as we stand a few feet apart, eyes held but saying nothing.

"Here, let me walk you home." He sets down his glass.

"That's not necessary. Really. It's not far."

"But it's dark."

"There's moonlight, and it's not like I don't know the way by heart." I take one step down the stairs.

"You sure?" He doesn't sound too convinced.

It's chivalrous and sweet of him to be concerned on my behalf, but it's unnecessary. I've faced much worse things than the night.

"I'm sure. Besides, isn't this what we were just talking about? Redemption Falls being safe?"

His gray eyes search mine. "Only if you're sure."

"I am." I offer another smile. "It was nice to meet you, Crew Madden."

"The pleasure was all mine, Tennyson West."

"Please tell the girls good night for me."

"I will." He nods, and I swear he wants to say something else, and what he does speak, it's not what's swimming in his eyes. "I'll come down this week and take a look at you."

"At me?" I laugh as he blushes and sputters.

"I mean your plumbing." He holds his hand up and shakes his head as I quirk a brow at the innuendo that has me laughing. "I mean your . . . I'll just stop now."

"You do that." I'm at the bottom of the steps now. "Good night."

And without another word, I make my way down the drive until the warm, summer night engulfs me in its darkness.

I hear the creak of the porch at my back. The giggle of the girls floating out from the upstairs window. The sounds of the night all around me.

Each step has me reliving the past two hours. The laughter. The ease. Crew's constant use of the word *we*. There was no *me*, there was no *the girls*, it was always *we*.

And something about that struck me.

I miss being a part of a *we*. Being something to someone, enough so, that they refer to you in the plural. Stupid? Yes. True? Sadly.

Before I turn at the bend in the road, I stop next to the big oak tree and look back toward the house. Crew is still standing there, shoulder against the porch post, hands shoved in his jeans pockets, staring in my direction.

There's something about him doing that—him watching me when I'm sure he can probably no longer see me but doing it anyway to make sure I'm okay—that has chills chasing over my skin in the best of ways.

I shake my arms as if that will rid them of the feeling, but it doesn't shake away.

What's not to like about Crew Madden? He's kind, funny, interesting, clearly a good father, and can most definitely roll with the punches.

But he's a cop.

While I don't know how that makes me feel, I don't have a choice in the matter, do I? It's not like he doesn't already know what I look like. That's the only thing that could trace me back to my old life, to the old me.

And even still knowing that, all I can think about as my cottage comes into view is how truly easy the conversation was between us. Normally, I feel like I struggle to keep my guard up while at the same time appearing that it's down.

It's the constant battle of letting people in just enough while my foot is out the door to prevent them from pushing it open too far.

But the thought never crossed my mind tonight. It felt . . . normal.

Is that what it was? Is that why it felt so strange? Just two people talking without expectation—unless you count the twins', of course.

Normal.

I repeat the word in my head as I turn my key in the security screen door.

The idea shouldn't be foreign after all this time, but it is.

Is that why I stayed at their house longer than I normally do? Is that why my excuses to leave remained muted while I laughed and ate Oreos and wine for dinner?

"Hi, bud," I say to Hani as he greets me at the front door, running his flank against my calves. I toss my keys and phone on the table, and the pink of Bobbi Jo's letter catches my eye.

How did I go from being spooked out of my mind to having one of the most enjoyable evenings I've had in a long time?

If I hadn't said yes, if I had let the misguided fear own me, if the girls hadn't twisted my arm, I would have missed out on everything about tonight—the laughter, the lightheartedness I carried home with me, the promise to get my plumbing fixed.

And even that brings a smile to my lips, considering how flustered Crew was over the innuendo.

I pick up the letter and toy with its edges as I read it again.

You haven't been living, Tenny.

This is not my forte—organizing a town event. Not even close.

You've been merely existing.

I look at the letter again. At the harsh pink of it—Bobbi Jo's signature color—and before I can stop myself, I sit down to my computer and type up an email telling her I'd be happy to be on the committee and take part.

I'm sick of being scared. Of living in and scared of every shadow I come across.

I hit send before I can chicken out and delete it.

It's time to live again.

Chapter Six

Crew

THERE'S SERENITY IN THE CHAOS.

Paige.

An order in the confusion.

Addy.

Every second is measured in heartbeats. In ragged breaths. In the blink of my eyes to try and process and assess and react.

Fuck.

The room. Smoke weighs down the air and creates some kind of magical art as it swirls and dances through the single sliver of light from the barely closed door across the family room.

My ears ring.

My mind races.

The smell. Metallic mixed with gunpowder. Two scents you never want mixed. One I'll never forget.

My body shakes as the adrenaline owns me. As it overshadows the pain. The helplessness. The desperation.

I press harder against my lower abdomen just below my vest. The warm stickiness of blood coats my fingers while my other hand aches from its tight grip on my Glock's trigger.

My lifeline right now.

Gut wounds. Bacteria. Sepsis. Infections.

My mind reels with the things I know, and none of them are fucking good.

Addy.

Paige.

Their laughter.

They need me, goddamn it. Don't do this to me. *They need me.*

A noise to my left has me straining to hear more—to place it—in the screaming silence.

I squeeze my eyes shut and grit my teeth to try and breathe through the pain.

I promise I'm coming home to you.

Justin groans from where he's lying in the middle of the room. No cover. No help.

I can see his feet from my position where I'm slumped against the kitchen wall. My cell phone is across the dingy carpet against the opposing wall. It must have gotten knocked off my hip when I dove for cover. It keeps vibrating.

They're trying to call me.

Trying to get info on how to get this bastard.

Think, Crew.

Think.

We need to get the fuck out of here.

"Hold on there, buddy. Backup is here. Outside." Each whispered word is a painful pant. A statement I'm not sure is true.

There's no flash of red and blue from the light bar coming in through the window.

But I know they're coming.

I know they must be outside staging to save us. No man left behind.

They have to be.

But Justin's dying. I'm not far fucking behind.

He groans again. My lungs rattle with each breath, and my pulse pounding in my ears almost drowns the sound out.

We're fucking trapped in here. Trapped with nowhere to go. A madman behind the closed but splintered bedroom door who has nothing to lose.

He's already shot two cops.

He's already going to prison.

Why stop now?

The baby cries again. Somewhere.

I think.

I don't know.

Am I hallucinating?

No. It's real.

Is it real?

That's why I hesitated.

That's why when Justin stepped forward, when I saw the gun, I hesitated. *The fucking baby.* I shudder as I relive the image of Justin taking the first barrage of bullets. His body jerking. His barked yelp. The sound of his body thumping as it crumbled to the floor.

"Justin," I say as quietly as I can to avoid giving our location away. But we're in his apartment. He shot us. It's not like there are many places we can hide at this point. "Think of Sheila. She's going to be so pissed at you if you don't make it home and finish that bathroom remodel." I try to engage him. To continue the conversation we had earlier today before everything went to shit. Before my mind becomes so foggy I can't remember anymore. "You can't let her be right. You have to pull—"

A slam on the other side of the closed bedroom door on the far side of the room has me jolting in fear, my finger tightening on my trigger.

He's coming to finish us off.

He's—

"Crew?"

"Here. I'm here."

"I don't want to die."

Tears burn in my eyes at the blatant fear in my partner's—my best friend's—whisper. "You're not. We're going to get out of here, and when we do, I'll let you take me to that shitty taco truck you swear by and—"

"I can't feel . . ."

"What? You can't feel what?" I beg him to keep talking to me.

To fight.

To live.

But silence falls again.

I squeeze my eyes shut. The girls fought this morning. I yelled at them. Told them they drove me crazy. I didn't tell them I loved them. I didn't say goodbye.

My chest aches from the thought. It hurts more from that than from whatever damage this goddamn bullet has done.

Another noise to my left. I shift to look and the motion sends a lightning rod of pain through my body. Shadows play over the closed blinds.

My vision blurs and my head dizzies again, but my hope soars.

They're here.

They're coming.

I brace myself for the battering ram. For the door to splinter.
Then . . .

Bang. Bang. Bang. Bang. Bang.

∽

I jolt awake. My breathing's ragged. My bed's soaked in sweat. My heart's a fucking freight train in my chest. There's an ache in my shoulder where the second bullet hit me.

Pressing my hands against the mattress on either side of me, I force myself to take in my surroundings. To acknowledge where I am.

Not in that apartment.

Not slumped against a wall.

Not slowly dying.

There are shadows here too. But these shadows are from the trees swaying outside in the breeze, not from SWAT about to breach the door.

I need to move. To work through the adrenaline coursing through my body. My throat is dry, but the last thing I think about is taking a drink.

One foot in front of the other, Crew. I watch my feet as I move. Count my steps. I get to twenty and then start again.

Repetition.

Deep breaths.

Focus my mind elsewhere.

I work through the process the therapist devised for me. The one we've practiced. The one that I thought was total bullshit because I refused to believe my mind was as fucked up as my body—but it's even worse.

And that's the fucking bullshit in all this.

The blood has been washed away. The darkened scars have begun to fade. But my goddamn head isn't right.

Post-traumatic stress disorder is the official diagnosis from the department therapist. The same damn therapist who has refused to allow me back on the force because I'm not fit to serve yet. Because my body is healed, but apparently my head is not.

"Fuck." The nausea hits me just like it always does. Forcing me to stop my pacing. To brace my hands on the windowsill and practice my breathing.

Two breaths in.

One long, slow exhale out.

I practice my breathing. Two breaths in. One long, slow exhale out.

Where's the crying coming from?

Where's the baby?

Bang. Bang. Bang. Bang.

Fuck!

Justin. No.

Stop.

Practice your breathing, Madden.

His laugh. That's what is the soundtrack to my nightmares most nights. The fucker's laugh as he waited in that room for us to die.

Two breaths in.

Stop thinking about it, Crew.

One long, slow exhale out.

Focus on something else.

Another deep breath as I scrub a hand over my face and then through my hair.

I look out the window over the driveway.

What do I focus on?

The oak tree at the bend.

How about one Tennyson West?

Talk about a welcome . . . distraction? Surprise? Maybe a little bit of both.

I've hooked up with women since Brittney left. I'm a guy. Sex is a necessity. A way to ease the adrenaline rush after a crazy night at work. But it's only happened a couple of times, and only when the girls went on sleepovers to friends or my sister's house.

For thirteen years, I came home to the same woman. Made memories with her. Did for better and for worse with her. And slept in the same bed with her. And although I do not miss Brittney, I do miss that connection. I miss the shared jokes, the easy company, the familiarity, and the having someone to talk to about your day.

The irony is that I thought we still had that when she up and left. Either I was blind, or she was good at pretending. Maybe a little of both.

Hookups are temporary and quick. Fun but fleeting with the promise of more never even considered.

But for the first time in a long time, I had an inkling of what I've missed when I laughed with Tenny earlier tonight.

Sure, the lust part fired good and well enough, but there was something more with Tenny. Something added.

And I have no fucking clue what it is or whether she felt it or not . . . but I know I want more of it.

Chapter Seven

Tennyson

"THIS IS JUST THE BEST DAY EVER." BOBBI JO CLASPS HER HANDS over her chest as her accent gets a bit thicker with each second. "I told Calliope that there was no way in H-E double hockey sticks that *the* Tennyson West was going to accept my invitation to help with our Founder's Day events. That she—meaning *you*—has turned down every other invitation to get involved in town. Lo and behold, you emailed me and did just that. Two years. You've lived here for almost two years, and this is the first time you've joined us, and we couldn't be more thrilled." She winks and leans over, her platinum-blonde hair falling over her shoulder as she lowers her voice. "Not only did you make my night, but you also made me look oh-so-brilliant to the girls on the committee, so *thank* you."

She smiles at me with a cute shrug before moving a stack of fliers from one table to another, her heels clicking on the varnished floor of the community center's convention area—if you can even call the small space that.

"I mean, we were all sitting there at Wine Wednesday, wondering how to infuse fresh ideas into our annual festivities, and we thought that maybe you, being a woman from the city and having experienced the world beyond Redemption Falls, might just have some to give."

"Like I said, I can't guarantee that I have brilliant ideas, but I have able hands and will definitely give all the help I can give."

She reaches out and pats my hand. "We are so very grateful for that."

She clickety-clacks her heels to the opposite side of the gym where she proceeds to direct and instruct the volunteers there.

I thought her sugary sweetness was going to annoy the hell out of me. That her niceness was going to drive me batty. That her overly cheerful demeanor would get old after three hours of hearing it infused in her south-ern twang, but to be honest, it hasn't been all that bad so far.

But I'm reserving judgment.

With that said, I'm more than certain I'll have reached the limits of my extroversion sooner rather than later.

I'm already trying to find a way to extricate myself when I'm done so that I don't end up getting roped into going out for cocktails like they are all talking about.

An introvert can only handle so much people-ing.

I get back to work on finishing up stuffing the envelopes I've been tasked with completing. The letters will be mailed out to a set radius of the town's addresses warning the property owners that fireworks will be going off on Founder's Day so they can move their animals inside.

"So tell me about that dreamy neighbor of yours," Alma—I think her name is Alma—says as she scoots into the chair beside me. Her personality matches her frame—large and unapologetic—as she winks with an expect-ant look on her face.

"Dreamy neighbor?" I ask nonchalantly when I damn well know she's talking about the man I've thought about more times than I'd like to admit over the past forty-eight hours.

"Yes. Crew? Isn't that his name? The nephew or something or other liv-ing out in old Ian Madden's house by you?" She mock fans herself and sighs but continues on before I can even answer her questions. "That man is the definition of sexy. Dark hair. Dangerous looking tattoos. A nice ass. That smile that makes your lady bits take notice. No woman in this town is com-plaining about our new visitor, I'll tell you that much."

"I'm sure they aren't," I say, biting back a laugh.

"Nothing is better than a man who screams bad boy but is actually nice and polite," Tanya says as she leans over her side of the table, obviously excited to contribute to our conversation. She waves a hand in indifference. "Best of both worlds if you ask me and Millie—you know Millie? The owner of Redemption Falls Annex? She said when he stopped in the other day that he was just that."

"Is it true?" Alma asks. Two eager sets of eyes stare at me. I'm certain there are a few more pairs of ears straining to overhear this conversation as well.

"I've only met him once." I can practically hear their hopes of learning some juicy tidbit deflating with that comment. "But I can confirm what Millie said. Crew is definitely genuine and kind. Or at least from what I've seen. Add to that, his girls clearly adore him as he does them."

"What do you think happened to his wife? A widower, don't you think? What woman would leave that man and those gorgeous girls of his behind?" Alma adds before looking at me for the answers that aren't mine to give.

"Sometimes things just don't work out—"

"Alma? Alma, *honey*? Can I get your help over here for a bit?" Bobbi Jo yells across the gym.

Alma huffs at the interruption but rises from her seat, clearly pleased at being called over for help.

"Saved by the bell," Tanya says when Alma is out of hearing range. "I love that woman to pieces, but she's known for questioning you to death, and then only taking the information she wants from it to help bolster the gossip she spreads."

"Thanks for the warning," I say with a smile.

"We all mean well, here. I promise." She pats my arm as Bobbi Jo's laughter carries over to us. "We're all just a little overbearing—that comes from knowing each other since we were basically born—but I assure you that's a good thing. Overbearing means we like you."

"Well, it's always nice to be liked," I say and begin stuffing my envelopes again.

"It is indeed. So, New York, huh?"

"New York?" I ask.

"Rumor is that's where you're from?"

"Sure am. It's been quite some time since I've been there, though."

"Cold Spring?" she asks, and my smile falters slightly.

"Correct. We lived there a couple of years while growing up."

"It's a beautiful town. Perfectly located—rural but close enough to the city."

"You know it then?" I ask of a town I've never lived in but that I know from research.

"Sure do. My sister and her boys live there. Been there more times than I can count. When were you there? Maybe you know her, or we crossed paths at some point. Wouldn't that be something?"

"Army brat here." I raise my hand and offer a warmer smile. "We moved around a lot, so much so that the years get all confused at some point."

"Sorry to be the bearer of bad news, but it only gets worse as the years add on." She pats my hand. "Take it from someone who knows. Now if you'll excuse me, I need to go see if Jess needs help calling food vendors." She reaches out, puts her arm around my shoulders, and gives me a quick and unexpected squeeze. "This is just so exciting."

I watch Tanya head in Jess's direction as I draw in a deep breath and take in the scene around me. There are pods of people working on projects. Vendor sponsorships, town decorations, carnival booth ideas, and the list goes on and on. Per Bobbi Jo, we are in the *assessing* phase of planning. What do we have? What do we need? What do we want?

Once we figure those three things out, we can go from there.

Lucky for me, I'm in the envelope stuffing phase where I can put my head down and avoid as much local gossip as possible.

Or rather, doing something that would make me become the local gossip.

Which is why I kept the bouquet of wild daisies I found on my front porch this morning to myself.

No doubt they were from the girls, and no doubt Alma could have spun a little tidbit like that into a whole damn love affair that doesn't exist simply because she could.

But those flowers . . . they brightened my day and made me think way too much about our non-dinner, dinner. The whole thing is silly really—the me thinking about it more than I should part—because it's not like it was the first time I'd ever had a disaster of an evening.

But it's still on my mind—Crew and the girls are still front and center—because it got me here. Out in the public. Pushing me out of my comfort zone that I've been hiding in for the past two years.

No one here knows the truth about who I am or anything about my past. I'm just Tennyson West, the anti-social book editor who lives in the cottage out on old Ian Madden's farm because she decided she wanted a slower-paced, quieter life than the one she had in New York City.

And yet the doubt is always there in the back of my mind. The fear of being found out is a constant thought.

The reassurances I've been given can't fully erase my knowledge of the power, the influence, and the thirst for revenge that Kaleo has—even when he thinks I'm dead.

We were a couple who lived in the public eye. Our faces were known to many—for good and bad. The change in my hair color can't exactly erase what I physically look like or who I am. A change in location, a change in name, can't alter that.

And so, I've lived my life since that day on the yacht years ago, constantly looking over my shoulder. Always wondering. Competently knowing that even from behind bars, Kaleo still calls the shots over his empire. What deals to make. What orders to be completed. What hits to make.

My hope is that in time, the worry and fear will dissipate and that I'll be able to live a normal life just like everybody else in this gym.

Normal.

Wouldn't that be something?

The thought stays with me as I finish my envelopes and am bidding everyone goodbye for the afternoon, trying to find a way to extricate myself from getting roped into going out for cocktails like everyone is talking about doing.

"Are you sure you don't want to come out with us?" Bobbi Jo asks, lips in full pout.

"No. Thank you." I've already stepped out of my comfort zone enough today. "I'd love to, but like I said, I already have plans tonight."

"Oooohhhh." Her eyes fire with mischief, the implication that I have a date hangs in the air.

"Not those kinds of plans."

"Oh." Another pout followed by a wink. "Too bad. Those are the best kinds of plans. But don't you worry. I'm not taking no for an answer. We'll get you out with us. Then we'll ply you with drinks till you spill all your secrets so we can know you better."

Not a chance in hell.

"Sounds like a plan." I hook my purse over my shoulder in a show to prove I'm really not budging. "I'm sure you will all have a great time."

The change in my routine, the different scenery than my normal cottage, was more welcome than I had anticipated. At the same time, I didn't realize how much I felt like I was being held under a microscope while stuffing envelopes until I step out of the community center.

Everyone is just curious about me—the woman who has lived here for two years but who has preferred to remain on the outskirts of the community—and it seems, excited that I'm helping. I get that. I understand that. But it doesn't mean that it has made the furtive glances any less noticeable.

But I did my deed and now with each step I take distancing myself from them, I feel like I can breathe a little easier. Like I can relax a bit more.

Silly, but true.

Redemption Falls is beautiful. I'll definitely give it that. Perfectly plotted flowerbeds teeming with different colors line the street. Sandwich boards dot the sidewalk announcing sales or specials for the day. Ornate light posts are set every so often. Banners hang from them announcing a town event, the high school athletes celebrated for the week, and town businesses.

It's the definition of quaint and idyllic.

A place many would dream of calling home. *Home?* Is that what Redemption Falls is to me? Has it become that for me yet?

I'm not sure. Bits and pieces of it feel like it at times. And at others, not so much. But all I know is that while its small-town quirks have taken some time to get used to, I think I can definitively say I *am* happy.

And after the shit I've been through, that's more than enough for me.

Chapter Eight

Crew

"**G**IRLS. YOU DO REMEMBER WE'RE GOING TO BE HERE FOR THE NEXT four months, right? There's no need to go into every single shop—"

"They're called *boutiques*, Dad," Paige says with a huff and a roll of her eyes. She pushes open the door of the current *boutique* we're in . . . without holding the door for me so that I'm hit squarely in the shoulder, smashing the bags my hands are loaded down with.

"I'll rephrase." The smart aleck. "We don't have to stop in every *boutique* today. We have weeks to do that. *Hell*, we've already been in half of them as it is." I set the bags down on one of the many benches that line the little shopping district of town, my ass beside them, and blow out a sigh. No doubt these shops are for the tourists who frequent here, and per my wallet, they definitely charge the tourist markup.

"If we've already worn you out, we can go into the next one on our own. You can just stay here. All we'll need is your credit card," Addy says.

"And so it begins," I grumble more to myself than to anyone. I've been warned about having girls. About how expensive they become when they reach a certain age.

I think we've just hit that age.

Paige narrows her eyes at my comment, but her smile remains. "So what'll it be?"

"How about *no*, you're not getting my credit card, and while you're at it, how about a few more *thank yous* and *pleases* get thrown in the mix, huh?" I say, internally waging that forever constant parental battle of whether I'm spoiling them or not.

And with the thought of spoiling comes the notion that I'm using this trip to make up for their mother's revelation today via email that she isn't going to make it back to the States for their birthday after all.

No friends in this new town to celebrate with. No mother coming to help fill that void. My sister is taking care of my mom fresh off hip replacement surgery so either of them visiting is out of the picture.

You're batting a thousand here in the parenting department, Crew. Taking them away from those who could help me shower them with attention to ease the sting of Brittney and her selfishness was a major parent fail.

It's at times like this that I appreciate my mom and the special bond the girls have with her. I realize also that I deprived them of contact with her when I picked up and came here. Sure, I thought texts and FaceTime was enough—but that was before I knew their mother was bailing on them.

Now it's up to me to fill the void their mother has left.

Then again, isn't that what I've been doing?

"Earth to Dad. We did say thank you," Paige adds. "You were just too busy flirting with the owner to notice."

"I was not," I sputter, looking from one pair of eyes to the next. "Girls. Talking and being nice to someone does not constitute flirting with them."

"Well, she sure liked you." Paige looks at Addy, and they both snicker.

I groan internally. "Out with it."

"When we were in the dressing room and you were sitting in the chair at the front by the window, we heard her whispering to her helper about how the rumors were true. That you are *hot*."

A round of giggles sounds off as my cheeks heat in embarrassment. *Jesus.* While it does boost my ego, the last thing I need is the girls hearing it.

Welcome to the small-town fishbowl.

"Well, what do you have to say?" Addy asks. A million things to say go through my head, but I decide to go with the one that will have the path of least resistance.

And the most laughter.

"Let's face it, girls." I blow on my knuckles and polish them against my chest. "Your old man *is* hot."

"Oh please," Paige says as Addy makes gagging noises.

"Gross. My ears did not need to hear that," Addy says. "I'm *so* going to tell Nana you said that."

Dear God. *No.* The last thing I need is my mom, bored to tears while recovering from surgery, to have that thought idling around in her head. I'll be bombarded with well-meaning but pushy texts and calls asking if I've asked the salesclerk out. Followed by *why haven't I asked her out.* Then to be smothered with reasons why I shouldn't give up on love because of that *trollop Brittney* until I call my sister to take her phone away from her.

It's like with our dad's passing a few years back, her new hobby has become being a sounding board in my sisters' and my life.

I love the woman to death but being smothered by love is not a way I'd like to go.

"No, you won't," I say.

"If you're going to make my ears burn, then I'm going to have her call you nonstop until your ears burn."

Jesus. The kid should be a hostage negotiator when she grows up.

Time to pull out the big guns.

"You send that text, and I'll buy more of that vegetable lasagna for you." I chuckle, trying to come up with what would be the ultimate deterrent for her. "*And—*"

"You wouldn't dare." She makes a gagging noise as Paige backs away, shaking her head.

"*And . . .* no swimming pool for you all summer."

"That's not fair," Addy says, launching herself at me, trying to tickle me until I renege on my threat.

"What's not fair?"

All three of us look up from our laughing fit to see Tennyson standing there, purse slung over her shoulder, a bemused smile on her face, and her eyebrows lifted.

Jesus.

That's my first thought.

She's even prettier than I remember.

Today, it's jeans and a red T-shirt with her hair pulled back in a conservative ponytail. But that smile. That smile is still the same. It lights up her face *and* affects me.

I rise from my seat on the bench. "Well, I was just telling the girls that their old man is in fact ho—"

"No. Please no. Our ears can't handle hearing it again," Paige says, and with her flair for the dramatics, she drops down on the bench I just vacated and pretends to have passed out.

"That bad, huh?" Tennyson asks.

"That bad," Addy says with a grimace. "Dad just said that he was *hot*. Ew."

"Ice cream, anyone?" I ask, cutting off Addy before she makes more of an ass out of me than she just did. "Please. Anything. Something to prevent me from having to explain why I made that comment in the first place."

Tennyson's throaty laugh rings out, and her head angles to the side while she studies me. "Why, Crew Madden . . . are you blushing?"

"Me. Never." I know I don't pull it off, and I honestly don't care because the subject has changed and hopefully been forgotten. "Real men don't blush."

"Uh-huh." Her smile widens. *Fuck, she's gorgeous.*

"Ice cream?" Paige asks. "Are you serious? I thought you said we'd eaten enough *crap* today and no more."

Leave it to kids to make you cringe as they repeat your own words back to you. "I did . . . but—"

"But anything to prevent you from having to explain to Tenny why you think you're hot, right, Dad?"

"Thanks, Addy." I give her the side-eye. "I appreciate you repeating that."

"No problem." She smiles cheekily before turning to Tennyson. "The ladies in the boutique thought Dad was *hot*."

"Like I said, ice cream anyone?" I ask through a laugh as I start grabbing the shopping bags. "Sundaes? A new car? A trip to Hawaii?"

The girls giggle, and Tennyson does right along with them. And that sight—of my girls having fun with someone they've really only met once before—is a stark reminder of what they're missing. A female influence that I can't give them no matter how hard I try.

Fucking Brittney.

"Wow. Now I know if I want my plumbing fixed, all I have to do is tell you you're hot because then you start promising irrational things," Tennyson says and smirks.

"Cute. Funny. Way to kick a man when he's down." I ruffle Addy's hair to which I get a huffed response. I keep forgetting they are into their hair and looks now and that I can't do that.

Tennyson's and my eyes meet over the girls' heads and for a brief second, I forget what we were talking about and the promise I just made because all sorts of irrational and inappropriate thoughts flicker through my head.

How her lips taste.

What her skin smells like.

What she would feel like sliding against me.

"So, ice cream?" Paige asks, eyebrows raised, clearly confused over the brief lull in conversation.

I will the thoughts away I'm not certain I want willed away. "Ice cream. Yes. Of course. I assure you I'm not that old that I already forgot."

"That's debatable," Paige says before squealing as she jumps out of range for me to push her shoulder.

"Hey. Easy now." I chuckle.

"You're coming with us?" Addy asks Tennyson.

Tennyson sputters over a response as she looks from Paige to Addy then to me.

"You can say no," I offer while silently wanting her to say yes.

"I'm going to start getting my feelings hurt if you keep saying that," she teases.

I lift my hands up. "No obligation required is all I'm saying."

She smiles softly at me and then at the girls. "I'd love to, but I have other—"

"C'mon. Pretty please," Paige says.

"I'm sorry, but—"

"And here I thought you were lying to avoid us," a voice with a southern drawl says to our left so that we all shift to look at the woman standing there. She's dressed head to toe in varying shades of pink. Her hair is big and the eyes she's blatantly devouring me with are even bigger. "But you weren't. Here you are keeping secrets from us. It appears that Miss Tennyson West definitely does have plans tonight."

Chapter Nine

Tennyson

SECRETS?

Can I die a quick death now?

Crew's going to think I've been talking about him—or even worse—lying about having plans with him.

I look from an expectant Bobbi Jo to a bemused Crew. I'm caught in no man's land—not wanting to say yes to ice cream because I've come to the conclusion after seeing that adorable blush on his cheeks that I like Crew more than I'd like to admit. That and now he clearly thinks I've been talking about him.

And at the same time, I'm unable to say no because then Bobbi Jo would catch me in a lie.

I'm damned if I do and damned if I don't.

Lucky—or unlucky—for me, Crew senses something and steps forward. "She does. *We do*," he says, my eyes narrowing as I try to figure out where he's going with this and why he'd step forward. "Crew Madden."

Bobbi Jo looks at the hand Crew holds out, her smile turning sultry as she shakes slowly. "Bobbi Jo Simmons. Nice to finally meet the new man in town I've heard so very much about."

His return smile is stilted at best as he draws his hand back. "Hopefully all good."

"Definitely all good," Bobbi Jo says, completely transfixed by Crew.

"And we've actually met before. I'd say a good twenty years ago if memory serves me correctly."

"There's no way. I know I'd remember a man such as yourself." She giggles. Freaking giggles and shifts on her feet as if she's the Belle of the Ball.

"Twenty years ago, I wasn't a man." He winks. "That's probably why." Crew looks to us and then back to Bobbi Jo. "Now, if you'll excuse us. I was just tak-ing the girls for a little pre-birthday shopping while we waited for Tenny to meet up with us for some ice cream."

"How lovely. Don't let me keep you then." She takes a few steps away, giv-ing one long last look at Crew. "Enjoy yourselves."

The four of us stand there and watch her click her heels down the side-walk as she lifts her cell phone to her ear.

"I can't imagine what rumors we just started with that little encounter," I mutter.

Crew snorts. "Would you have rather let her know you lied? You think those rumors would have been any better?"

"How do you know I lied?" I turn and face him, mock offended.

"You're not a very good liar, West," Crew says.

"He's right. You're not," Paige pipes in.

"Hey, you're supposed to be on my side," I say to Paige and pull her against my side and squeeze her.

"I'm on your side," Addy, with her adorable freckles, says, making sure to get equal snuggles as she sidles up against my other side.

"You can thank me for saving your ass from the pink paraphernalia party I'm sure she was about to badger you into attending," Crew says.

"How did you know that?" I ask.

He shrugs as if it were a good guess. "Do you think she sleeps in pink too?"

The girls burst out laughing, and thank God they do, because my sudden jolt at Crew placing his hand on my lower back to steer us toward Cups and Cones goes unnoticed.

"Ice cream awaits, ladies," he says.

I try to exhale the breath I'm holding softly as we make our way a few stores down the mall area.

It takes a few minutes to order our ice cream, for me to argue with Crew over not letting me pay for mine, and for us to get settled in the back corner of the local hangout.

The girls are chatty and giggly and quickly make me forget Bobbi Jo and the rumors that I'm sure are flying right now.

And honestly, why do I even care? There could be worse things or people I'm rumored to be with.

"So, did I hear the word birthday?" I ask.

"Technically, not—" Crew starts.

"Not yet, but out of the blue today, Dad declared that since there are two of us, we get to celebrate it for the whole summer," Addy says before taking a heaping bite of ice cream.

"The *whole* summer? Wow. You girls are lucky. What's on the agenda?" I ask.

"Shopping. Finishing our influencer room. More shopping. And dinner, our choice somewhere, but we don't know where yet since we've only been here a few days," Paige says.

"Sounds like a plan many would envy," I say.

"We know." Paige shrugs. "We're lucky we have Dad wrapped around our fingers."

Crew barks out a laugh and gives a sharp shake of his head. "You girls couldn't make me look any less masculine if you tried."

"What does that mean?" Addy asks.

"Here." Crew digs some quarters from his pocket and pushes them across the table, motioning to the old-fashioned jukebox in the corner. "Go pick out some music."

We both watch them head toward it, already bickering over what songs to pick, before falling into a comfortable silence.

"What has you out and about today and meeting up with the all-knowing Bobbi Jo?"

"You know her?" I ask.

"I knew the nine-year-old version of her the last time I was here. She clearly doesn't remember me, but I do her. I don't think one can quite forget her." He chuckles.

"She's a little extra. Nice, but extra." I take a lick of my ice cream and want to groan at how good it is. Cups and Cones definitely has a superior product to the numerous gallons I've tasted from the grocery store.

"Definitely extra." He chuckles.

"I was invited to help with Founder's Day this year. If I'm honest, I've been invited to help before, but this is the first time I've ever agreed to help."

"What changed? Why'd you say yes this time?" he asks.

I shrug. "No reason."

"I'm not buying that. C'mon. Why'd you say yes?"

I twist my lips as I look at the girls still deciding which songs, then slowly nod. "I've pretty much kept to myself for the two years I've lived here. I figured it's as good a time as any to be a part of the community versus its outlier, cat lady."

He licks his ice cream slowly as his eyes hold mine. It's not done in a seductive nature, but Jesus, parts of my body fire with tingles that shouldn't be firing in an ice cream parlor. "He hurt you that bad, huh?"

Crew's comment startles me so much that my chortled laugh sounds borderline hysterical. "What do you mean?"

"Running to a small town. Choosing to keep to yourself. Reveling in being off the grid for a bit while you collect the pieces of yourself off the floor." He shrugs. "I might know a thing or two about that too."

His honesty is completely unexpected and wholeheartedly welcome. And while that's not the whole reason I picked Redemption Falls, it is a big part of it. Because regardless of the man I found Kaleo out to be, he was still the love of my life at the time. He was still my person. And finding out the truths about him only made his betrayal of my heart and mind that much worse.

It only made me question myself and my judgment that much more. *And mourn what he took from me.*

Crew's eyes don't hide the hurt that has settled there. I'm not used to someone being so transparent with me. It's refreshing. It's terrifying.

And it makes me want to know more.

"How long has it been?" I ask.

He looks at his girls, a ghost of a smile on his lips. He keeps his focus there as he explains. "It's been a little over a year. Eighteen months to be exact because this is the second birthday of theirs she'll have missed."

"I'm sorry. For the three of you. I can't imagine . . . I mean, at least with us, with me—he didn't want kids yet, so it was just me who was devastated."

His smile is tight. "Don't be sorry. You know how it goes. You go into every relationship knowing shit could go south—even when you never think it could or is." He falls quiet for a beat as the girls dance around to a pop song. "Simply put, she loved herself more than she loved us. And now she's in Greece living what she thinks is her best life with some resort manager when the best thing in her life is those two right there." Not to mention Crew himself.

How could a mother and wife leave them?

"I don't even know what to say." And I don't.

"There's nothing to say. It's hard to hang the moon on someone and then realize they didn't do the same in return. Am I bitter? Of course I am, but the bitterness has helped cauterize that heartbreak a lot quicker than if I weren't." He shrugs and looks back to me for the first time. I see sadness there, anger, but I also see a resolve that is more than admirable. "She emailed today to tell me she wasn't going to make their birthday. After missing last year, she promised she'd come. She sent an email because it goes to me, and she's too chickenshit to text or call them and say it face to face, so to speak."

It all clicks for me. The ridiculous number of bags sitting on the floor beside us. Today's declaration of a birthday celebration lasting the whole summer. "They don't know yet, do they?"

His Adam's apple bobs. "I didn't have the heart to tell them. Instead, I'm going to spoil them rotten. It won't replace them not having their mom, but it might distract them for a bit."

"You're a good man, Crew."

He snorts. "I'm just trying to do the best I can. I'm not going to lie, it's felt like the year from hell for us. She left, then just as we were getting settled without her, the shit went down at work. Brittney not being there just made it ten times harder for the girls. They wondered if something happened to me, what would happen to them. That kind of shit." He blows out a sigh and runs a hand through his hair. "You know what? I'm sorry. This isn't exactly an *over ice-cream* discussion. A bit heavy."

"Don't apologize at all. I get it. I do."

Crew gets the cutest smile on his lips as he reaches out and taps his cone gently against mine. "Cheers."

"Cheers?" I ask.

"Yes. Cheers. We survived our exes. We're figuring our shit out. And we survived another day—you with Bobbi Jo and me with the terribly terrific twosome—and that, in and of itself, is worth celebrating."

"Agreed. Cheers."

He nods before turning to laugh at his girls as they come back to the table. Crew was right.

He is hot.

And kind.

And endearing in so many ways.

You're not supposed to be that, Crew Madden. You're supposed to be the asshole landlord who won't repair my place. The grumpy prick who lives in the house up the drive who prefers to be left alone.

You're not supposed to be you with your charm and your devotion to your girls.

You made promises to yourself, Tenny.

Huge promises. Ones you can't break.

And anything other than a friendship with Crew would do just that.

Chapter Ten

Tennyson

I<small>T'S ONLY BECAUSE YOU WANT TO HELP MAKE THE GIRLS' BIRTHDAY SPECIAL.</small>

It has nothing to do with wanting to see Crew again.

Absolutely nothing.

Then why do I suddenly feel nervous as I walk up the dirt drive toward the Madden house?

And why did I do my hair and makeup if I'm just dropping these gifts off?

My push of the doorbell rings hollow even though Crew's truck is sitting in the driveway. Déjà vu hits me of the last time I knocked without an answer. *A shirtless Crew.* Not saying I'd mind that visual again, but at the same time, it's a bit different if I poke around now versus when I did before.

I ring the bell again, uncertain what to do with two massive balloon bouquets bumping around from the slight but welcome breeze.

"Tenny?" Crew's voice crackles through the camera I didn't notice mounted in the top corner of the porch.

Oh shit. Has that always been there?

"Crew?" I ask hesitantly, looking up to the camera.

"We're in the pool. Come around to the back."

"No. It's okay. I don't want to disturb you. I'll just—"

"Now it's me who's going to get my feelings hurt," he teases. "Come around."

The hum of the connection clicks off, leaving me no other choice but to follow my footsteps around to the backside of the house like I did the first time I came up here.

Laughter rings out, followed by the unmistakable sound of splashing. The sounds of summer.

The irony is that when I clear the corner of the house, I'm met with a similar sight as I was that first time. But this time, Crew isn't only just shirt-less, he's also wearing shorts that cling to every inch of him, and he's dripping wet as he climbs out of the pool.

The smile he offers me is brighter than the sun as he scrubs a hand through his hair that sends droplets of water spraying every which way.

Hellos come from the girls but are quickly drowned out by the oohs and aahs as they scramble out of the pool when they process the mass of balloons. They fire questions off immediately. I welcome the distraction. The required focus that is needed on them because it prevents me from staring at—cor-rection, *ogling*—Crew in all his gorgeously sculpted glory.

"What are the balloons for?"

"What did you bring us?"

"Ladies," Crew warns as he runs a towel over his chest and shoulders. I catch myself staring for a beat, and when I meet his raised eyebrows over his amused eyes, I know I've been caught.

Embarrassed, I put all my attention back on the girls while attempting to ignore my body's immediate reaction to him.

"Well, since there is an ongoing celebration for your birthdays, I figured I'd bring over your gifts now."

"You brought us gifts?" Addy squeals.

"That wasn't necessary," Crew says, but I hold up my hand in his direc-tion to shush him.

"I know it wasn't, but I couldn't resist."

Both girls look at me as I hand them each a bundle of balloons with an envelope attached to the bottoms of each. "Can we open them now?" Paige asks.

"You may." I nod as they start to open their individual envelopes. My knowledge of what girls their age like is untested, but I did my best in pick-ing something I think they'll truly get something out of.

Oh my God. I just sounded like the old grandma who offers toothbrushes on Halloween for trick or treating instead of candy.

Envelopes rip as the balloon bundles and their weighted strings sink to the ground.

"Seriously?"

"Oh my God."

"No way."

"Sooo cool."

The twins speak in their own language back and forth as they read the certificate in their envelope and then swap so their sister can see what their gift was.

"Are you freaking kidding me?" Addy asks excitedly, but when her eyes meet mine, there are tears swimming in them that make my heart constrict.

"Language," Crew warns but is shushed by a squeal and the sudden launching of two girls hugging my midsection. *Two very wet girls.*

I'm overwhelmed by their reaction to the point that it takes me a second to speak without emotion clogging my throat.

"You like them?" I ask.

Thank yous rain down on me as Crew stares perplexed at what two simple envelopes could hold.

"Is someone going to fill me in here?" he asks, stepping forward. "Or am I going to be left in the dark?"

"Tenny got me a gift certificate to a month's worth of dance lessons at the studio in town," Addy says.

"And me art lessons," Paige adds.

"It's nothing much," I try to explain. "I just thought it would help them feel . . ." For a brief moment I fear I've overstepped. That my aspirations to help ease the pain of their mother missing their birthday and being in a strange town was a little overboard.

I mistake Crew's silence for him being pissed off, but when I glance his way and see emotion swimming in his eyes, I know I'm wrong.

Our gazes hold as he subtly shakes his head and mouths thank you.

For some reason, I'm overwhelmed by the quiet gratitude in those two words and the awed expression on his face.

"Girls?" He clears his throat. "Why don't you run upstairs and put your balloons and certificates in your rooms so they stay out of the ceiling fans—"

"We had a balloon casualty once," Addy says and snickers.

"The ribbons got wrapped around the fan and . . . it was a disaster," Paige says, fighting a smile. "Dad said it wasn't funny, but it kind of was."

"Okay, smart alecks." He sighs but there is no frustration in it. Just resignation that he is never going to live anything down, and he might secretly like it. "Up to your rooms. The pizza should be here soon."

"Pizza?" Addy asks.

"You ordered pizza?" Paige parrots.

"I did. Yes. Call me the lazy dad."

"No way. That's not lazy. *That's awesome.*" Addy grabs her balloons.

"House rule is we only get to eat out once a week," Paige says to me. "This will be twice." She turns to Crew. "Are you feeling okay?"

"Clearly I'm not," Crew says drolly. "Go get changed before I change my mind. And whoever leaves a wet towel on the floor doesn't get any."

"Yes, sir," Paige says before bolting up the porch stairs, but I notice Addy hanging back, fingers twisting while rocking back on her heels.

So does Crew. "What's up, kiddo?"

She rolls her eyes at the term but also lights up at it too. And when Crew realizes she wants to say something to him, he moves over to her and squats down in front of her.

"What's wrong, Add?" he asks softly.

"I really want to go to these lessons." Her eyes dart my way, followed by a nervous smile. "But I won't know anyone. What if I'm not as good as them? What if—"

"You're going to be awesome," Crew murmurs. "You rock the studio back home."

Addy just looks at him and nods.

"I'll sit there at every lesson if you want. Trust fall."

Her smile is hesitant but stronger. "Trust fall," she says back to him, her spine a little straighter now.

And just like that, I feel like a voyeur with these two, but I'm in the same space so it's not like I can avoid hearing the conversation.

"That's my girl. Now go get changed," Crew says and ruffles her hair.

"*Dad.*" She bats his hand away. "Stop. I'm not a little kid anymore."

He chuckles but stands with his hand on the railing and watches as she runs up the stairs.

"I'm sorry," I say. "I didn't mean to cause a problem with—"

"It's not a problem at all. It's just Addy being Addy. She's super outgoing, but she doubts herself when it comes to dance. All she needs is a little reassurance and then she's good to go."

"You sure? I can get her something else instead—"

"Don't be ridiculous."

"Okay." Trust fall. I wonder how that started. "*Trust fall?* What does that mean? If you don't mind me asking."

"It's silly really, but . . . it serves its purpose." Crew scrubs a hand through his hair and chuckles. "When everything happened with their mom, they struggled for a while. We had a rough couple of weeks at one point, and one night to try and change things up, I got this ridiculous idea to do trust falls in the family room."

"You mean like—"

"Yes, I mean like they fall back and trust that I will catch them kind of trust falls." He shrugs. "While it was silly and ended up being the first time I heard them really laugh in what felt like forever, I was also trying to prove a point to them. That no matter what happens, they can trust that I'll always be there for them."

"That you'll always catch them if they fall," I whisper as my heart swells in my chest.

He nods. "Exactly. I'm a guy. I don't have fancy words or know how to say things to girls, but I knew how to show them that I wouldn't let them fall . . . whether it be trying something new or simply figuring out how to deal with what life had thrown at them. So now it's become our thing when I want them to know I'm there. That I've got them in case they need me too."

I simply stare at Crew, enamored at how hard he tries to be a good father. At how much I would have killed for my parents to have an iota of his drive to be better and do better for his girls.

He reaches out and runs a hand down my arm, effectively lighting every nerve ending on fire. "Thank you again for the gifts. You didn't have to do that."

"I know I didn't. I wanted to give them something they love and a place where they can become better at it. Plus, I thought it might give you a little break from being on the clock."

He lowers his head for a beat and nods. "It's appreciated. The thoughtfulness. You trying to help. I promise I didn't unload everything on you the other day to make you feel responsible to help fill in for their mom."

"Oh my God." I hold my hands up. "I promise I wasn't trying to take her place." I put the heel of my hand against my forehead. Is that what it looked like I was doing?

"No. Tennyson. I didn't think you were. I just wanted you to know that . . . hell, I don't even know what I wanted you to know if I'm honest." He sits down in the chair beside me, and leans back, his towel still clutched against his abdomen as he does.

"We're a pair, aren't we? Both apologizing when—"

"When there's nothing to apologize for," he finishes for me with a half-cocked ghost of a smile on his lips.

"Yes. Something like that." I smile. I suddenly have more interest than

I should in the paint chipping off my fingernails. "Look. These gifts weren't meant to burden you with more obligations. My plan was to take them to their lessons. To give you a respite of sorts . . . if you want."

Crew reaches out and places his hand over mine. A current of electricity jolts through my body despite going completely still. "Thank you. Truly. It was thoughtful and perfect and way better than shopping trips for clothes that will be forgotten in the back of the closet before the summer is over."

"No need to thank me. They're good kids." My words are soft, suddenly feeling shy under the intensity of his gray eyes and the feel of his hand on mine.

"Besides, if those lessons mean I get a break for a few hours from watching YouTube tutorials on how to cut the perfect cat eye with eyeliner—or whatever the hell that means—then Jesus, I'm here for it with bells on."

I burst out laughing. He has this uncanny knack for adding levity when we get caught in that awkward trap of attraction.

Or at least on my end it feels that way.

"I can't help you there. I'm a little clueless about the current trends, and my YouTube watching is limited in scope—*oh*."

It's all I can think to say when he moves his hand from mine and shifts so that his towel falls off his lap. I'm greeted by the sight of an angry red scar that mars the lower right side of his abdomen.

I have no idea how I didn't see it before. Obviously, I was too distracted by his physique and looking at the sexy tattoos the one other time I saw him shirtless—dirty and sweaty and hauling wood—that I never noticed the scars.

He was hurt in the line of duty.

Those scars show a lot more than hurt had happened.

"Crew." His name is a mixture of disbelief and sympathy.

He smiles but it's shaky at best before that charm of his kicks back in to mask it. "Just a few battle scars, is all."

"You said you were injured at work. I'm sorry. I don't know why I thought it was something less horrific." Every word that comes out of my mouth makes me feel more and more like the idiot I am.

"Don't apologize. It's hard to think otherwise when I'm healthy . . . but if this whole situation has taught me one thing, it's that sometimes the physical is way easier to heal than the mental." He pauses briefly, averting his eyes as he does, and the expression on his face guts me.

He's a proud man, and I have a feeling that admission of weakness, so to speak, just cost him. It's in the way he shoves up out of his seat and moves about the patio—picking up swim goggles, moving a patio chair back to its rightful spot, pulling a raft out of the pool.

My heart breaks for him and whatever he has gone through and is still going through. There are so many things I could say, but I opt to sit in silence and let him have his moment.

I study him as I do. The scars call to me to look and wonder about their story, much like his tattoos do.

But I don't look there. I don't stare and ogle and make him feel any more uncomfortable than he already does.

Instead, I sit in the quiet around us. I catch a hint of the girls talking out of their open bedroom windows or the sound of a beetle making that buzzing sound I hear often. It's only after Crew has picked up and reorganized everything that he can, that he moves back toward where I'm seated.

"I didn't mean to make you talk about it," I say softly.

"You didn't. I volunteered." He huffs out a self-deprecating laugh that does nothing to dissipate what feels like the sudden weight of the world on his shoulders. He meets my eyes as he absently runs a hand over the scar. "Just your average maniac looking to shoot to kill. Lucky for me, his aim was a little off that day." He winks at me while I stare at him, lips lax. "Relax. It's okay. I'm still here, maybe with a foot less of my intestines and some fragments lodged in some precarious positions."

"And you're joking about it."

He dips his chin for a beat. "I have to. Besides, I couldn't let the girls see how real shit got. They'd just lost their mother. The last thing they needed to think about was losing me too."

And it's that statement right there that sticks with me long after the girls run outside, unknowingly interrupting a deeper conversation than what looked like a poolside chat, and convinces me to check out the progress on their influencer studio. I examine the new ring light, their backdrop options of choice, and even let them show me a makeup tutorial or two, all while marveling about Crew and how open he is.

All the men I've known in my life have hidden their vulnerabilities. Would never admit that they've been affected by an event like that.

Then again, I'm starting to learn that Crew Madden is nothing like most men.

And I'm not quite sure what to do with that information.

Chapter Eleven

Crew

"YOUR SPIN DIDN'T GO," ADDY SAYS, JUMPING OVER TO THE SPINNER where Tennyson is trying to flick it with her outstretched hand. "I've got it for you."

"Can we be done with this game yet?" I groan out of fatherly obligation while secretly enjoying how much laughter has been ringing through this house over the past two hours.

"No," Paige says. "We want to see who will win between the two of you."

I eye her as I have one foot on a yellow spot and another on a red spot, my legs already spread way farther than is natural for an inflexible man such as myself.

"That's not exactly fair considering she's a dancer and I'm . . . me," I say to another round of laughter.

"Exactly. You always win." Paige crosses her arms over her chest and smiles smugly. "It'll be nice to see you lose for once."

"Aren't you supposed to be on my side—"

"Red," Addy shouts and adds a little jump of excitement when the spinner lands on the color.

Tenny snorts as she looks at the current placement of her first foot and where her other foot has to go, directly in front of me. There's no way her small frame can cover that distance.

But the smack of Tenny's hands and her rubbing them together tells me her competitive streak is just as stubborn as mine is.

And she's just about to lose some of that sass of hers to a spot on the board.

"You're mine, Madden," she says playfully as she snakes one leg in front of mine.

My chuckle turns into a sucked-in breath as her body slides in front of mine with her back to my front.

Warmth.

That's my current focus as the warmth of her body heats up my own skin. At least that's what I try to stay focused on because it's pretty fucking hard to have our bodies lined up, pressing against each other's like this, and to not have a clear physical reaction.

That's to say I'm trying to make sure my dick doesn't go hard at the feel of her nestled right up against my cock, in an innocent game with my girls standing there watching.

I'm going to hell.

That's where my mind thinks I should be going with the thoughts I can't stop from running through my head.

"You're going down," Tenny playfully says over her shoulder. She has no idea how much I wish she were right. Me going down. *On her.*

I shake my head to rid the thought but only serve to lose my balance with the action and fall farther into her.

"Not on your life," I grit out.

"Do you want us to spin for you, Dad?" Addy asks, bringing me back to my own twisted, comedic reality.

"Sure. How about a green?" I ask for my own sanity's sake as that would move me away from Tenny.

I hear the flick of Addy's finger on the spinner. The sound of the plastic scraping against the cardboard holder. And then the laughter as the two girls see what my fate is.

"Red," they both say in unison as I groan.

"How in the hell am I supposed to—"

"Language," Paige says sarcastically. I glare at her.

"Funny," I mutter.

"What's going to be funnier is seeing how you'll wrap yourself around me and put some part of you on that red dot," Tenny says, pointing to the one in front of her.

More body-to-body contact with her. That's just what I need when I'm already struggling to stop my mind from wishing the girls were at a friend's house and I could act on the thoughts I'm having.

"You're about to see the master at work here," I say and wiggle my fingers as if I know exactly what I'm doing.

But I don't.

Not in the least. I attempt to replace my one hand where my foot was, which gives me a face full of Tennyson's very nice ass. And as awkward and distracting as that is, when I try to wrap my arm around her to reach the only red dot to claim, I end up with the side of my face pressed very squarely against the side of her chest.

We're talking nose to nipple.

This is a cruel, cruel . . . incredible game.

Tenny's sharp hiss is enough to make me lose my concentration. My feet slip out from under me, and I fall, my legs sweeping against hers as I go.

My barked-out curse is followed by Tenny's yelp seconds before she lands squarely on top of me. And if I thought pressing against her back was temptation, then her lying on top of me, her lips so close I can feel the flutter of her breath against my own, is torturous in all the best ways possible.

I think we're both stunned. Rather, I know I am because there's no rapid scramble to move off each other. There's a brief moment where our eyes meet and our smiles widen, and then laughter bubbles up and over. I hate when she rolls off me to collapse on the floor beside me because that moment of enjoying the feel of her weight on top of me is over before I can truly appreciate it.

"How do we judge that?" Addy asks Paige as Tenny and I lie beside each other, staring at the ceiling and not speaking.

Is she thinking what I'm thinking?

"What do you mean how do we judge that?" Paige asks.

How easy it would have been to kiss her? How much I wanted to?

"I mean, who's the winner?"

"Tenny is," Paige says. "She was the last man standing."

"I demand an instant replay," I say, raising my hand as I push up to a sitting position. "My opponent plays dirty and hip-checked me so I'd go down first because she knew I was going to win."

Tenny snorts out a laugh as she rolls on her side and stands. "Cheaters never prosper, Madden. Didn't you know that?"

I snort. "Right, West. Whatever you say."

Chapter Twelve

Crew

TENNY STAYED.

It's all I can think about later when we sit on the back patio as the girls swim. If this is the result of losing to her, I'm perfectly fucking fine with it.

She came to bring the girls gifts, and she stayed. Not because the girls badgered her to have a slice of pizza, but because I asked her to this time. And truth be fucking told, I really wanted her to.

Because this woman is doing things to me that I'm not sure I want undone.

First, she is incredible with the girls.

Second, she's fucking hot.

Genuine.

And ... *nothing* like Brittney.

Is that my requirement now? That not a single thing reminds me of *her*? Am I that pathetic?

"Do you miss it?" Tennyson asks.

I know what she's asking right away as before the girls returned to the pool, they were telling Tenny some of the funny—and PG rated—things I've come across as a cop over my tenure. The job. The adrenaline. The life that goes with being a police officer. I take a sip of my beer and stare at the bottle as I contemplate my answer. "I thought I would. I mean, I have and I do ... but at the same time, a weird part of me breathes a bit easier now."

"What do you mean?" she asks with a sincerity that tells me she really wants to know.

"Lightning rarely strikes twice, right? So now that I've been through all this, then I don't have to worry about it happening again." I shrug and meet the compassion in her eyes. "Or at least that's what I tell myself to help me put one foot in front of the other some days."

"Was the recovery long?"

My long exhale is a sound of triumph and frustration combined. "It's going on six months now. Not gonna lie, the first two were pretty fucking brutal. I was in and out of surgery a lot. Chained to a bed—or at least that's what it felt like. The girls felt like they were a million miles away." I cringe, thinking back to the frustration, the pain, the unknown. "Then it was making sure what they sewed up stayed that way and that we staved off infections. Now it's . . . now it's making sure I can still handle the job and not jump at my own fucking shadow."

"I'd think jumping at shadows is to be expected when you were swallowed whole by one for some time."

Her words hit me hard. Not being cleared to go back on the force has been hard enough—especially when it's because of the PTSD.

But truth be told, the guilt is even harder.

How can I protect and serve when I couldn't even protect my own partner? When I hesitated long enough for him to get hit?

"Yeah, but if you'd asked me a year ago if I believed the head takes longer to heal than the body, I'd tell you that you're full of shit. And my department is full of guys just like the old me. They don't understand, and I don't ask them to. For all they know, I'm still dealing with the aftermath of the surgeries." I shrug and smile as Addy calls for us to watch a dive she makes.

We hoot and clap in encouragement at her wonky dive.

"What happens after?"

"After, as in if I don't get cleared, or after as in when I collect my pension after my time served?"

"Take your pick."

I blow out a long sigh and shift in my seat. I don't talk to people about this part of my life. My aspirations. My goals. They're mine, and I often feel ridiculous putting a voice to them, but for some reason, I want to tell Tenny. "At first, I thought maybe I wanted to delve into cybersecurity. I did a stint in it and enjoyed myself. The trying to copy footprints and find hidden information. But I soon found out that my skills are amateur compared to what is needed to get the job done properly."

"So if not cybersecurity, then what?"

"Personal security."

"Like . . . bodyguards? That type of thing?"

I nod. "Yep. Like that kind of thing."

"That is most definitely not what I was expecting you to say." She laughs, and it melds with the sound of the girls' in a way that makes me stop and take notice.

This feels more natural than it should.

"Why's that?"

"Doesn't that mean famous people? Dignitaries? Notorious criminals?"

"Something like that."

She gives me a look that says she's trying to place the person who might do that with the man she sees before her. And truth be told, I don't see it either, but I know it's what my future holds.

Helping people is in my blood. *My calling.* And if I can't be on the force doing it, then this would afford me the opportunity to be behind the scenes facilitating when people need help the most.

"Tell me about it," she says.

"Why do I feel like I'm answering all the questions here?" I lean back and put my feet on the chair across from me and cross my ankles. "What about you?"

"You're way more interesting than me." She taps her wine glass to my bottle neck. "Going back to the cybercrime for a minute. Was that a warning that I need better passcodes to my laptop so you can't break in and see all the nasty emails I'm saving up for my landlord?"

"Yes. You should. And if you did open your email, then you'd see that your *landlord* sent you one saying I'm waiting for the plumber to get back with me, but it most likely will be next week sometime."

"Remind me to tell my landlord thank you." She offers me this shy smile that shouldn't be a seduction, in and of itself, but that somehow is as she sits there with moonlight dancing in the strands of her hair.

"Will do."

"So, I'm intrigued, Crew. I want to know more about what interests you about personal protection. Why that avenue? And more so, why do you seem so hesitant to talk about it?"

I stare at her, at this woman who has gently walked into my life and has made me want to answer questions I usually hide from.

And by hide, I mean not talk about it yet to many people because I'm not one to *talk* until I'm ready to act. When I say I'm going to do something, I damn well will be doing it.

My mom, two sisters, late father, and Justin. Those are the only people who know about this pipe dream of mine. These are the people I trust the most. My support system. The ones who will do anything to help me succeed.

I always knew this, but Brittney leaving me only served to reinforce that. They were the ones who listened to my late-night ramblings when the pain, loneliness, and despair became too much to bear. They were the ones who commiserated with me when I'm sure they had much more important things to do. They were the ones who took the girls for a bit so they wouldn't see their father at his worst.

My tribe.

And now, for some reason, I've just let Tenny in too. I'm so comfortable with her that I seem to have let her in without really thinking about it.

"Why this field? Because my sister tried her hand in Hollywood and became the someone she wanted to be, only to end up being stalked to the point that it paralyzed her from enjoying everything she'd worked so hard to have."

"That's horrible." Tenny's eyes widen. "My God."

I nod, thinking of the eldest of my two sisters and her shining star that almost burned out because of the man who terrorized her every move. The helplessness I felt as I tried to watch and bond and enjoy every moment with my two newborn babies while crisscrossing the country to sleep on Vivian's couch to try and help ease her fear somehow. Coordinating off-duty cops and security personnel to provide a constant cocoon around her to give her some semblance of safety.

"Eventually his obsession pushed him to act, get caught, and land him in prison. While it eased Viv's day-to-day fear, it still affected her long term."

"How could it not? I can only . . ." She just shakes her head in a way that has me looking closer at her. *What isn't she saying?* "And how is she now?" Another redirection.

"She's good. She has a recurring role on a sitcom. She's become an advocate for victims' rights. She's now a mom." I think of my nephew and smile. "The whole process taught me that there isn't much the police can do until someone physically acts and that there is nothing like the fear of having another person hunt you down."

She stares at me. Her lips opening and closing in a way that gives me pause. I've seen that flash of fear in someone's eyes before. *My sister's.* And

I suddenly have a feeling that Tennyson's continual avoidance of questions about her life, uprooting herself and moving herself here, has a lot more to do with that flash of panic than it does wanting a simple change of scenery and a slower pace of life.

Between Viv's situation and my on-the-job experience, I've learned that someone who exhibits these reactions—their inherent need for peace— doesn't like being prodded. Prodding can make them pull away further. *And honestly, sometimes it's safer not to prod.*

Fuck.

Here she is asking about me, wanting to know more about me. And here I am debating how to ask about her, to show her I'm interested and want to know her better, all while struggling over if the innocent questions will make her uncomfortable by putting her on the spot. *By prodding.*

"And so that led you to wanting to be a bodyguard?" she asks, pulling me from my thoughts.

"Not me personally, no. God, that would be a disaster," I say and chuckle to cover my own shortfall.

Who wants a bodyguard who hesitates?

I shove the ghosts from my mind and force a smile to hide the tinge of pain from what used to be my dream. How can someone trust you with their life if you don't even trust yourself anymore?

"I tried it once. Vivian's friend needed help because her own personal security had gotten sick. I was in town, so I helped out." I shake my head. "Watching paint dry is more exciting, and that's coming from a man who has sat for hours on end in a car on a stakeout."

"I can imagine. So what aspect of it are you interested in then? Managing it all? More of a macro level type thing?"

"Exactly. I'd be present in my girls' lives while still allowing myself to keep my foot in the game, so to speak. I have the connections through Viv and the people I met when I helped her. And I'm thinking more along the lines of an agency that specializes in being called in when there are specific threats—such as a stalker. Not the day-to-day sit outside of a house type of thing. Because of my background and my experience coaching her through it all, I know the red tape and how to get under it if a problem arises."

Tenny angles her head to the side and studies me. "It makes perfect sense to me. You've spent your whole life protecting and serving. Leaving it behind would be hard, so this would allow you to keep your foot in the world, while at the same time trying your hand at something new."

It's weird to actually talk about it more than just in passing with Justin or while talking *what-ifs* over a beer after our shift.

"It's just a pipe dream." One I've thought about more and more while being forcibly sidelined by the department.

"Pipe dreams can become a reality," she says, and I respond with a chuckle laden with doubt. "Leaps are hard. Scary. Disconcerting. I get that, I've been there, but it doesn't mean you won't land on two feet."

"What about you?" I ask, more than fine switching the subject off me. "Tell me about your job. Have you always wanted to be an editor?"

There's that hesitation again. That invisible wall that prevents her from saying more.

It's subtle, and she's good at keeping her guard up, but I've made a living catching nuances, and she most definitely has some.

"Yes. No. Like most things in life, it was never something I expected to be doing. I took some courses at a junior college. Assisted an editor who doled out small jobs to me so I could learn and she could critique my work. She thought I had a great eye and encouraged some of her clients to use me when her schedule was full. Besides, who doesn't love to get lost in fictional worlds?" She watches the girls, her profile all I can see to decipher her expression. "Reading was my escape for the longest time."

"Escape from what?"

Her smile is quick, and her chuckle is tinged with the slightest hint of nerves. "Good one, Paige," Tenny says in regards to another dive before rising from her chair and grabbing a towel that Paige asks for.

One I could have easily tossed her way if Tenny hadn't gotten up so quickly to have a reason to avoid the question.

I watch her sit on the side of the pool, her legs slipping into the water as she dangles them over the edge. The girls light up as she asks them questions about the game they're playing.

There's a reason she's here in Redemption Falls.

Just like there's a reason I'm here.

I guess we're all escaping something in our lives at some point.

I have a feeling hers is significantly more than most. My guess is an abusive or demanding ex. Someone she clearly fears. But at the same time, that is such a contrast to the confident and carefree vibe she emits that I could be wrong.

Maybe she's gained some of that back in her time here just as I'm looking to do.

But the unspoken answer circles in my mind the rest of the night as we finish our drinks and the girls finish swimming.

"I didn't mean to avoid your question," Tenny says as I walk her out to go home.

"What question is that?"

She levels me with a look that says *don't be an idiot*. I laugh. I can't help it. She joins me for a beat before her expression falls, and her eyes grow serious in the darkened night. She opens her mouth to speak and then closes it a few times. It takes everything I have not to tell her it's okay, that she doesn't have to speak—

Either that or kiss the hell out of those lips and tell her that way.

But after all the freaking months I've had to spend in therapy, I know more now than ever that people have to talk in their own time. Pushing them is selfish.

I reach out to hold her hand. It's the simplest of touches but that doesn't mean it doesn't light every one of my nerve endings on fire and beg me to act on the urge to kiss her.

"You don't have to answer the question, Tenny. I was just trying to get to know you better."

She looks down at our hands, and when she looks back up, emotion I can't name is swimming in her eyes. "I *was* escaping something, Crew. Something that might seem like nothing to others but that really affected me." She sucks in a shaky breath and then continues. "I'm not ready to talk about it yet. I might not ever be. But rather than lie about it to you, like I normally would others, I feel like you deserve the truth. The problem is, I'm not ready to put the truth out into the world yet. *Okay?*"

The *okay* kills me. The hitch in her breath. The break in the syllables. The hope that I'll understand woven in it. All three kill me. *Who the fuck hurt her and how?*

"Okay," I murmur and, without thinking, pull her into me and wrap my arms around her.

It's meant to be a friendly hug. One offering comfort and support to a friend who clearly needs it.

But it only takes a split second to notice the way she fits perfectly against me. The smell of shampoo in her hair and the scent of the summer sun on her skin. The feel of her arms wrapping around my waist, and her hands pressing into my back as she hugs me back.

And the way her body tenses when I can only assume she suddenly feels the same awareness as I do.

"I'm sorry," she whispers and goes to step back but doesn't fully commit to the movement.

The two of us are in that awkward state of being too close while I look down and she looks up to me.

I can feel the warmth of her breath on my lips again. Can see the widening of her eyes. Can feel the tightening of her hands on my flank.

"I'm sorry. I didn't mean to . . ." I don't finish the words because I damn well meant to.

I want this kiss.

I want her.

Giggles erupt at my back. When the two of us jolt away from each other, I know exactly what I'll find when I look behind us.

And I'm right.

Two matching faces, eyes wide and noses smashed into odd positions against the screen.

A creak has me looking back to see Tenny halfway down the steps. "Good night, Maddens," Tenny says with a chuckle as she heads down the drive toward her house.

Every part of me wants to follow. Wants to finish what I think I'm trying to start.

Every part of me needs to find a damn babysitter.

Chapter Thirteen

Tennyson

I CAN'T FOCUS.

On my newest manuscript in front of me.

On the documentary I tried to watch after that.

On the book I tried to pick up only to reread the starting paragraph ten times and still not remember what it said when I finished it.

I can't focus on shit because there were two times tonight when all I thought about was kissing Crew Madden. Two times when I felt his breath on my lips and the heat of his body against mine. Two times where I had to remind myself that I don't deserve a kiss from Crew Madden.

It was a lot easier to be restless when we lived in the city. There were things to do and places to go to ease your agitation. An empty Lombard Street to hike up and down when insomnia hit. A tough workout at the gym to work through my thoughts. A late-night diner to gorge on ridiculously bad-for-you food that I'd pay for the next day when teaching my students.

The anonymity was welcome. The diversity of options endless.

But here in Redemption Falls, the only distractions are empty trails through night-darkened woods or a drive into town where your visit will become town fodder.

Not exactly two attractive options right now.

"Tennyson?"

I jump at the sound of the voice and at Crew standing on the other side of my security screen door.

"Crew? Is everything okay?" The words come out in a whoosh of air as I move to the door, noting the clock on the wall reads well past midnight. When I pull open the screen, he's standing there in the same clothes he had on earlier—swim trunks and T-shirt—hair a mess, jaw slightly unshaven, eyes intense. "The girls?"

"They're asleep. Locked in the house. Note on the counter that I'm down here in case they wake up. Alarm set."

"Oh. Okay. Then what . . ." My heart pounds in my chest, the cool night air doing nothing to abate the sudden warmth spreading through my body.

His smile is half-cocked and sexy as hell. "If we're not going to lie to each other, then I figure I might as well say it."

"Say what?"

"I'm not sorry." He takes a step toward me, my hands still on the screen door handle, my head angling up to hold his eyes.

"Not sorry about what?"

His Adam's apple bobs. "About hugging you earlier."

"Oh."

His eyes roam slowly down my body. Each second feels like an eternity as my chills chase his gaze almost as if he's touching me. When they meet back to mine, the gray of his eyes is a little darker, the tic in his clenched jaw a tad more pronounced. "About wanting to kiss you."

"Crew." His name is breathless and sounds weak, but the thought is erased as Crew steps forward, sliding one hand to the back of my head and the other to the small of my back in one swift motion as he lowers his lips to mine.

Crew tastes like mint and desire. His lips are soft. His stubble just enough that its scrape against my skin tells me that this is real. That he is kissing me.

I could say I'm startled by the action, but that would be a lie.

I'm ready for it.

I want it.

Hell, I think I've wanted it since that first day I spied on him working in his yard.

And his kiss? It's the perfect combination of demand and tenderness. Of us both wanting and taking.

I get lost in the sensations while memorizing every single thing about it.

The cool night breeze.

His warm, smooth skin.

The soft groan in the back of his throat.

His hand fisting in my hair.

His thigh pressed between the V of my legs.

The hard wood of the doorjamb at my back.

His heart racing beneath my palm as I run it down to fist in the hem of his shirt.

Crew ends the kiss, his strangled breath of restraint melding with the crickets chirping around us.

We stay that way for a moment—our faces an inch apart, our hands on each other, and anticipation vibrating between us—before he steps back. And not only does he step back, but he jogs down my porch onto my driveway.

"Wait. Crew. What . . . what was that?"

He turns to look at me, that disarming grin owning the parts of me he just heated up.

"I don't know, but it sure felt good and . . ."

"And . . ."

He scrubs a hand through his hair, that smile of his lopsided now. "And I figure I should give you fair warning . . . I'm pretty fucking sure that just once isn't going to be enough for me."

"You already knew that, or was this a decision made on the fly?" I ask as I cross my arms over my chest and lift a brow.

"On the fly." He winks and takes a step backwards. "I'm quick on my feet."

"Is that so?"

"It is." He turns on his heel to walk down my driveway and calls over his shoulder, "Good night, Tenny."

"Good night, Crew."

He whistles as he walks, and you bet your ass I watch him until I can't see him anymore with a goofy grin on my lips and my head in the clouds.

Crew kissed me.

Whew.

Third time is a charm, I guess.

Chapter Fourteen

Tennyson / Tessa

Four Years Earlier

"Tessa." Kaleo's tone is one I've never heard him use before with me—more threat than warning—and it stops me in my tracks. I stare at him, quite the picture against the dark night sky. His eyes glint and hands clench and unclench.

The party continues on the decks below us. The music is loud and the laughter even more so. I can't help but feel like it's all a ruse. That something is going on. The same something that has made me feel so uneasy over the past few days.

"Are you going to tell me what's going on?"

"It's just work, Ku'uipo. I know you're tired. Why don't you go to bed?"

Chills chase the length of my spine, but they have nothing to do with the cool breeze coming off the ocean. His words may be a question, but they are definitely a demand.

He no longer wants me at the party.

So many things from the past few months flash through my mind. The late-night meetings. The constant phone calls he needs privacy to take. His sudden need to be back in Hawaii more than our penthouse in San Francisco.

The agitation and stress that never seems to lift from his shoulders.

Most women would fear that her husband was having an affair. They'd say I'm naïve in thinking he wasn't. Not me. Not with Kaleo. We have a bond that is indescribable. One that was forged the night we met and that hasn't stopped in the three years we've been together.

"No," I say.

Anger flashes in his eyes. If there is one thing my husband doesn't like, it's being disobeyed by his employees.

But I'm not his employee.

I'm his wife.

And I want answers.

"Tessa," he says as he types something on his phone before setting it down on the table beside him. I now have his undivided attention. Something I haven't had all day. "I need to finish up some business. Have some conversations with my guests downstairs before the night grows too long, before they drink too much, and before they leave."

"You control the tenders back to the shore, so I don't think they'll be going anywhere until you say so."

"Now is not the time to be difficult," he says. "Please give me the time to do what I need to do."

"What's wrong this time?" I ask, the beads on my dress causing reflections to shine on the yacht's deck all around me as I throw my hands up. My patience and curiosity have been exhausted. "The shipments aren't on time and your customers are pissed?" Isn't this the same excuse he's been giving me over and over the past few months? "What's the excuse as to why you tore me away from the studio without any notice and demanded that I be here? *With you.* If I'm here to schmooze or keep up pretenses for your clients at these ridiculous parties, the least you can do is tell me the truth. But no, you want to send me off to bed like an errant child. I'm your wife."

He pinches the bridge of his nose in an obvious show of frustration. But I've been patient long enough. "You've thrown one hell of a party here tonight. Thank you."

"That's not the answer I'm looking for."

"You're right. I'm sorry." His sigh mingles and melds with the sounds of the ocean lapping at the boat's hull as he crosses the distance to me. He reaches out and pulls me against him, resting his chin on my head. This is where I belong, where I fit best, and I hate feeling like something is between us when I don't know what it is.

"I think I need to record that so I can replay it," I say, the words muffled from my cheek pressed against his chest as I soak in everything about him. "It's not often Kaleo Makani admits wrongdoing."

"Just this once," he murmurs, the heat of his breath hitting the crown of my head. "Look, I apologize. It was selfish and arrogant of me to pull you away from your students, but you're right, there have been problems. Ships aren't arriving on time. Clients are angry over it. The union is threatening to strike. The truckers are down our necks since they're losing time waiting for the cargo. Then there are issues with the warehouses in Los Angeles. To say it's been a shitshow is an understatement."

And now I feel like the asshole for not knowing this. For being so busy with my own passion that I haven't been paying attention to the details and the problems that weigh on him. Not that he normally says much. He's been so adamant since we married to "leave work at the office" so to speak. Perhaps that's why I've struggled over the last few months. He's been so . . . distracted.

"I'm sorry. I didn't—"

He shushes my apologies by pressing his lips to mine in a possessive kiss that I love. My nipples harden as the ache between my thighs begins to burn. Kaleo knows this. He knows what he does to me, so when he pulls up the hem of my skirt to dip into the wetness there, he hums in appreciation.

"How could you have known?" Another kiss. "I needed you here with me. I wanted you here with me." His fingers rub ever so gently. "Thank you for playing the part. For throwing the parties. For helping me make it seem like everything is perfectly under control. People are watching, always watching, and if you're here, then they know everything is okay."

"Kal—there are people downstairs. Don't you need to deal with them first?" *Say no, please say no. Your touch is magic.*

"What people?" he teases, my breath catching as he tucks a finger into me, the heel of his hand rubbing at my clit. He chuckles against my lips, and it rumbles through me. "Let me finish what I need to finish and then I'll make it up to you. Tonight. You know I make good on my promises."

I nod, my breath stolen temporarily as he makes me forget about the many guests and the possibility of being caught, and shows me more hints of exactly what he's promising. And I know from experience he definitely makes good on them. "Okay. Fine. Yes."

"There's my girl." His lips find mine again as my body aches for more of his touch. "I'll wake you when I come to bed, yes?" He presses a kiss to my forehead and smirks in the way only he can. "Until then, rest up because you're going to need it."

He walks back to the table, picks up his phone, and then disappears around the side of the boat where the stairs lead to the decks below and no doubt the bodyguards waiting to follow close behind.

It took some time, but I've gotten used to the bodyguards. To Kaleo's paranoia over certain things. To the gun he often carries with him for protection. They all went hand in hand after I took the Makani last name when I married Kaleo and his shipping magnate family. When money was no object, but threats were a constant.

And my safety, my protection, is something that Kaleo takes with the utmost seriousness. *Nothing is worth risking you, Ku'uipo. My sweetheart.* That's what he calls me in his native language, and it makes me smile, every time, without fail.

I glance over the railing and watch as Kaleo rejoins the party. His first step is toward his right-hand man, Rangi. They put their heads together for a beat, deep in discussion, before Kaleo steps back with a nod and heads toward the main group of our guests. The second he steps up to their circle, their body language changes immediately. Even after three years with Kaleo, it still marvels me, Tessa Miller, from a map dot town in Oregon, how the aura of money and power makes others react without question. Like how the men I'm currently watching give my husband the respect he demands and the attention someone of his authority requires without question.

All while I stand up here and get butterflies over the sight of and thought of him.

Is that why I stand here and watch their interaction I can see but not hear? Because while I'm pissed at him for pulling me away from my students at a crucial part of the course, I'm still hoping he can fix whatever needs to be fixed so we can salvage some of this time together. So we can enjoy each other without the worry that has been interfering over the past months.

"Mrs. Makani?"

I jump at the sound of one of the bodyguard's voices. "Yes, Carlo?"

"Mr. Makani wanted me to bring this to you." He moves across the deck with a glass in hand.

"What is it?"

He shrugs. "Just a little something to help you relax. *To take the edge off,* I believe were his words."

I peer into the glass. Another one of Kaleo's guava juice and rum drinks, most likely with a muscle relaxer dissolved into it. I appreciate my husband's thoughtfulness, but that's the last thing I want right now.

"Thank you," I say, but Carlo remains standing there. "Yes?"

"He told me to bring back the empty glass."

What? I chuckle. "Thanks, but I can manage my own dishes." And yet he remains standing there, legs spread, hands clasped in front, staring at me.

"Christ," I mutter. "I'll be right back." I stalk to our stateroom, irritated by Kaleo's want for control over all things for some reason when normally it doesn't bug me so much. Within seconds, I have the drink poured down the drain and am marching back to Carlo. "Happy?" I grit out.

His face is impassive when he meets my eyes. "I'm just doing my job, ma'am."

"Yes. I know. I'm sorry." I shake my head. "I love the man to death, but sometimes he drives me crazy."

That comment gets a slight smirk from Carlo as he takes the glass from me. "Couldn't agree more."

I chuckle and the irritation lessens knowing Kaleo is just trying to take care of me when that's something no one has ever really done for me before.

"Thank you," I murmur to Carlo as he heads back downstairs, leaving me to glance over the railing one more time at the most incredibly sweet, irritating, demanding, loving man I have ever met.

Seeing Kaleo in his element—wheeling and dealing and trying to ensure success so that we never have to worry about anything again fills me with a kind of pride and love I've never known.

I'm one lucky woman.

The thought stays with me as I head to our stateroom, as I take a shower and put on something sexy, and as I doze off to the sound of music on the deck below.

Shouting wakes me up.

At least I think it does. All I know is that uneasy feeling returns, crawling over me as I scramble out of bed, knot a robe around my waist, and shuffle toward the deck.

Kaleo should have been in by now. He should have woken me up and fulfilled his promise. He should have—

A gunshot pierces the silence. I don't even realize it's my own yelp that follows thereafter because I'm scrambling to the only protection I can find, the solid railing that lines the perimeter of the top deck.

My whole body trembles as I try to gain my wits, and it's only then that the thought hits me.

Kaleo.

He's hurt. One of the men here—

"Don't fucking lie to me again." I almost cry in relief when I hear my husband's voice, but that relief is followed by a cold trickle of fear. It's foreign and terrifying and begs for me to look all while wanting me to run. "Mercy is a funny thing," he says with a chuckle that chills my blood. "The longer you take to tell the truth, the less it will be shown."

With my heart in my throat, I peek my head up over the edge of the railing and bite back the gasp that hits at the scene below.

Kaleo stands with his gun aimed and an expression on his face that shakes me to the core. It's pure indifference as he points the gun at two men while another man is crumpled on the deck beside him with a pool of blood beneath him. Rangi stands behind Kaleo, a gun, clear as day in one hand and the same impassive expression that Kaleo holds etched in the lines of his own.

It's then that I see the rest—the sight of the man clearly dying or already dead so shocking that I missed the bags open on the deck. The bundles inside of them. The lone package cut open with powder spilling out.

I try to process. To comprehend. To believe what I'm seeing while denying it all at the same time.

"So, who's going to talk? Which one of you is playing both sides?" Kaleo moves the gun back and forth between the two men. The smile on his face amused in the scariest of ways. "FBI? DEA? Who are you with?"

"We're not. I've told you—"

The gunshot rings out and the man speaking staggers backward, hits a chair in his path, and collapses.

Fuck.

I jolt at the sound, my heart lodging itself in my throat, and my knees almost give way.

What just happened? This is like an out-of-body experience—a movie I'm watching and not my life. *My husband just shot an unarmed man.*

"He lied," Rangi says to the lone man standing, who is shaking so hard I can see it from where I'm watching. "Are you going to make the same mistake, Sebastian?"

Sebastian?

I know him. We had drinks with him and his associates last night. We laughed and . . . and I convinced him to stay tonight, to come to the party I was throwing, rather than fly home to Los Angeles.

He's here because of me.

They're all here because of me.

Their blood is on my hands.

I bite back the nausea that threatens. The dizziness that spins around me.

"There are only two answers you can give. Yes, you are an informant. Or yes, you stole product from me," Kaleo says and chuckles as he takes a step closer. "And neither of them makes me a happy man."

My hands are over my ears and my body tucked behind the railing when the third shot rings out. But I still jolt at its sound. This can't be happening. My husband can *not* be a . . . *killer.* He's Kaleo Makani. From a long line of Makanis.

Shipping.

Kaleo deals in shipping goods. Products. Merchandise. Customers who receive them.

But that bag? The white powder? Those are drugs.

There are drugs on the boat. A lot of drugs.

Does everyone on the boat know or just a select few?

Did they hear the gunshots, or with the other cabins being at the other end of the boat, were they too far?

This can't be real.

I've . . . I've lived with this man, I've loved this man, I thought I knew this man better than I knew myself and I've . . . been wrong.

It's all . . . all been a lie?

I stagger to the stateroom as my ears ring and my stomach pitches until I empty the contents of it into the toilet.

I'm in a fog. My thoughts are hazy. Disjointed. Never-ending in an eddy of disbelief.

The truth . . . I can't avoid it as much as I want to, and now that it's out there, it's so very different than the "truth" I believed.

It's all been a lie.

Who I married. The man he is. What he does. The money that supports the life I live.

All a lie that I've been too blinded and now feel so stupid that I didn't see. Or maybe I haven't been, and I've just ignored the truth because it was easier to turn a blind eye.

It takes forever for the tears to subside, for my body to stop shaking, for my mind to stop running in loops on how to get off this boat. On how anyone would believe I didn't know what was going on right under my nose. On what to do.

If Kaleo somehow finds out that I saw—*that I know*—will I end up like the men whose blood is staining the deck below?

The thought sends another fresh round of fear through me as the early morning hours slowly wear on.

I don't know what time it is when the door to the stateroom opens. When I hear the man I thought I knew sigh into the silence of the room after his *hard night*, and slowly begins to undress. The sound of shoes dropping. The slide of his tie through his collar as he takes it off. The snap of his slacks as he straightens them before laying them over the back of the chair.

If the lights were on, would I see blood splattered on those items now on the floor? On the skin of the man who wore them?

Each second feels like an hour.

The shower turns on.

Each minute feels like an eternity.

It turns off soon thereafter.

I have to brace myself when the bed dips. I steel myself not to jerk away when he reaches for me. When those hands of his that just killed seek to touch me.

His lips feel like poison on mine as I squeeze back the tears burning behind my closed eyes. As I try to turn my mind off and pretend I didn't just see him murder three people in cold blood. As I try to reconcile the fact that my husband is a drug lord probably using his shipping company to launder the profits.

And if my brain couldn't betray me anymore, my body does. Pleasure is a traitorous bitch even when it's for self-preservation.

That only makes me hate myself more.

"Tessa," he breathes out my name as he seats himself inside me as deep as he can. "Tessa," he repeats, forcing me to open my eyes and look at him.

But he has to see it. He has to know.

The look he gives me says it all. *This is who I am. This is who you married. This is who you love. And if you didn't see it sooner, then you were only fooling yourself.*

He knows I saw. He knows I know.

The little dip of his chin and those dark eyes boring into mine tell me so.

"Just us, Ku'uipo. Always. Just. Us."

"Always, Kaleo." The expected response falls from my lips while my heart shatters.

And then he begins to move, and the fairy tale I thought I lived in? The happily ever after I never dreamt of until I met him?

The fairy tale comes crashing down all around me.

Chapter Fifteen

Tennyson

"Look at you," Millie Buckman says as she moves behind the counter of Redemption Falls' only postal store. Her hands may be busy, but her attention and knowing smile is focused directly on me. "I feel like I should know what you're talking about."

"Don't be so coy." She waves a hand my way. "Everyone is talking about how great it is—that new man of yours has finally gotten you out and about. Lived here two whole years, ferreting away in that cottage while you tippety-typed on that keyboard, and then that handsome fellow comes into town, and all of a sudden you come alive. Volunteering with Bobbi Jo. Coming out—"

"I hate to disappoint the local rumor mill," I say, glancing around at the other patrons near the sundries who are probably listening in, "but there isn't a man, and I volunteered to help Bobbi Jo because for the first time in forever, I have a break in my schedule."

She eyes me over her bifocals and pushes a gray curl off her forehead. "You mean to tell me there's nothing there? No ice cream dates after shopping or buying more than usual when grocery shopping?"

"Nothing," I say with a straight face.

Nothing except a bone-melting kiss three nights ago that I haven't stopped thinking about.

She slides the books of stamps I'm here for across the counter. "It's okay," she whispers and winks. "Your secret's safe with me, but just know that everyone's talking about how you bought gifts for his girls the other day—"

"Well, it's not a crime to buy birthday presents for your neighbor's daughters." I finish my payment on the credit card machine.

"True. True. Those two sweethearts deserve a strong woman in their life such as yourself. That's what everyone is saying."

Well, everyone has lost their ever-loving—too nice, too nosy, too assuming—minds in this town, that's for sure.

I'm not strong.

I'm not who you all think I am.

I have blood on my hands that I'll never be able to wash away.

My smile is anything but genuine as I wait for my receipt and prepare to make my getaway. If she's glad I'm out and about in the town, then she might want to cool it on the pushy suppositions.

"Thank you. Have a great—"

"Speaking of that," Millie says when I've already taken two steps toward the door, freedom just beyond its hinges. I simply look over my shoulder and raise my eyebrows in question. "It's going to be such a struggle for Miss Junie, don't you think?"

My head spins at the whiplash as I try to follow her train of thought. A gift card for Addy to dance lessons. Miss Junie is the owner of the dance studio. Okay . . . what in the hell is she talking about?

Luckily, she likes to hear herself talk so much that she continues on without a response from me. "Forced to make a decision between going to her daughters to help take care of her grandbabies and leaving the place and business she's created over the last ten years. Just think . . ."

But I don't hear another word because I notice the screen of my phone.

Missed Call. Uncle Peter.

Twice.

I stare at the screen again and uncertainty washes through me. Missed calls are no big deal. In fact, I purposely miss a lot of calls because it's so much easier to text.

But not from "Uncle Peter."

Not unless I'm in danger.

I mutter a distracted thank you and hurry out of the Annex. No message was left—not that I expect there to be—but that makes it even worse. Within seconds, I'm behind the wheel of my car, doors locked, and calling the number back with trembling fingers.

But no one picks up the call.

Not the first time I dial.

Not the second time either.

"It's probably nothing," I mumble as I type in the name Kaleo Makani on my phone and hit enter.

It's never nothing if I'm called.

The screen populates with headline after headline about an attempt on the life of a former associate of Kaleo's. I scan the first article quickly as my heart races and my mouth grows dry. Phrases like "still in control," "ordered from his cell," "out for revenge," clutter the screen.

I stare at the search page until my eyes burn and my head spins and the need to get home to my own bubble owns my every thought.

Relief washes over me when I pull into my drive. For a few seconds, I rest my forehead on my hand on the steering wheel and draw in a few shaky breaths to calm myself. *Uncle Peter would call back if contact was critical.*

Stop jumping to conclusions, Ten.

Nothing has changed. Your life isn't hers anymore.

But when I start to get out of my Jeep, I notice the side door to my garage swung wide open. I freeze, one foot on the ground, one foot still in the car, as I look around.

The pots on my porch have been moved. *It should be three to the left and two to the right of the steps.*

The security door is open, the mat in front of it is askew. *I always have it straight, butted up against the jamb. Always.*

The panic I felt earlier from a simple missed call becomes full-fledged terror.

Get out of here, Tess. Go!

I slam the car door, start the engine, and floor it in reverse.

Tenny.

I'm Tenny now.

Someone slams on their horn, but the billowing cloud of dust I just dug up is too thick for me to see through. I'm trapped. Unable to leave my driveway. A bumper less than a foot from my driver's side door.

Terror streaks through me.

I'm trapped. *He has me trapped.*

My hands shake so hard that I drop my phone to the floor when I try to dial 911. Desperate and terrified, I climb over the console to the passenger side and fling the door open and nearly fall out.

Arms close around me, catching me, and I fight against them.

"Whoa!"

Crew.

It's Crew.

A strangled cry is all I can manage as sobs of relief wrack my body just as violently as the trembling does.

"Tennyson? What is it? What's wrong?"

All I can do is shake my head and try to stand on my own without him holding me up.

"It's okay. We didn't hit each other. No harm. No foul."

Embarrassed, more shaken than I care to admit, I finally have the courage to meet his eyes. "The house. I . . ."

"Dad?"

I jar at the sound of Paige's voice. "No," I murmur, shaking my head and immediately turning my back to hide my face from her.

"Is she okay?"

Crew takes a few steps away from me. "Yes. Just shaken. She thought we were going to hit her. Tell you what, why don't you and Addy head back to the house for me, *okay*? We'll go to the library later."

"No. P-please. You can t-take them. I'm f-fine." I stutter over the words. "*I promise.*"

Crew shakes his head. "Paige? Head back. I'll be there in a few minutes."

Paige looks my way, worry on her sweet face.

I muster a smile. "It's okay. I'm fine." I clear my throat. "Really. Take the girls, Crew."

"No." There is no arguing with him, and frankly I don't want to.

We watch both girls as they head up the driveway. They look back a few times before turning past the oak tree.

Crew walks past me and reaches across the seat of my Jeep to turn the ignition off and pockets my keys. When he steps back out of the doorway, I can't escape his questioning gaze. "You want to tell me what's going on? Why you're rushing out of here like a bat out of hell?"

My heart is still racing, and it feels like I have a huge lump in my throat. "My doors. Someone was here. I—"

"Shit." He takes a few steps back and runs a hand through his hair before putting his hands on my shoulders and stooping down so we're eye level. "That was me. I—"

"*You?*" It was him?

"Yes. Christ, I'm sorry. The plumber called and needed a part number so he can order it in before his appointment next week. I didn't think you'd mind if I grabbed it from the garage. But I noticed water trickling out from under the door to the mudroom and couldn't find a spare key under the pots, so I thought maybe the window was unlocked. When it wasn't, I turned the mainline off to the house and ran home to get a spare key and some tools. I was just on my way back."

"It was you," I repeat, forcing myself to hear myself. To believe the words. "I thought someone was inside. I thought . . ."

"I'm sorry." He pulls me against his chest, but I just stand there, hands at my sides, trying to calm myself down. "I should have called you. Let you know. I didn't—"

"It's fine. I'm fine." I take a step back, pushing against the comfort of his hug, mortified at my reaction. I can't imagine what he's thinking right now. "The house. Let me open it."

I walk toward the cottage, my thoughts so disjointed from the fear that just owned me that I don't register the fact that Crew just said my house is flooded. All I can think about is the feeling of being trapped. The sheer terror of thinking Kaleo had sent someone to come after me.

The door is locked. I try the handle, try to remember where my keys are, suddenly frantic to get inside. I yelp when Crew puts his hands on my shoulders to steady me. "Tennyson. Stop. It's okay," he says into the crown of my head. "I'm here. You're safe."

You're safe.

You're Tennyson. And you're safe.

Will I ever really feel that way again? *Safe?*

I draw in a slow, steadying breath and simply nod as he pulls my keys from his pocket and hands them to me to unlock the door. We're greeted by about an inch of water pooling through the kitchen and into the family room, its flow already stopped from him turning the mainline off.

"Right there," I say, pointing to a wall near the garage door where the drywall has deteriorated and looks like it's sliding down the wall. "Let me—"

"No," he says, taking my hand and moving me toward the couch that luckily is untouched by the water. "Sit." He looks around the kitchen. "Where's your hard stuff at?" I must stare at him with a dumbfounded look on my face. "Brandy. Scotch. Vodka. Where is it at?"

"Above the fridge," I say, and within seconds he has a glass in his hand and is bringing it to my lips.

"Drink."

The burn is there, dulled by the adrenaline subsiding through my veins, but still there. I close my eyes for a moment and try to figure out how to talk my way out of looking like an overreacting, mad woman.

"Better?"

"Yes. I totally overreacted like an idiot. I was literally listening to a true crime podcast on the way home. I pulled up and saw the doors open, feared life was imitating the story, and got spooked," I lie, my eyes focused on my hands wrapped around the tumbler, all the while feeling the weight of his stare on me.

"Uh-huh." It's all he says as he stands from his seat beside me and moves toward the kitchen.

"Crew."

"Don't." It's a one-word warning, and when I meet his gaze, I know I won't be challenging it.

Chapter Sixteen

Crew

TAKE MY TIME PUTTING A HAMMER THROUGH THE DRYWALL TO FIND the leak in the pipe. I work slowly as I soak up and then mop the freestanding water on Tenny's floor.

I need time for my temper to abate.

I need a moment to not shake the answers out of her.

Who did this to you?

Where can I find him?

Because the fear that was in her eyes, the abject terror someone must feel to crawl over a seat to escape a running vehicle, tells me there is a whole hell of a lot more going on here than being spooked by a true crime podcast.

All the signs tell me that she's the one who already survived one.

I've seen victims before. I know the telltale signs. The shell-shocked look. The stammering lies to cover the truth. The embarrassment after the fact.

And Tennyson West exhibits all of them.

With a deep breath, an almost dry floor, and a calmed temper, I head back to where she's still seated on the couch. Where despite her protests, I instructed her to remain while I did my best on the plumbing and its damage.

I take a seat on the coffee table in front of Tenny, my knees framing hers. "What's going on, Tenny? Are you going to be straight with me and tell me what really happened today, or are you going to keep feeding me bullshit lies?"

"I don't know what you're talking about," she says, pushing my knees out of the way and moving to the other side of the room where she unfolds and then refolds a blanket.

"I'm the good guy here," I say. "All I want to do is help you in any way I can."

"I'm fine. Everything is fine." Her words are clipped and the smile she offers me is strained when she glances my way. "The girls are waiting for you."

I nod slowly as I study her and wonder what the fuck the bastard did to her to elicit the reaction she had.

And all she works at is avoiding me. She straightens the magazines on the table. She collects Hani's toys and puts them in a basket next to the hearth. She puts the sopping towels from the floor into the washing machine in the mudroom.

I wait patiently for her—just in case she decides to talk—but the longer I sit here, the more I know she's not going to. She doesn't trust me.

Not yet anyway.

But I'm working on it, and the first part of that is not pressing her.

"Okay, then." I rise from the table and move into the kitchen where she's now wiping down already clean counters. "I'll leave you be, but we're going to have to figure out arrangements for you while your water is shut off."

"I'm fine," she repeats.

If I never hear those two words again, it will be too soon.

"No, you're not fine, but you can say it if it makes you feel better." She stills, sponge in one hand, but doesn't turn to face me. "You don't have running water here until Bobby comes out next week. Plus, I'm going to need to get the walls checked for mold. I have no idea how long that pipe has been leaking behind the drywall. I can put you up in a hotel since I'm to blame for this—"

"No need to. Like I said, I'm—"

"Fine, yes, we've established that fact." I sigh in frustration and then continue without really thinking through what I'm offering. "Or you're more than welcome to stay with us. We have two extra bedrooms just sitting there unused. The girls would love it. I'd stay out of your hair."

"I can manage."

"It's just a thought. Besides, I don't feel right leaving you here with an open wall and—"

"Thank you." Those two words delivered with a finality tell me there's no convincing her otherwise.

"You know you're stubborn as hell, right?"

C'mon, Tenny. Turn around and look at me. Let me see your eyes. Let me know you're really okay.

"I know."

I leave the house feeling unsettled and useless with offers to come back if she needs me. But Tenny's silence only makes the barrage of noise I open my front door to even louder.

Is Tenny okay?

Can we bake her a cake?

Should we make her a card?

Preoccupied with what just happened, my response is an all-around resounding yes as I make an excuse for why I need to make a call in my office.

And I need to make it before I second-guess myself and how I'm invading Tennyson's privacy.

Dusty picks up on the first ring. "Holy shit, as I live and breathe, Crew Madden is blessing me with his presence."

"Fuck off, man." My smile is automatic. The pang of how much I miss everyone even more so.

"How are things?"

"Good. The same. You?"

"Can't complain other than I'm having to pick up slack for your sorry ass not being here," Dusty teases. "But then again, I had to do that whether you were here or not."

The comradery is what I miss the most about not being active on the force.

"You're so full of shit."

"True, but you already knew that." His chuckle reverberates through the line. Someone in the background yells something about telling me hi before he continues. "So tell me, brother. Why am I being blessed with your presence? And it better not be for you to put a good word in with my sister. She's still off-limits to you."

I'm so glad he can't see my smirk or else he would know that off-limits or not, we hooked up a few months back. Two people meeting their needs and curiosity and then moving on. What he doesn't know won't hurt him.

"Noted," I lie.

"So?"

"I need you to run someone for me."

"Why? What did they do?"

"Nothing. It's just a new tenant I want to check out. Make sure she's on the up and up since she's offered to watch the girls for me." *And because I'm worried about her.*

"I hear you. Smart. Not a problem."

I take the next few minutes giving Dusty the small amount of information I have on Tennyson—her name, her license plate number, her bank account info I have off her rent that's direct deposited into Ian's account. It's not much, but it's enough for him to run a check.

"Now it's your turn," he says.

"My turn?"

"I need you to do that thing you do for me."

"Dude, you're going to get me in more trouble than I already am," I groan.

"Two things. *One*, you're not in trouble. You're just waiting for the department shrink to clear you. We all know she has a serious hard-on for you so she isn't because she just wants you to stay in her office longer. She's hoping in time you'll recognize your undying love for her."

"Bullshit." I cough the word out.

"And *two*, you're the one who can work magic finding the shit we need. Besides, Sarge may have even hinted for me to give you a call on this."

I look over at my computer setup and secretly itch to dig up the information he wants. Anything to stretch my mind and feel useful again when I haven't been able to.

"What's he need?" I ask.

"He just needs you to work your sources and figure out what we're missing on this big case we're working on. No one pieces together a trail of *almost* clues quite like you do."

"Send over what you need. As it is, I've got nothing but fucking time."

"Great. Will do. And three—"

"*Three?* You said two things."

"I lied." He laughs.

"Fuck off."

"When's the last time you talked to Justin?"

His words hit hard. The accusation woven in his tone even more so. Both have me sucking in a deep breath and scrubbing a hand through my hair, struggling for a response that I'm not embarrassed to give. "I—uh—texted him a few days ago."

"Texted?"

"Yep."

"That's fucked up, man. You guys rode together for over eight years. Spoke to each other every damn day and twice on your day off. And all you can do is text him?" He mutters a curse. "Don't you think this is when he needs you the most?"

Guilt. It hits me like a sledgehammer to the solar plexus. Or maybe the heart. Both are scarred but used to this feeling.

Usually, it's self-inflicted.

"Dusty—"

"No, man. It's fucked up, and you know it as well as I do. Pick up the fucking phone. He needs you. Or maybe he doesn't. All I know is that you're probably the only one who understands the nightmares you both have, and that fucking goes a long way."

I don't have a response. Pride. Embarrassment. Shame. All three block any excuse from rolling off my tongue.

"Talk to him, man. It might help get your head back where it needs to be so you can get your sorry ass back here."

"What's wrong with you? Usually, guys like me aren't wanted back. I'm a reminder of what can happen. Of the danger." It's so much easier to address this than to talk about Justin.

"You're right. We don't want you." I can imagine his sarcastic shrug and lift of his eyebrows on that ruddy face of his. "Or maybe it's you who doesn't want this. To be back. And that's okay, Crew. I get it. We'd all get it. You faced some serious shit. It shredded your body and fucked with your head. But don't use Justin as the excuse. He deserves better than that."

Easy to say when you're not the one who hesitated. When your two-second delay is the reason your partner, *your best friend*, has a bullet lodged against his spine and won't ever walk again.

They think they don't want me around as a reminder.

Well, maybe seeing Justin is that same fucking reminder about how I failed.

"I'll look at your stuff for you," I say, completely avoiding everything he just said.

"I'm sure you will."

When he hangs up, I stare at the wall with a sour taste in my mouth. He's right. Fucking right, and I need to be a man and suck it up.

I need to be the man I know I can be.

The thought prevails as I make my way downstairs, moody and worried and wondering how both Justin and Tennyson are doing.

"Whoa!" I say when I walk into a complete disaster in the kitchen. Addy has flour on her cheek and Paige is dumping unceremonious amounts of cocoa powder into a bowl filled with who knows what.

"What?" Paige asks with a bat of her lashes and an impish smirk, daring me to ask her to stop.

"I'm not a culinary wizard or anything, but I think that might be way too much cocoa powder." Its bitter smell fills the air.

"Why? The chocolatier the better, right?" Paige says.

Addy adds, "Momma says you can never have enough chocolate."

Or Greek assholes who steal wives, but hey, who am I to judge?

Oh yes. Right. I'm the abandoned husband. I have every right to judge.

"What?" I ask when I shake the thought to find two pairs of eyes narrowed at me.

"You got that weird look on your face like you're mad at us," Addy says, immediately making me feel guilty for ruining their fun with my bitter thoughts.

"Not mad. Not at all. Just wondering how that is going to taste."

"Like heaven," Paige says.

"We'll see about that," I tease and then yelp when Paige accidentally lifts the hand mixer from the bowl too far and batter flies everywhere. The walls. Her chest. The floor. *My face.*

Their quick inhales are audible. The fear that they are in trouble heavy as their wide eyes stare at me.

I have a split-second choice—get pissed at them for the mess I'm going to have to clean up, or show them I'm not the hard-ass they think I am.

"Really?" I warn with a playful grin on my face. "You think that's bad? How about this?" I ask as I reach out, dip my finger in the batter, and smear it across Addy's cheek. And as she shrieks and tries to evade me, I wrap an arm around Paige's waist and give her a big smack on the cheek, transferring all the batter from my face to hers.

"Ew."

"Gross."

"Dad, stop," Addy shrieks as she runs straight toward me, her laughter just as loud as her smile.

Paige holds up a spoon and flings more my way, the blob hitting me squarely on the chest.

"This. Is. War," I declare.

The statement was more than accurate because when all is said and done, when the girls have jumped in the shower to clean up, I'm left with my batter-slicked hands on my hips and an utter disaster to pick up.

But from Tenny earlier, Dusty calling me on the carpet, then my girls' giggles—their hugs? These are memories of not being perfect.

They're exactly what I needed.

What I need.

A simple reminder of what matters the most.

A reminder that I'm alive for a reason.

Chapter Seventeen

Tennyson

WHEN MY CELL RINGS, I JUMP AS IF IT ISN'T ALREADY IN MY HAND and I'm not desperately waiting for Peter to call.

"Hi. It's me. I'm here," I say, the adrenaline of the day coming out in those five simple words. "Peter?"

"You're good?"

What kind of question is that after he hasn't called me back for five hours. "Yes. No. You tell me." I chuckle nervously. "You called me."

"I did. I just wanted to tell you that you might see some stories in the news about some things possibly tied to *him*," he says, not mentioning Kaleo's name as is protocol. "I just wanted to reassure you that everything is still okay. That *you're* still okay."

"How can you be so sure? The articles said that—"

"I know what they said, but *that* person ceased to exist. There are no records saying otherwise."

"Databases can be hacked. They can—"

"And if they are, what will be found are images of the mangled car, autopsy photos of charred remains, dental records confirming *that* person died."

Chills blanket my skin as they do every time I think of my death being documented like this.

"His reach is endless, Peter. We both know that."

"It's only endless if he thinks *that* person is still alive—and to the rest of the world, she's not."

My sigh is long and shaky as I try to take his words to heart. As I try to hold on to them.

"Look. I understand why you're uncomfortable, why you doubt, but I'm telling you that I am the only person who knows your whereabouts and so forth." He pauses for a beat. "You're allowed to be scared."

I'm terrified.

I'm sick of being terrified.

And just when I felt like I could start breathing again, just when I decided to start participating in life, I'm shocked back to reality.

To the truth.

To knowing that regardless how safe "Peter" says I am, I'll probably be looking over my shoulder the rest of my life.

"Does it ever get any easier?" I ask him, not exactly expecting him to answer. "You deal with other people like me. Does it ever get any easier for them?"

"At first, no." His sigh is reticent, his pause weighted. "It's not easy learning how to move on. To forget who and what you were in order to be this new person you've been allowed the chance to be. Through it all, fear is the one constant, but that too, will fade over time. One day you'll wake up and suddenly realize the fear hasn't been there for a while. It's then you'll realize that you really are Tennyson West."

"Okay," I say more to myself than to him.

"You're safe, Tenny. It's okay to live your new life."

"Thank you."

"Goodbye."

I sit with my phone in my hand, almost as if I need to decompress after waiting all afternoon and night to get that call. My eyes are closed, my ears listening to each creak and crack of the house around me, as if to memorize them so I won't be scared when I lie in bed later tonight.

This is my safe space.

Kaleo can't find me. He can't reach me. For all he knows, the fire-warped wedding ring he received in a Ziplock bag is all he has left of me.

The minute I drift off, a text on my phone jolts me awake.

Crew: That's me climbing the steps to your porch. Didn't want to scare you. Can I come in?

I scramble off the couch and to the door without thinking about the hot mess I must look like right now. Between the freak-out in front of him and then the tear fest as my emotions deescalated after he left, I'm more than certain I'd cringe if I looked in a mirror.

But all those thoughts vanish when I open the door and see Crew standing there. He has a grin on his lips and is holding a plate of cupcakes, each one with a different letter on them. They spell out "Get Well Son."

I angle my head to read them again to make sure I didn't miss something.

"I might have dropped one with an O on it the dirt on the way over here," he says with an unapologetic shrug. "These are from the girls. From me. They wanted to do something to make you feel better."

It's been years since someone did something *just because* for me. I almost forgot what it felt like to be on the receiving end of a sweet gesture such as this.

"I'm touched."

"And I promise we know how to spell."

"Says he to the editor." I chuckle as he shakes his head. "Come in. Please. And thank you." I take the cupcakes, turn my back to him, and walk in, blinking to clear the tears that just welled in my eyes.

Crew has seen enough crazy from me today to last a lifetime.

His feet clomp on the floor behind me as he follows me to the kitchen. "It's still wet in here."

"As expected. Coke? Water? Brandy?"

"How about the latter?"

"Sounds good," I say, pouring him a glass as he takes a seat at the table.

"I was at Millie's this morning," he says. "Before . . . earlier."

Appreciating his knack for talking around my freak-out earlier, I opt for humor. "Such a brave soul going into the Annex all by your lonesome."

"Jesus," he barks out. "That's for sure."

"If you're telling me that you were at the unofficial Redemption Falls gossip hub, should I worry that it's for a reason?" I ask, reveling in this normal conversation with him. Or as normal as can be with torn-apart drywall, wet floors, and no water.

"It's like estrogen overload the minute I walk in there with gossip leading the way." He gives a quick shake of his head and chuckles. "Apparently, you and I are shacking up. Having a torrid affair at that." He hooks his arm over the back of the chair next to him and just smiles when I meet his eyes.

The question is, did Crew set them straight like I tried to . . . or did he let them run wild with their imaginations?

And why am I hoping it's the latter of the two?

"Gotta love small towns."

"True. Thanks." He takes a sip from the glass I set in front of him. His hum of appreciation does things to my insides a simple sound shouldn't do. "Cheers." He taps a cupcake to mine and takes a bite.

And after two chews, he spits it out with a sputtering sound and an, "Oh God, that's gross," before wiping his mouth.

I wait for him to tell me it's a joke, but by the look on his face, it most definitely is not. He takes a long drink of his brandy to wash the taste from his mouth and then grimaces from the burn.

"Salt."

"What?" I ask, getting up to get him salt for some odd reason. "You need—"

"No. Salt. The girls distracted me. I think I mixed up the measurements for salt and sugar." His eyes bug out of his head as he takes another sip.

Laughter bubbles up as I put the "G" cupcake back on the plate. "How can you mess that up?"

"Don't ask," he says and then proceeds to explain the food fight with the girls. How he cleaned up the disaster while they showered. Then got interrupted by a text that came in and lost track of what and where he was in the recipe.

I simply stare at him. *He made me cupcakes.* Well, tried to, anyway. But the thought was there. The intention was there. After the first batch was ruined, he didn't have to make more. I would have never known the difference.

That, and he is seriously a cool dad. Never in a million years would my parents have allowed a food fight to take place. Then again, they were busy drinking themselves to death so they might not have noticed either way.

"What?" he asks when he notices me staring at him.

"This is becoming a theme here. Between the two of us. Bad food. Spitting it out. Laughing." I shrug. "At least I know I don't have to worry about gaining weight around you."

"Funny. Laughing is never a bad thing, Tennyson." His eyes hold mine, and I feel like there is so much more he's trying to say with those words. I want to believe him, but I'm always afraid to hope.

"I know," I say softly and fiddle with the cupcake wrapper. It's easier to look there than at him. "Thank you for today. *For earlier.*" I put my hand on his forearm and squeeze.

There's something about the simple touch that has us both jolting subtly with awareness. I open my mouth and close it, my lips remembering all too well what his kiss tasted the other night.

"There's no need to thank me."

"I haven't had a panic attack like that in a long time."

Silence fills the kitchen, and it's only when I look up that he responds. He has a way of doing that so I know I'm heard.

"They're brutal. When you're in the middle of one, it's like you're underwater and desperate for air. And even when you get that first breath, you're still terrified it's going to be taken away."

"You've had them?" I ask, surprised at how accurate his description of the feeling is.

He nods slowly, and it strikes me that this is the first person I've ever let see this part of me. *The new me anyway.* And it feels so damn good to share it with someone. To have someone understand me and empathize with me.

It sounds stupid, but it only serves to reinforce how very alone I've been.

"I have," he murmurs as he studies me. "I've experienced a lot of things. More than most to be honest. As of late, more bad than good. I just hope that next time you have one, you'll trust me to be there for you."

The need to offer a better explanation for my reaction earlier lingers in my mind. While saying I had a panic attack is partially right, it's far from the whole truth.

I open my mouth to say something, anything, but end up blurting out something that has nothing to do with the topic. "Work."

Damn nerves.

"Work?" He furrows his brow and chuckles. "What about it?"

"I don't know." I stand abruptly, needing to move, to walk, anything other than crawling into Crew's lap and holding on.

I'm a strong person. I learned through this whole experience that I don't need anyone. But I've also never met a man who wears his thoughts and heart on his sleeve as easily and as genuinely as Crew does.

And after today, after feeling so vulnerable, his sincerity over how I should trust him and let him be there for me gets to me.

It makes me want him that much more.

He tried to make me cupcakes.

He had his first parenting breather without his girls, and he chose to come and check on me.

Crew's chair scrapes on the floor as he stands and follows me the short distance into the family room.

"What departments or squads or whatever you call it did you work in?"

I reach down and pet Hani, who is staring at Crew like *who is this man in my house?*

"Cybercrime. Homicide. Sexual assault. Narcotics. A little bit of everything over the years."

Narcotics.

Of course, he worked narcotics.

I'd like to pretend that Kaleo was based out of San Francisco so a cop from Chicago might have no clue who he was, but his trial was covered nationally. His collar was a huge feather in the DEA's cap, and they wanted the US citizens to know it.

"What else about my *work* do you want to know?"

"Tell me about a memorable call." I adjust the blinds and turn to face him. He's taken a seat on the arm of the couch, a curious look on his face as he tries to read me.

Good luck with that one.

"That's what you want to know? A memorable call?"

"Yep. A funny one."

He darts his tongue out to wet his lower lip, and again, my brain—and other parts of my body—go into overdrive.

"We responded to a call in an upper-class, suburban neighborhood. A lady called, frantic. She swore her neighbor was being assaulted. *Murdered* is what she told the 911 operator. She said she heard some yelling, some weird noises, then her male neighbor screaming for help. She was too scared to try the doors and go in, afraid the perp might still be there."

"I'm afraid to ask what you found."

"We roll up, breach the door, and"—he starts chuckling—"we'll just say that the owners of the house had been having some *fun.* She was tied up to the four corners of the bed. Consensual, nothing criminal there, but apparently, mid-stroke, the husband's back went out. He was laid out on top of her and couldn't move in all his latex-clad glory."

"Oh. My. God."

"Yep." He chuckles like he still can't believe it even now. "Needless to say, we let the paramedics handle the . . . dismount, so to speak. And we waited for a female officer to untie the wife."

I'm blushing for the couple.

I'm also noticing the firmness of his thighs and how they frame the arm of the couch.

"I would die."

He quirks an eyebrow, eyes locked on mine as a crooked smile ghosts his lips. "It's just sex, right? Everybody does it."

His words hang in the air between us, my tongue suddenly heavy.

"Where are the girls?"

Classic, awkward Tennyson is back.

"Phoebe, one of the friends they made the other day when I took them to the park, called. Or texted rather, because who calls anyone these days?" He rolls his eyes dramatically just like the girls do, and I laugh. "I met her mom—I actually remember her from the last time I was here *when I was ten.* They invited the girls to go to the movies with them."

"That was nice of them."

"It was. I hemmed and hawed over it, called Uncle Ian to make sure the family was okay and that he knew them, and then figured what did it hurt? Besides, with the rumor mill in this town, if the girls misbehaved or something bad happened, I'm sure I'd hear about it before they got home."

"Ever the police officer checking backgrounds," I tease and then wonder if he's done the same of mine. I wouldn't put it past him. It's not like he's going to find anything interesting.

"What can I say? It's a habit."

"Wait. Does that mean you get time to yourself?"

"Four glorious hours." His eyes dart down to my breasts and then back up to mine as I take a few steps toward him.

"Four, huh?"

"Four." He nods.

I can think of a lot of things that can be done in four hours. Things that would erase this terrible day from my head. Things that would occupy my body so I didn't have a chance to think.

And by the look on Crew's face, his thoughts align with mine.

"Crew." I step in between his knees. With my height and his position, we're almost eye to eye.

"Hmm?"

"Thank you for today." I place my hands on his thighs. Feel them tense.

He angles his head to the side and studies me. "I think we covered the thank yous already."

I lean in and love the hitch of his breath as I bring my lips to his ear and say, "It's been a rough day. *Distract me.*"

I take the initiative this time. Desperate to feel. Needing to shut out the noise. Wanting him in a way I haven't wanted anyone since I started this life as Tennyson West.

Our lips meet. Slow at first. Searching. Feeling each other out as his hands slide around and span the width of my back. They feel so big there, so commanding, when his kiss is quite the opposite. It's tenderness laced with a simmering hunger. Desire edged with a restrained desperation.

I like the feel of his chest beneath my palms. The coarseness of his stubble as my hands run against his jaw and over his shoulders so I can thread my fingers through his hair. The intoxicating groan that begins in the back of his throat as our tongues meet and our bodies melt against one another's.

His hands slide up my back until one is in my hair, tugging my head back so our kiss breaks. "I'm going to hate myself for saying this." Another brush of his lips against mine. The kiss so potent that my entire body leans into him, against him, wanting more from him. He scrunches his face up briefly before sighing. "I feel . . . today was a rough day. I didn't come here for this. I don't want you to think I'm taking advantage of you because of it. That I'm the type of guy who would—"

"You are not taking advantage of me, Crew."

"Tennyson . . ." My name is a strained string of syllables. "How can I be sure?"

I reach out and run my hand over his cock, his whole body tensing at the contact. "Because I'm going to be the one taking advantage here." I run my tongue over his bottom lip.

"You are?"

"Uh-huh. I'm going to use this, *use you*, to make me forget my day." I meet his eyes and love seeing them darken with the lust his hardened cock reacts to. "Are you going to keep me waiting?"

I pull my shirt over my head and let it hang on the end of my finger before lifting an eyebrow and walking down the hallway to my bedroom.

Chapter Eighteen

Tennyson

I DON'T EVEN REACH THE DOOR BEFORE CREW'S HANDS WRAP AROUND my waist and pull me against him. His lips find the curve of my neck and the warmth of them mixed with the scrape of his stubble sends my nerves into overdrive.

"You think that's all it takes to drive me wild?" A kiss to my bare skin there. "You're sadly mistaken." A gentle nip.

"No?" I murmur as I sink into the feel of him pressed against my back. "Then what does it take?"

"All you had to do was open the door."

I bark out a laugh that turns into a yelp when he uses my belt loops as a means to spin me around so I'm forced to face him.

God, he's gorgeous.

And shirtless.

Guess I'm not the only one who took their shirt off and walked down the hall.

"The door? That's it?"

"The door. Oreos on a porch. Toasting our ice cream cones. Your smile." He jostles his head from side to side and grins. "Basically, just you."

"Lucky for me then."

"I think I'm the lucky one."

And with those words, Crew dives his hands into my hair and brings his mouth to mine. It's a soul-searing, body-heating, panty-wetting kiss that leaves me gasping for air when his lips break from mine.

"Jesus, Ten. You kiss me like that again, and you just might end up being thrown on the bed and taken advantage of."

"Yes. Please." It's my turn to return the favor. My hand at the back of his neck. His hard, jean-clad cock pressed firmly against me. The sweet, oak taste of his brandy as our tongues dance with each other's. The soft slide of his hands as they move up my back and begin unclasping my bra.

"I'm warning you," he murmurs between kisses before doing just what he threatened to do. In one fell swoop, with our mouths barely breaking from the kiss, Crew scoops me up with his hands on my ass and my legs wrapped around his waist before diving onto the bed.

Both of us together.

We land with a thud accentuated by our laughter and then emphasized with my moan as his lips close around one of my nipples and his hand kneads at the other.

"Not very graceful," he says as he looks up at me from between my breasts, "but when you're as desperate as I am to be inside of you . . . grace goes out the fucking window."

My body aches for more of his touch. For more of his taste. To feel every inch of him—inside and out.

His mouth closes around my other nipple, and I emit a laugh-filled moan. "I don't need grace, Madden. I just need you." An arch of my back as his teeth scrape over a sensitive peak. "And for us to have been smarter and taken our jeans off before we lay down."

Crew's laugh rings out. "Are you doubting my skills?"

He's up and off the bed in seconds, his hands on my ankles and yanking me toward its edge. With our eyes on each other's, we both fumble with our own buttons and zippers. But whereas I'm unable to pull my pants off because he's standing between my legs, Crew does just that.

He pushes his jeans down, and when he stands up, I'm rendered speechless. Yes, I've seen the man shirtless and know just what I'm getting myself into . . . but seeing him like this—the entirety of him—is on a whole other level.

Those chiseled muscles continue everywhere his clothes normally cover. To the deep V of his hips and the darkened scar that only serves to highlight his otherwise perfection. To the firmness of his thighs that I crave to feel pressed against mine.

And let me not forget to acknowledge his incredibly impressive cock standing at attention.

No woman would see it for the first time and not acknowledge that it's a thing of beauty.

Least of all a woman who's been in a dry spell and is about to get pleasured by it.

When I look back up to meet his eyes, the half-cocked smirk he gives me, highlighted by his lust-darkened eyes, is a seduction in and of itself.

I itch to touch him. To taste him. To run my tongue over every dig and striation of those well-earned muscles. To feel them tense as he's about to come.

"My turn," he murmurs as he begins to tug at the waist of my jeans. I lift my hips as he tugs them down and off. His breath and the graze of his eyes over my body ignites a tiny thousand fires beneath my skin. "Christ."

It's a lone, groaned word that holds so much dark promise.

"Do you know what I've dreamt of doing to you? The places I want to kiss? The things I want to lick? The pleasure I want to give? The sounds I want you to make? *Do you, Tenny?*"

Chills chase over my bared skin at his words. At the look in his eye and the taunting smile on his lips.

"You're not the only one."

His smile widens, tempts and teases, as he crawls over me. A kiss to my knee. A slide of a hand up my other thigh. A kiss to the dent of my hip. A brushed thumb over my clit that has me arching my back and fisting the sheets.

"Tell me how it feels," he murmurs, his lips pressed to the curve between my hip and my thigh. "Tell me what you want."

"You. God. *You.*"

The anticipation has been so high, the want building day by day, the desperation I have for his touch so fraught, that I know I won't take much to detonate.

He lifts his head so that our eyes meet as his fingers find me. Arouse me. Seduce me with their deft dexterity and the buttons they push. A tease of friction on my clit. A slide to my slickness beneath. A guttural groan from him as he tucks two fingers inside my wet core followed by my blissful moan as his slow and steady movements hit each and every spot I need to be hit.

Crew watches me. Every sensation that flickers over my face. Every stuttered moan I emit. Every flutter of my lashes as I sink into the bliss his fingers give.

There's an intimacy in the look. In his touch. In this darkened room and our soft sighs.

"You're gorgeous." He kisses his way up my torso. "Stunning." His lips take their time to taste my nipples once again. "Sexy." They slide to the curve of my neck and then to the tip of my earlobe, his warm breath sliding over my skin. "I want to make you come." His lips find mine again. "I want to make you lose yourself so you can forget everything about today except for this." Another kiss. "*Except for me.*"

My body burns bright. From the tease of his kiss to the skill of his hand.

"Crew." His name is a plea to give me the one thing I want. His chuckle lets me know I've been heard.

Within seconds, Crew protects us and positions himself back between my legs, his hands on my thighs as he pushes his way ever so pleasurably, slowly into me.

Our joint moans of satisfaction fill the room as I stretch to accommodate him, and he fights to control the carnal need to race to the finish.

Crew leans forward, cupping the back of my neck, and kisses me. He takes a sip from them, his tongue sliding in and out of my mouth as he begins to do the same with his cock.

"Jesus, Tenny. You feel incredible," he murmurs against my lips. Our groans become one as he moves slowly at first, his exhale my next inhale. Our hands roam—over sweat-misted, chill-chased skin, gripping and grabbing and needing the feel of our fingertips over each other. Our bodies meet in the most carnal of ways. In. Out. Gripped hair and curled toes. Hips lifted and backs arched. Gazes met and teeth sunk into bottom lips.

"Crew . . ." The next push in steals my breath. "Feels so good."

The pleasure builds then Crew eases up so it floats back down. A lull of tenderness before he pushes us back up again with a quickened pace and a grind with his next thrust in.

"You're going to be the death of me," he laughs out as I squeeze around him, milking his orgasm to come. "Wouldn't I be so lucky to go like this."

Our lips meet again. Our hips slap together as he picks up the pace, driving us into oblivion. Our bodies tense as we edge toward the precipice.

And then the pleasure surges like a tidal wave. Bigger. More powerful. Undeniable until it pulls me under and swallows me whole. My breath held. My muscles taut. A charge of electricity jolting through me that feels like it never stops resonating.

The surge hits over and over.

Harder then softer, then an undertone that pulses through me.

I'm lost in myself. In the way Crew has made me feel—mentally and physically—that it takes Crew's own guttural groaned "*Fuck*," to pull me from the haze of my orgasm.

I watch him as he comes. Shoulders tense, tattoos dancing with the flex of his biceps, tendons in his neck taut as he throws his head back and pistons his hips into me as he chases his own release.

He's a sight to behold.

And watching what I do to him turns me on all over again. But it's the way he comes down from his high that's even sexier.

It's the skim of his hands back up my hips. To my waist. To beneath my back so he can bring me against him so that when he collapses on the bed, he's able to pull my body on top of his.

My head is on his chest, and his hand plays with my hair as our hearts decelerate.

As we soak each other and the moment in.

As we realize from here on out, nothing will stay the same.

Chapter Nineteen

Crew

JESUS.

That was . . . unexpected. Heaven. *Fucking incredible.*

I mean . . . if that's what baking Tennyson some cupcakes will do, I'll start looking for a place in town to buy her a whole fucking bakery.

I move from the window where, *yep*, I'm staring in the direction of her house. I can't see it, but hell if that doesn't stop me from thinking about her and reliving every dick-hardening moment of the past few hours.

Truth be told, isn't that what I've been fantasizing about doing with her for the past few weeks? Of course, it is. Was it better than what my imagination had thought it would be? Most definitely.

And if it weren't for the girls coming home soon, I probably would have found a way to extend those hours to have more time with her.

The best part? There was no awkwardness when I kissed her goodbye at the doorway. No moment of regret. Just a look back over my shoulder and a sigh as I tried to process how damn incredible she is. It was.

And possibly how much I want to do it all over again.

I read the text from Dusty again. "She's squeaky clean. Never married. No kids. Not even an unpaid parking ticket or missed jury duty to her name. You're good to go with her."

Never married.

Was I hoping that she had been? That there was an ex-husband I could look up so I could make his life miserable for whatever damage has been done to Tenny? So I had someone to place the blame on?

But then that would mean she'd had a husband. That she'd loved someone else enough to take their name and promise her future with.

You're talking crazy shit, Crew.

You have a past. One with a shit ton of baggage. Clearly, she has one too.

And why am I even thinking any of this? You had sex. She's a great person. You enjoy her company.

That's it.

My cell rings with the girls' specific ringtone. "How was the movie?" I ask.

"Awesome. The wizard won in the end but . . ." Addy drones on and gives me the entire plot in the way kids do even though I lost track of everything after the first minute.

"Sounds great," I say.

"So we have a question."

"Go on."

"Phoebe asked us if we could spend the night at her house. Her mom said it's okay, and you can talk to her to make sure, but please, Dad? Can we?"

I chuckle. Of course, they ask after I've already left Tenny's house. Seems perfectly accurate when it comes to the sex life of a single parent.

"Sure, you can stay. Do I need to run you over some clothes? Toothbrushes? That kind of thing?"

A muffled conversation takes place that I can't make out. "No. We're good. She has extra toothbrushes. We brought sweatshirts since the theater was cold and can wear those tomorrow."

"You sure?" My parent mind goes to things like clean underwear and sports bras, hairbrushes, and deodorant.

"We're sure."

I spend the next few minutes playing cell phone tag as I talk to Phoebe's mother, verifying the invitation, then to both Paige and Addy about being on their best behavior.

When I hang up, I look around the house a little lost. I can't remember the last time I actually had an entire night to myself. Since the incident, the girls have been super clingy, always afraid to leave me alone.

There have been the few times that my mom or sister have talked them into staying over, but that came with several phone calls throughout the night to make sure that I was okay. To make sure I was still here.

This is progress. Wanting to stay away. Not fearing that I'm going to get hurt or leave them since they've had a lot of both things in the past eighteen months.

Maybe my decision to come here, to give them a change of scenery, and our family a chance to heal without any reminders of my ordeal or their mother picking up and leaving, was the right move. God knows I stressed over it.

But a few weeks here and they're already fine with spending the night at someone's house.

It's one of the rare times as a parent that I actually feel like I made the right decision.

I know the feeling won't last long, so I'll soak it up while I can.

Well, Dusty did his deed for me. Since I have an empty house, it's either sit and think about Tenny all night or return the favor.

I know which one I'd prefer.

The knock on the door is unexpected. Especially since I didn't see any headlights come up the drive.

That means it should only be one person.

And I'm not disappointed when I swing open the door to find Tenny standing there with a sheepish smile. Her hair is pulled up in a messy bun, and her lips are still slightly swollen from earlier. From me. The caveman in me loves seeing it and knowing I did that.

"Hi." My grin is automatic. Having her on my porch is way more exciting than a deep dive into someone's cyber activity.

"Hi." That coy smile of hers has my balls drawing up. "It seems a pipe burst in my place, and I figured maybe I could come take a shower in yours."

God. Damn.

"You did, did you?"

"I did." She nods slowly and looks over my shoulder, presumably to see if the girls are around.

"Good thing I have all my showers free since I just found out the girls are spending the night at their new friend's house."

Her eyes fire, and her smile widens. "So your four hours just became twelve?"

I nod and take a step backwards. "They did indeed."

She steps forward. "A lot can be done in twelve hours, you know."

"It can."

My eyes sweep up and down the length of her body as her sweatshirt slips off her bare shoulder sans any bra strap.

The strangled moan she emitted earlier when I closed my mouth over her nipple echoes in my head, and I'm already getting hard.

She runs a finger down the middle of my chest as she steps even closer. "I don't mean to be forward, but . . ."

"Why stop now?" I pull her against me, our lips inches apart, our breaths mingling together. "I'm a strong man, Tenny, and I don't get offended by a woman taking what she wants. In fact, I find it to be quite the turn-on."

"In that case"—her lips brush over mine—"time's a wasting."

Chapter Twenty

Tennyson

STUDY CREW IN THE EARLY MORNING HOURS JUST BEFORE THE GRAY sky puts on a show with its soft pastels and then bright oranges. He's facing me, his head on the pillow, his body uncovered down to his hip, and his lips with the barest hint of a smile as he dreams whatever it is he's dreaming.

I wonder if it's of me.

The thought comes easily. Naturally. And when I normally would over-analyze everything about that thought, somehow I don't. Instead, I sink into the pillow, enjoy the feeling of having him beside me, the contentment of some damn good sex, and relive everything about last night.

Sitting in my house last night, wishing Crew could have stayed and then realizing no car had come up the driveway to drop the girls off. Then summoning up the moxie to come up here, and if I'm honest, ask for more.

I scrunch my nose at the thought.

I've never been that forward in my life. I've never wanted to be . . . and yet with Crew . . . it just feels like things are different. In the short time I've known him, he's made it okay to be both strong and weak. To own both.

My eyes trace over the tattoo that goes from his bicep to his shoulder. The one that masterfully covers the scar of a bullet wound. One I would have never noticed unless my own tongue hadn't slid over it. One my own mouth hadn't kissed.

Because the shower was nice. Soapy, slippery hands. A cold shower wall against my back. A seat he hoisted one of my legs up on to open me up while he used his mouth to explore and pleasure and masterfully destroy my senses.

Then the conversation after when we were wrapped in towels, sitting cross-legged on the bed with glasses of wine in hand.

"So much for sticking to my guns," Crew says as he eyes me above the rim of his glass. His hair is half dry with its wavy locks falling every which way, the corners of his mouth curling up.

"About?"

"You."

"Me?" I say in mock surprise while secretly wanting to know more.

"Yes, you." He huffs out a laugh. "I'm pretty sure I wanted this to happen from that first bite of horrible pea-ridden lasagna, but I swore I couldn't let it happen. That I couldn't complicate my life more than it already is."

"Should I be offended that you're calling me a complication?" I say and laugh.

"In all the best ways."

Crew leans forward and kisses me with a casualness that seems so natural I don't give it a second thought.

"Truth?"

"Truth."

"I may have had the same thoughts as we ate Oreos on the front porch." I purse my lips and nod. "And I also might have told myself it was ridiculous to want the hot landlord."

"Well, good." He gives a resolute nod. "At least we both know we suck at resisting each other."

"They do say resistance is futile."

"Tell whoever they are, that they're right because I'm going to want a lot more of this," he says and then smothers my laugh when he leans forward and presses his lips to mine. He tastes of wine and desire, and my insides melt from the sensation overload of the last few hours.

"No complaints about that on my end."

"Good to know." He kisses me again.

"Another truth?"

"Lay it on me."

"I convinced myself I didn't need this, that it didn't matter . . . but after tonight, I've been proven wrong."

"Care to define this and it for me?" He narrows his eyes, and his playful smile makes butterflies take flight.

I take the hand he holds out and twist my fingers with his. "Sex. Physicality. Companionship. Connection."

"Everybody needs it." He squeezes. "Why would you want to deny yourself that?"

I shrug and try to explain it the only way I can. "The past has a way of screwing with you."

"Don't I know it." The wink he gives me makes me feel less stupid for admitting it. "Which, truth be told, is probably the same reason I was trying to stick to my guns and avoid you."

"I'm glad you didn't."

"Me too." Another kiss that ends with his hand on the side of my face and our foreheads resting against each other's. "Since we're putting it all out there, I do need to address the elephant in the room."

I lean back so I can meet his eyes. "What's that?"

"The girls." His sigh is reticent. "I wouldn't be a good father if I didn't talk about . . ."

"About?"

"I know I might be jumping the gun in saying this because this has just happened and who knows what happens next, but they really like you, Tenny. Like they talk about you all the time, like you."

"Okay." I say the word but silently revel in hearing this. It's always nice to be liked—but by tween girls? That's a feat in and of itself.

Teaching people in their late teens and early twenties at the studio was one thing. I could relate easily to them. But being an only child and never really having a chance to babysit or interact with younger kids, I never knew how I'd be.

To say I wanted kids with Kaleo is an understatement. It was one of the only things we argued over. He wanted to wait. He tried to tell me that my dancing and teaching days would be over if I got pregnant and that we should hold off.

But that never lessened my desire to have them. Lucky for me, we didn't.

Like they talk about you all the time, like you.

My smile grows even wider.

"They may seem well-adjusted, but they've been through a lot in the last eighteen months. Me in the hospital, their mom up and leaving them. I just don't want them to get too attached to you, to think that we're more than we are, and then get hurt again and think yet another person they love is leaving them."

"The fact that this even crosses your mind makes me like you even more, Crew Madden." I set my wine glass down and crawl over his lap so my thighs are on either side of his. "It makes you even sexier than you already are."

"I thought the word you used earlier was hot."

"That too." I wrap my arms around his neck while his hands cup my ass.

"We'll keep this from the girls until you want to say something, if you ever do. As for now, we're just . . . friendly neighbors."

I'm not sure why it hits so hard that even if we wanted more—which is insane to even think about after only one night together—that's all we'll ever really be able to be. Friendly neighbors. *He's here for the summer, and I have my whole host of baggage I can't burden someone else with.*

So we both better get used to being—

I suck in a breath, completely distracted from my overthinking, as his lips close over the spot right beneath my ear.

"Hey, neighbor?" he murmurs.

"Hmm," I practically moan.

"I'm about to borrow some of your sugar. I hope you don't mind."

His lips close over the peak of my breast. "Borrow away."

I don't fight my smile because while no one else can see it right now, it feels good to do it. To have a reason to do it.

And I definitely don't stop myself from visually tracing the lines of his ridiculous abs to where the sheet rests at the very end of his happy trail. Even scarred and sewn back together, Crew is beautiful.

The man definitely knows how to change things up. Each time we came together last night was different. We did the *greedy, needy* sex. The *slowed down and take a bit more time* sex. The *this is funny, we've bumped our heads, we've misaimed where things need to go, we can't stop laughing* sex.

Maybe I enjoyed all the phases of the night because the last time I had sex was with Kaleo. For a month, the act was a necessary evil to endure. Until he was arrested, it was a way to survive without him knowing of *my* betrayal. An improvisation of epic means to hide my repulsion when the man I'd stopped loving wanted to touch and pleasure me.

I was terrified each time he touched me that I'd hesitate and he'd somehow know.

I shiver at the memories I'd much rather erase from my brain.

But right now, in this moment, that time feels so far away. So long ago. Especially when I'm staring at a man I thought would be a hard-ass but is really anything but.

"You should stay here." He pants the words out as we come down from our last orgasm.

"What do you mean I should stay here?"

"At the house. Here. In the room down the hall."

"Um . . . I don't even know what to say about that."

"They're going to have to tear up the hardwood floor. Cut out the drywall. The water will be off for some time while this all happens. It would just be easier if you and Hani stayed here."

I'm not exactly sure how I'm supposed to respond. It's one thing to have an incredible night of sex with someone, but it's a whole other thing to move in with them. It makes finding out what drives you crazy about them that much quicker. It makes the newness wear off that much faster. It makes—

"I can hear you overthinking from here, Tennyson. I'm not asking you to move in for the summer or anything permanent like that. Just while they fix the shit that broke in your house because I didn't get down there in time." He reaches out and rests a hand on my lower abdomen. A casual gesture that somehow feels so very intimate. "The girls would love it. It'd be nice to have some intelligent adult conversation on things other than what's trending and how to do a Swedish braid."

"You mean Dutch braid?"

"Yeah. That." He chuckles. "See? I need more adult interaction. That, and you'd get more horrible cooking and baking. That's all. Nothing else."

"Nothing else?" I ask, suggestion laced in those two words.

"Well"—I can hear his smile in his voice—"unless you want something else."

"It might complicate things with the girls under the same roof."

"Or it might make it more fun." He leans over and kisses my bare shoulder. "Think about it."

Chapter Twenty-One

Tennyson

"**T**HE GIRLS."

I awake to Crew's startled words, followed by the sound of a car door slamming. We both bolt out of bed, half-awake and seriously sleep deprived from all our exertions last night.

Laughter bubbles up. I can't help it when in the chaos of trying to find my clothes, I look up and see Crew. He's standing in the middle of the room, hair rumpled, a pillow crease on his cheek, and morning wood flying full-staff.

"Get dressed," I say and yelp when my foot gets hooked in the waist of my shorts. I fall over, landing with a resounding thud that has both of us laughing despite the frenzy we're both in the midst of.

Already with his shorts on, Crew effortlessly hauls me up from the floor and shoves the rest of my clothes into my hands. "Here."

Fighting more laughter, I start toward the bedroom door only to hear the front door open and a chorus of "Dad!" rings out and up the stairs.

Crew freezes, eyes wide, and mouth open. "I didn't lock the door," he mumbles. "Or set the fucking alarm." Then he looks around the room in panic. "The closet," he whisper-yells as he scoops up my shoes and purse and pushes me toward his closet.

"The closet?"

"Yes. *Please.*" He presses a brusque, appeasing kiss to my lips. "I'll figure something out. Give me a few minutes," he says seconds before I'm bathed in darkness when he closes the louvered doors.

Through the angled slats, I watch Crew rush out of the room while pulling a T-shirt over his head.

Oh my God.

The visual of Crew naked and panicked hits me again, and I have to hold a hand over my mouth to smother the laughter I've lost the battle fighting.

This is really happening. I never snuck around with boys when I was a teenager, so I guess I'm crossing off that rite of passage a little later in life.

Thirty years old and I'm hiding in a closet. Talk about new experiences.

I do my best to finish getting dressed without falling or making any sounds, but it's damn hard in the small space. That and the hilarity of the situation hits me at the oddest times, and I struggle with more laughter.

Time passes in the clomps of feet up the stairs. In the sounds of voices drifting down the hall. In the car driving away. In the text that Crew sends telling me to wait just a few more minutes. *Thank God my phone was on silent.*

And while I know what's going on, those minutes feel like hours. I've scrolled through social media. I've checked my email. I've played a few games.

I freeze when the girls walk down the hall. "Dad didn't make his bed?" Addy says, stopping to look inside the bedroom. "That's a first."

"He's acting weird," Paige says. "Guess that means we don't have to make ours then."

"Dream on," Crew says, his footsteps heavy on the stairs. "Go on. Take your showers and get cleaned up."

"Can't we just jump in the pool?" one of them asks.

"Nope. Showers. Now."

Some grumbling follows, but a few minutes later I can hear the pipes creak as the water turns on.

Crew waits a few minutes before jogging into the bedroom and opening the doors. He laughs when he sees me standing there, framed by his clothes. "I'm so sorry," he whispers, glancing over his shoulder, his grin still there. "They're in the shower. The mom fed them kale pancakes or some shit like that, so I promised them breakfast in town. Let's get you out of here while they're getting ready."

Within a minute, we're down the stairs, and he's ushering me out the front door. "I'm sorry it ended like this." He holds my face in his hands and presses his lips to mine as his curve up in a smile. "But damn it was fun."

"It was." I step back, our fingers linked as I take a few steps away. "See you later."

"Later, Crew."

I walk down the driveway with the goofiest of grins on my face.

I've never had a walk of shame like this before.

Best part about it? There's no shame at all.

Chapter Twenty-Two

Crew

"**D**AD?"

"Hmm?" I'm distracted and for good measure. While the French toast at The Diner is some of the best I've had in a long time, and you won't find me complaining about my breakfast guests, my mind keeps flashing back to last night. To this morning.

And to the woman I was with and the casual intensity of it all.

"Why was Tenny's sweatshirt on the back of the couch this morning?" Addy asks, her stare unwavering.

I choke on my sip of coffee and then blame it on the temperature. "God, that's hot," I lie as I try to recover. "She um . . . she came up last night to brush her teeth and stuff since she doesn't have any water at her place."

"Oh. *Huh*," Paige says and looks over to Addy.

Are they buying it?

Do they believe me?

"We were curious because you put that camera app on our phone. It went off last night when we were at Phoebe's, and we saw her walking up the driveway. It just never alerted that she left."

Mother. Fucker.

My mouth goes dry as I fumble for a reasonable explanation, all the while freaking out over what the hell they might have seen this morning on their phone when she left.

Our kiss? Tenny disheveled and laughing as she walked down the driveway?

"Really?" I ask. "She wasn't there long. Maybe the app needs to be updated. Let me see your phones for a sec."

My palms grow clammy as both girls hand over their phones. With them staring at me, I stealthily go into the app on each phone and delete the motion alert this morning which, plain as day, shows Tenny walking down the driveway toward her house.

Evidence erased; I hand them back. "There. I updated them for you. They should be good to go now."

Note to self: pause the cameras next time Tenny comes over so you don't get caught.

Because there will be a next time.

"Speaking of Tenny," I say. "I wanted to run something by you."

"Like what?"

"I've offered for her to come and stay in one of the spare bedrooms for a few days. The repairs on the cottage might take a bit of time and she—"

"Did she say yes?" Addy asks, eyes wide, excitement evident.

"I don't know. I haven't talked to her today." Another lie. I'm definitely going to hell. "I put the offer out there to her. We'll see if she takes me up on it."

"Please make her take it," Addy says.

"We might get some decent cooking then."

I throw my balled-up napkin at Paige. "Hey."

"I know, I know. You do your best." Paige rolls her eyes. "But I mean . . ."

"I never claimed to be a chef. Not by any means. Your mom . . ." I clear my throat to cover for my stall. "Your mom was the culinary wizard. Not me."

Silence falls over the table, and I wonder if I'm doing them a disservice by not talking about their mom more. It just seems like every time I do, they grow sullen and it takes more than a while to snap them out of it.

The department therapist tells me this is normal. But am I doing enough for them? Am I doing it all wrong? Am I fucking them up more than their mom's desertion did?

That's the shitty thing about parenting. You only know if you did it right about twenty years too late.

Both of their heads are angled down, looking at their plates of food.

Fuck.

"So uh, girls. Look at me, please." Both reluctantly lift their eyes to me. "I know I've said this before, but it's okay to talk about your mom. It's okay to be happy over memories we had. It's normal to want it to be like it used to be. And it's perfectly normal to be angry and pissed at the both of us too—"

"Why would we be mad at you?" Paige asks. I know they act old, but right now, in this moment, it hits me how young they are, and the upheaval—the trauma—they've experienced in such a short amount of time.

It takes me a second to find the words. To swallow the acrid bitterness toward a woman I once loved and now despise for doing this to our family. To be mature and honest even when it pains me to a fault. "It takes two people to make a marriage work, and it takes two people to make one not work. We're both at fault, so it's okay to be mad at me too."

Damn you, Brittney. Damn you for making me have the hard discussions with them and explain why they didn't mean enough for you to stay.

They both nod quietly.

"I also don't want you to think that if you want to see her, it's going to hurt my feelings. Okay?"

"Okay," they say in unison.

My heart is heavy as I focus on my food, darting glances at them, every few seconds to see that they are doing the same.

I've failed them in so many ways on this.

This isn't a scraped knee I can bandage up and then kiss to make it feel better. This is a defining moment in my girls' lives that I can't fix for them no matter how much I smile or love them or try to.

"Dad," Paige murmurs.

I look up to see both girls staring at me with those eyes of theirs that have owned me since the first time they looked into mine in the delivery room.

"Trust fall," Addy whispers, to which they both nod.

Emotion lodges in my throat as I look at my girls telling me to trust them. Telling me that no matter how far I fall, they too will catch me.

Jesus. When did they become such incredible human beings?

"Trust fall," I say back to them with a ghost of a smile and a heart bursting with love.

The silence lasts only a few seconds longer before they return to their chatty selves as I try to decipher every word and every look between them to make sure they are really okay and not just pretending for my sake.

Talk turns to their birthday party as we head toward the car. The kind of cake they want. The few new friends they've made that they want to invite. Over whether they should throw it before or after Founder's Day.

Chatter on the way home covers their first art and dance lessons Tenny has offered to take them to this week. To the new book series they want to read. To if they think they can talk Tenny into staying with us and bringing Hani with her when she does.

I act indifferent but hell if I'm not rooting for the same thing too.

And a few minutes after we get home, we get our answer.

Tenny drives up and parks her Jeep next to my truck. "Does the offer still stand?" she asks as she stares at me out the window, Hani in a carrier on the seat beside her.

By the cheer the girls emit, I think she has her answer.

"We'll bring Hani's stuff in," they say as they carry the carrier and a bag of items into the house.

"I guess they're excited," she murmurs around her smile.

"They're not the only ones," I say, fighting the urge to kiss her. "It's going to be harder than hell keeping my hands off you."

Her laugh floats through the air. "You invited this torture on yourself, and I intend to have so much fun tormenting you with it."

Chapter Twenty-Three

Tennyson / Tessa

Four Years Earlier

A TRIP TO PANAMA.

Two days later as we docked the yacht in the harbor, while I worried about where the men's bodies disappeared to and where the drugs were currently being held, he told me he had to leave for an urgent trip to Panama. Something about cargo on a barge that was being held up, and he was the only one who could fix the situation. Lies I'm sure, but I went along with them and acted upset while silently counting down the minutes until he climbed aboard our private jet and it taxied down the runway.

"Just us, Ku'uipo. Always. Just. Us."

"Always, Kaleo."

His parting words. His reminder that there is no way out for me now. His hold over me is still strong, but in such a contradicting way now.

But his absence offers me a reprieve. A moment where I no longer have to hide my complete and utter devastation. A respite where I don't have to force a smile on my lips or welcome the touch of a man I no longer know. A man I no longer want to know.

But leaving Kaleo Makani, divorcing him, is not an option.

That much I know.

And every time I think of a way leaving him might be possible, I hear Sebastian begging. I hear the echoed gunshot and the *thud* of his body collapsing. I hear Kaleo's chuckle as Sebastian lay there dying.

I can't continue to live this life. To live this lie. To have the media and the public—*my friends*—look at us and think he's just a shipping magnate and I'm just a ballerina who teaches at the San Francisco Ballet School.

Hell, he's leaving for Panama. How many other people's lives are now in danger when he arrives there? How many other people's lives is he poisoning with the drugs he's making? Distributing? Hell if I know how he gets them.

But those are the what-ifs when all I can deal in is the knowns. Like how do I live with myself knowing I'm the reason those three men are dead? I asked them to stay. I convinced them to attend my party when they wanted otherwise.

I could have called out. Distracted Kaleo somehow. Maybe saved one of them from their fates?

Even I know that's unrealistic, but it doesn't stop the second-guessing and the reliving of the images in my head from playing.

Guilt.

Shock.

Disbelief.

Desperation.

All four have shared the never-ending eddy of thoughts in my head since the moment I peeked over that railing. The echoes of the gunshots still jolt me awake in a cold sweat at night.

I sit at the kitchen table, my food untouched, and a killer view of the Pacific out the window in front of me, but I don't see it. The fog is still there. The shock of what I witnessed still jarring. The implosion of my whole world still a dust cloud.

"Ma'am?"

I look up to see Rangi in the kitchen. He's just as imposing as Kaleo, maybe even more so with his broad shoulders, dark brown hair, and silent observation of every situation. The difference between him and Kaleo is that I know Kaleo won't hurt me. He may be a murdering bastard, but he still loves me.

Rangi, on the other hand, has no loyalty except to Kaleo.

Maybe that's why he left him here with me. To keep me in line. To make sure I don't do what I really want to do—*bolt*.

"Yes?" I finally respond.

"Kaleo thinks it's best if you stay at the house while he's gone. If you need anything—nails, hair, groceries—we'll have the technicians come here, or it'll be delivered."

I take a sip of my coffee. I don't flinch from its scalding temperature and the burn it inflicts because I deserve so much worse.

"Why?" I don't back down with my stare. Am I in danger because of what happened, or is Kaleo afraid I'm going to do what any sane person would do—go to the authorities?

"Just following orders." Rangi offers a barely-there smile that dares me to ask more. "I'll be in his office if you need me."

I nod and track him as he walks out of the kitchen door, down the long, floor-to-ceiling windowed hallway, to the opposite side of the house where Kaleo keeps an office when we're here in Maui.

"You don't like it?" Rose, our cook and head house manager, asks as she walks back into the kitchen and notices my untouched plate. I'm not the only one who's not a fan of Rangi. She makes sure to be where he's not.

I think of the blood seeping out onto the deck of the boat. "I don't seem to have an appetite these past few days."

"Can I hope that's because a little Makani is on the way?" she says with an excited shake of her shoulders.

"Afraid to disappoint you, Rose, but Kaleo isn't there yet."

"But you are." She pats my shoulder. "He'll get the bug. Don't you worry."

I offer a smile as I excuse myself and wander from room to room in the house. This house and all the memories in it are built on deception, manipulation, smoke and mirrors. On sleight of hand that I should have recognized but somehow . . . didn't connect the dots to.

Does our staff know the truth? There are at least twenty people we employ here—gardeners and staff and assistants—do they all know and laugh at me behind my back? Or worse, do they assume I know and am okay with it all?

The thought eats at me and pushes me to head upstairs to our quarters where a very select few are allowed to enter.

Just as I reach the top of the stairs, a phone rings in our bedroom. A ring I've never heard before. I move toward it, toward the cell phone sitting on the edge of my nightstand—right next to my cell phone.

I glance around as if this is some kind of practical joke. But the only proof that anyone has been in my room is the open balcony doors and its curtains billowing in the ocean breeze.

If I wasn't already on edge, now I'm on edge and paranoid.

With trembling hands, I pick up the cell phone and answer it. "Hello?"

"Blood is on your hands." The voice is deep and baritone, and his words have the hair standing up on the back of my neck.

"Who is this?" I whisper-yell as I look over my shoulder toward the hallway. No one is there.

He chuckles, and I focus on its sound as I try to steady my heartbeat. "All three of them dead, and you did nothing to stop them?" He tsks. "Did you help hide the bodies? Weigh them down so they became fish food? What about the drugs? Did you know you just transported five million in cocaine via that fancy yacht of yours?"

"Who. Is. This?" The words burn in my throat, and my mind races.

"You're in a world of trouble, Mrs. Makani."

Tears spill as my world turns over again for the second time in a few days. This cell phone. How did it get in my bedroom? Who put it here? Who am I talking to?

"Your silence tells me you already know that." A pregnant pause where my pulse is pounding in my ears is the only thing I hear. "There is a way to save yourself. To get out of the shitstorm you just landed in . . . or have you always known? Are you an accomplice to so much more?"

"I don't know what you're talking about," I eek out in an unsteady voice and wipe the tears off my cheeks.

"Yes, you do. The question you need to ask yourself is: who is more important? You? Kaleo? The men who died?"

"Everything okay?" I whip my gaze toward where Rangi is standing at the top of the landing, his eyes loaded with curiosity. Does he see my cell on the nightstand? Does he suspect something?

"Yes. Fine. It's . . . it's just one of my students." Don't over-explain. "She needs some personal advice on how to deal with another instructor."

He holds my gaze for a beat longer before nodding subtly and walking away.

"You there?" I ask when I'm met with silence.

"Interesting. *You lied for me.* That means you're scared. That means you want to do the right thing."

"What do you want?"

"You have what I need, and I have what you need."

"And what's that?"

"A way out. Immunity. *Protection*." I can practically feel this mystery man's smirk when he pauses. "I'll be in touch."

The call ends, and I sit down on my bed and wonder what in the fuck is going on.

"The question you need to ask yourself is who is more important? You? Kaleo? The men who died?"

How the hell did he know how to reach me?

Is there really a way to be free?

Chapter Twenty-Four

Tennyson

"SO YOU TWO MOVED IN TOGETHER?" BOBBI JO SMILES LIKE THE cat that ate the canary. "Well, *that* was quick. And to think you two were hiding this right under our noses all this time."

First. *Wow.* I've been there for a whole four days and the town already knows? The girls must have told someone who told someone who told someone.

Second, the Maddens have been in Redemption Falls for a few weeks. She acts like we've been having a fling for months.

"Good to see the rumor mill is still alive and strong and *wrong*," I say with a placating smile on my face but don't care to elaborate. The last thing I owe anyone, let alone Bobbi Jo, is answers to the question she's asking without putting words to—*is it true? Are you and Crew an item?*

Let her stew on it.

Let her guess.

Next, the town will say I'm knocked up with twins or something like that.

"Don't be so shy about it. We're all just a little jealous is all. It's not often we get new, handsome bachelors around here to gawk at." She taps my arm. "Now, where were you on securing sponsorships for the banners?"

I fill her in on the phone calls I've made and the vendors who have agreed to buy a banner to help sponsor and pay for some of the Founder's Day expenses. It's a cake job, really. Most vendors do it every year, and so it's merely a matter of doing the paperwork and collecting payments.

"Good. That's fabulous. I knew you'd be a great addition to the team."

"Thank you. Now where are the old banners again? I'd like to go through them and see if we have any we can reuse. We're getting short on time to get them made, so I need to take inventory."

"They're upstairs in the storage area. It's a total disaster up there." She mock shivers. "Stuff everywhere. It makes my OCD go absolutely haywire. *Hives. And. All.* I can always send one of the guys up there for you if you want."

"I'll figure it out. I'm resourceful."

"Of course, you are. I'll leave you to it then," she says, the clickety-clack of her heels following her as she goes.

I glance across the community center to where I've convinced Crew to come help build booths for the day. He's standing outside through the open doors, and I'm a tad distracted watching him work the hammer. With every swing, those muscles I know all too well contract and flex. I'd be lying if I said I haven't caught almost every other woman in here noticing it either.

Crew glances up, and his eyes meet mine. The look he gives me and the flash of his lightning-quick grin has that slow fire we've had on simmer start to burn.

To say living under the same roof with him is difficult would be a lie. In fact, the first week has been quite seamless. I edit during the morning hours while he plays handyman doing some of Ian's tasks. The girls swim and shoot and reshoot and then reshoot again their tutorials. Their laughter as they make them floats to wherever I'm working, and rather than distracting me, makes me smile.

In fact, after having lived on my own for the last two years, I thought living with someone else—let alone two eleven-year-old girls—might be sensation overload. Truth be told, I've been pleasantly surprised how much I've enjoyed having people and their noise around me.

Laughter. I never realized how much I've missed the sound of it, even if just in my periphery, until now. Until I'm working and I hear the deep rumble of Crew and the girls' higher-pitched tone. While it may be muted through my closed door, it brings an automatic smile to my face. It gives me something to look forward to when I'm done working.

And that is something I haven't had in the longest time.

It's welcome.

It's wanted.

And while the days have had an order that's kept me sane—work, the girls, mealtime—the nights have been more challenging as Crew and I have to be clandestine with our flirting. Glances across the room that are held longer than one would deem platonic. The brush of a hand over my lower back as he walks past me. An innuendo made that flies over the girls' heads.

But the following through on what that flirting promises has yet to happen. A stomachache one night led Addy to want Crew's attention. A late-night movie marathon hindered another. An excitement over me being there and a sleepover downstairs in a homemade fort another.

The lack of opportunity for us to have sex again has made the desire that much stronger. Has made this burn so much more intense.

To have the dessert you want right at your fingertips but not be able to taste it is a torture in and of itself.

So when Crew looks at me like he does across the distance, every part of me dares him to find some dark closet and have at it.

Desperation and me are becoming good friends.

"Tenny?"

"What? I'm sorry. I was lost in thought," I say, turning to find Tanya standing there with a smile on her lips. "What did you need?"

"It's photo time."

"Photo time?" I look around and see everyone being rounded up, including Crew and the guys working outside. "What for?"

"Can you believe Bobbi Jo got the *Daily Sentinel* to do a feature on Founder's Day?" she says with a little flutter clap. "It's the biggest newspaper in the state. Its circulation is . . . geez, I can't even imagine, but it's about ten thousand times more than the population of Redemption Falls."

"That's great news for all the vendors."

"Don't you know it. I told my hubby that we need to order extra *everything* for our booth." Her eyes light up with an excitement that is more than endearing. Clearly this is a much bigger deal than I thought it to be. "It's not often Redemption Falls gets any kind of love, so we're just over the moon with this development."

"It's great for the town and the festival."

She smiles and motions for me to follow her. "C'mon then."

"For what?"

"To be in the photo, silly. The paper wants all of us volunteers in the shot."

The smile I give her is strained. "That's okay. I don't need to be in the photo. It really should be all of you who have done this year after year."

"That's nonsense." She grabs my hand and pulls me to go over to the group of volunteers being staged for the photo.

The last thing I need is for my face to be splashed on some newspaper and website. My hair color may be different, but everything else is the same. Most people would be able to spot someone they'd lived with day in, day out, been intimate with, and woke up next to for years.

Crew catches my arm as I try to head toward the back row where I'm hoping I can successfully hide myself behind other volunteers.

"Hey. Where are you going?"

"I'll be right back. I just need to ask Kelly something real quick," I say and immediately hate myself for lying.

Crew gives me a confused look but releases my arm.

I purposely get lost in the confusion as the photographer stages people. The process takes so long that I silently slip away before the actual photo is taken, heading up the stairs to the storage room to find the banners.

Bobbi Jo was right. The storage room is a vast cavern of chaos. I can't find the light switch, but there's enough light coming in from the numerous skylights that I can see well enough.

There is row after row of shelving units. Some are overflowing with random items ranging from sports equipment to theater props to catering equipment. As I walk aisle by aisle, it's clear that there is no rhyme or reason to the haphazard placement of what looks like a decade's worth of stuff.

And that's going to make finding the banners a difficult task, seeing as how they could be rolled up or folded and pushed to the back of a shelf where they can't be seen.

Since I'm already halfway into the room, I decide I'll start my search at the far end and make my way back toward the door. I'm only in my second aisle, opening the drawers of a long, low-profile cabinet, when I hear footsteps in the hallway. I tense for some reason, even though it's not like the boogeyman frequents the community center.

"Tennyson?"

I release the breath I was holding at the sound of Crew's voice. "Back here," I say.

His footsteps come closer until he clears the end of the aisle, his eyes narrowed and smile curious as he looks at me. "Are you hiding up here from the pink princess and her demands?"

"No. Yes." I throw my hands up. "Just trying to find old banners in this shitshow of a storage room."

"It is a mess," he says as he closes the distance toward me. "A big, disorganized mess. One that say, if you were missing for a few extra minutes, might be expected since it'll take some time to go through."

"Is that so?" I ask as he puts his hand on my back and pulls me against him.

"It is," he murmurs before closing his mouth over mine.

It feels like forever since we've kissed when, in reality, it's only been a couple of days. But I'm reminded immediately why those couple of days have been a struggle because this man . . . *his kiss* . . . is absolutely addictive.

In a matter of seconds, I'm drugged by the taste of him. By the feel of his hands running down my sides, cupping my ass, fingers grazing ever so slightly over my slit as he does before lifting me onto the cabinet I was just searching through.

"God, how I've been wanting to do this all day. Every day. The girls. They're everywhere." Each sentence said between demanding kisses. "Fuuuucck." He groans when I cup his rock-hard erection. And that one word spoken in his guttural growl is like an audible seduction when frankly, I don't need to be seduced at all.

Because he's right.

I've been wanting and waiting and desperate to have him again. To taste him in any capacity beyond a stolen kiss in the pantry. A subtle slide of a hand over my lower back. A salacious look across the dinner table when the girls aren't watching.

"I want you, Tenny. I haven't stopped wanting you or your kiss or *this*."

My hands making quick work of his button and zipper give him *my* answer. I want him too. He shudders as my hands grip the velvety hardness of his cock and pull him toward me.

"Have I ever told you how much I like your cock?"

His chuckle is a rumble through me as he steps back to push his pants down and then sucks in a hissed breath when I drop to my knees before him.

I take him into my mouth without warning, all the way to the back of my throat. His strangled groan and fingers twisting in my hair are all I need to know that he doesn't mind this little detour on the way to sex.

"Tenny. We're going to get caught."

I look up at him, his gray eyes burning bright, and say around him, "Do you want me to stop?"

"God. No. Definitely no." And those are the last words he can manage as I hollow out my cheeks and tighten my suction over him. His head falls back and thighs pull tight as I work him. Sensation chasing sensation. Tongue sliding over him after my lips release him momentarily. Hands pumping the base of his shaft as my warm mouth controls not only the moment, the act, but *him* too.

He begins fucking my mouth. I don't even think it's a conscious decision, but rather him getting lost in the pleasure I'm providing.

I can feel him growing harder, his balls tightening up, and then, without warning, he hauls me up and kisses me with reckless abandon. Like a man drowning and I'm his air. Like a man about to lose all his control.

And I revel in knowing I've done that to him. That I can make him feel just as incredible as he makes me feel.

"I want you, Ten. I need you. Now." Our mouths break apart as I shift back to sit on the cabinet, pull my maxi skirt up around my hips, and spread my legs for him.

I'm not sure if the groan he emits now or the one he gave when I wrapped my lips around his cock is sexier, but hell if I'm going to argue with either.

"Have I ever told you how much I like skirts?" he murmurs, his mouth in a crooked smile, and his eyes darkened from lust. He bends over so his face is between my positioned thighs and inhales. His groan has my nipples hardening to painful peaks. "You smell incredible." And before I can respond or process or react to those words, to the way they arouse every part of me, he closes his mouth over my fabric covered clit and sucks on it. The muted sensation is heaven and hell all in the same breath. It's a tease of what I want and the barrier preventing me from getting it.

"Crew. *Please.*" I say the words. Maybe I think them. All I know is they are screaming in my head over and over as his chuckle rumbles against me. Through me.

"I want this later." He pats a hand against my clit that sends shock waves of pleasure through me in a way I've never felt before.

"Promise?" I pant out.

"Oh, baby, you have no idea the things I'll promise to do to this body of yours."

Yes.

Please.

The sound of hollering downstairs through the closed door reaches us and breaks through our intimate fog. It reminds us that we're not alone. That we could easily get caught.

And fuck if that doesn't make this whole situation even hotter.

Crew stands to full height, his eyes focused on my wet panties before lifting to meet mine, one eyebrow raised. "You call this underwear?"

"You can call them whatever you want so long as you pull them to the side and fuck me right now."

"Yes, ma'am." He chuckles and then pushes into me, my strangled cry echoing off the dust floating through the air. "Christ," he mutters, dropping his forehead to my shoulder for a beat as sensations, as pleasure, as the feel of me wrapped around him, overwhelms him.

It's the scrape of my nails over his hips that brings him out of his desirous coma. It's the plea of his name that urges him to move. It's the clenching of my muscles around his cock that snaps him to the here. To the now. To the need that I have and the greed that I willingly admit to.

Within seconds, we're a fast and furious mess of nipped lips, my fingers digging into his biceps and his into my hips, and traitorous bodies trying to prolong the buildup before the fall but failing miserably.

We come in a torrent of hushed words.

Quiet.

Oh my God.

Shh.

Harder.

Faster.

Fuck me, Crew.

Hold on, Tenny.

I can't wait.

Come for me.

It's my riotous mewl that fills the room. It's his hand that covers my mouth to muffle the sound as he pounds into me, the table shaking beneath us as Crew's climax slams into him seconds after mine does me.

And it's then—when we're both riding the peak of pleasure, trying to stay quiet but turned on even more by the thought of being caught—that the table leg breaks beneath me.

Our yelps fill the empty room when in an instant the table slants and we both go tumbling into each other.

And then it's laughter. Pure, unfiltered laughter edged by the high of our orgasms, as Crew lies on top of me as I slide down and off the table, legs in the air, arms flailing.

We land in a thump on the ground, half undressed, cheeks flushed, bodies still climaxing, breaths panting, and laughter still slipping from our mouths.

Crew presses a kiss to my lips. A delve of the tongue. A nip of my bottom lip. "Promise me you'll wear those panties again later."

"I'll wear anything you want so long as you make me come like that again."

"Quickies are overrated," he murmurs and presses another kiss to my lips before standing and pulling me up off the floor.

"Definitely overrated."

"Tenny?" The call of my name and the sound of the door shoving open has the two of us shrieking quietly. He quickly shoves his cock back into his jeans, while I try to straighten my skirt and put my breast back into my bra that somehow Crew had pulled out in our crazed frenzy.

"Back here," I call out as the two of us fall into another fit of giggles.

"I was just helping her find those banners," Crew calls out as the clickety-clack of Bobbi Jo's shoes draws closer.

"Look at you," she says when she meets the end of our aisle. "Always so helpful."

We fight the urge to laugh again, but damn is it hard with the taste of his kiss still on my tongue, the ache he caused still present between my thighs, and the knowing smirk on his lips.

Quickies are definitely overrated.

Chapter Twenty-Five

Tennyson

THIS CHAPTER IS A MESS. GRAMMAR-WISE, IT SEEMS LIKE MY AUTHOR was drunk when she wrote it. And plot-wise, there are holes so big you could drive a truck through.

I lean back in my chair and stare at the screen until the words blur and the muted sounds of the girls filming a video is all I hear.

"Knock. Knock."

"Hey." I swivel around in my chair to find Crew standing in the doorway. His hands are shoved in his jean pockets, his feet are bare, and his shoulder is resting against the doorjamb.

I'm sucker-punched by the sight of him. I shouldn't be, considering I see him every day now, but there's something about the moment, about the look on his face, and his presence in general, that makes me sit back and admire the whole of him.

I know this won't last—it can't with the complication that is my life—and yet I know, if I had my pick of a guy I'd want, he would be just like Crew.

He would be Crew.

"It's a nice night. Want to take a walk?"

"Um, sure." This is a first.

But rather than grabbing the girls like I expect him to, Crew sets the alarm and then shuts the door behind us. "They're fine without it, but they like to have it on when I'm not here," he explains.

I nod and follow his lead as we head down one of the nearby horse trails. Once we're out of eyesight of the house, he links his fingers with mine.

We walk in comfortable silence as the summer sun slowly makes its way toward the horizon. Its shine highlights the tall grass, giving it a halo of sorts, as it sways in the evening breeze. The trees stand tall around us with their birds chirping and flitting around from branch to branch.

"Thank you for inviting me today to help out. It was a lot of fun meeting people and helping build the stands."

"You're not mad at me for subjecting you to the ogling eyes of the Redemption Falls women's club?"

"A little ogling every now and again does good for a man's ego."

"Oh, please. As if every time you step into town, you're not followed around like you're the Pied Piper and they're just hoping to get your attention."

"Whatever." He laughs good-naturedly and swings our joined hands. "If I had to hear one more time what a great body and throaty laugh you had, I might have swung the hammer and accidentally missed and hit someone."

"Throaty laugh? Who says that?"

"Well, me. I was checking out one of those romance novels you edit. Picked it up at the library. I figured that's as good of an adjective as any to pick up and use. Besides, you do have a throaty laugh, and it's sexy as hell."

"Hmph."

We walk a bit more, laughing at two squirrels on the path that are fighting over the same piece of food.

"So are you glad you chose to help with Founder's Day this year? Was it everything you hoped for in small-town living?" he asks.

I stare out toward the horizon and take a moment to figure out where this question is coming from. I grew up in a small town. Well, not Tennyson West, but Tessa Miller did. And thanks to my parents' bad reputation and known alcoholism, I couldn't wait to get as far away from it and them as possible. To have a fresh start where no one knew my family. Where I could simply be Tessa Miller, the new girl without any stigma attached to my name.

But of course, I can't tell Crew that.

"It's been fun helping out. Feeling a part of things here. I grew up as an army brat, and probably still am one at heart because I'm not used to putting down roots. Every time I start to, there's that voice in the back of my mind telling me I shouldn't. Giving in to the fear. Afraid that if I do,

I'll be uprooted, and it'll hurt more if I'm attached to the people and the place."

"So what would you consider this? The helping out? Are you trying to put down roots now?"

I nod. "I guess. It's silly to be scared to, but I figured I had to at least try."

"Hmm," he says, and I'm not exactly thrilled with the sound. "So you plan on moving on then?"

"No. Not really. Old habits die hard, I guess."

"So you're not running from something, then?"

His words catch me off guard, my whole body faltering at his question. "No. Why would you ask something like that?" I give a mock laugh and roll of my eyes. "That's ridiculous."

"Is it? I mean, it's okay if you are. Everyone is running from something. Hell, look at me. I'm here because I'm running from the implosion of my life over the past year and a half, so there's nothing to be ashamed of. I just thought it was an important thing for me to know."

I try not to sputter a response, but he has completely taken me by surprise. Instead, I opt for silence because right now, that might be a better option for me.

We walk for a few feet, and I can feel his doubt weighing everything down.

"Crew." I sigh softly, figuring it's better to face this than hide from it. At least that way, I can control the narrative as best as I can. "Just come out and ask what you want to ask."

He nods, but the silence that follows is slightly unnerving. Does he know who I am? Has he connected dots I didn't even know were sitting there? Did he use his police intel to somehow beat the system?

Each second that passes feels like an hour while I have to act like I'm taking a stroll with my lover, and I'm not internally rioting with anxiety.

"I'm a cop, Tenny. I notice things others don't," he finally says softly.

"Like?"

"Like the security door on the cottage you had installed on your own. Like your avoidance of being in the picture today. Don't think I didn't notice you slip away before it was even taken. Like your evasiveness any time we talk about you. It's not lost on me that you have a way of turning the topic back to me. And yes, I get you have truths you don't want to say yet, but we're also a little further into this thing now. You're owning my thoughts more than not. You're around my girls constantly. You've become a part of our lives. Don't you think maybe I deserve a bit more than you've given?"

Fear, panic, dread—all three lodge in my throat and have me struggling to answer. A simple, "You're right," falls from my lips. "You do deserve more, but . . ."

"Tell me about him." He squeezes my hand again and tugs me to sit down beside him, the pond in front of us, the sun's rays dancing off its ripples.

"About who?"

Crew studies me for a beat and then simply nods without saying anything more. I know who he means, and he knows it. The man who terrifies me even in his absence.

He may not know the why or the who, but clearly, I suck at hiding it from his well-trained eyes.

"I went on many calls, Tenny. I've seen a lot of things." He puts an arm around me and pulls me closer so that my head rests on his shoulder.

"Then you'll understand that sometimes things get to be too . . . much, and you need a fresh start. A place where there are no demons to chase you. A place where no one knows the old you."

"Whoever he is, he's not going to find you," he murmurs into the crown of my head.

I swallow forcibly to hide my surprise. "Who said I ran away?"

"No one. And for the record, leaving isn't running away. It's called saving yourself." He presses a kiss to my temple with an ease and an honesty that frankly I don't deserve.

"I couldn't live the life we had anymore. Not without compromising who I was and everything I thought I was. Strong. Independent. Honest. Safe." I run a hand up and down my thigh, needing something, anything, to do with my hands so that I can ease the discord I have over saying anything at all. But he deserves this much. Hell, truth be told, he deserves so much more.

Because he's right. I'm living under his roof. I'm currently part of his girls' lives when they are his everything. If I were in his shoes, I'd be asking a hell of a lot more questions than he is.

And I'd be demanding answers.

"I've spent many nights rolling up to a scene to find the woman terrified of her husband or boyfriend. Women who knew it didn't matter how far they ran, he would do everything in his power to ensure his terror would follow her. You have the same look in your eyes sometimes. The same skittishness about things. I hope that I'm wrong, but if I'm not, just know that it's okay. I'm not like that. I'm not like *him. And you're safe.*"

Tears spring to my eyes, and I do my best to blink them away.

And you're safe.

How long has it been since I've really felt that way? Twenty-six months, ten days, and eight hours to be exact. Forty months, ten days, and thirteen hours since I walked without looking over my shoulder or fearing what might be hiding in the shadows.

An even crazier question is why does Crew's presence make me feel like this can be a reality? That I can be safe? That I can walk and live and laugh without always worrying about what if?

And you're safe.

Those words. This man. He might be wrong about the context of everything, but the lasting, scarring effects are basically the same.

I am running from a man whose identity terrorized me. A man I thought was my future but found out I didn't really know at all.

"Thank you," I whisper. They're the only words I can manage to say that keep my voice, and the dam holding back the tears, from breaking.

We fall quiet as we sit there with the sun slowly setting and the tall grass rippling like a moving tide around us. I appreciate that he is giving me a moment or two to digest this conversation. It's a door I didn't want to open but am grateful I was able to at least stick my toes in it so he feels like I'm opening up.

"I blamed myself when Brittney up and left after thirteen years of marriage. No warning. No nothing. I was blindsided and dumbfounded." He chuckles. "I know most guys are dense and don't pick up on shit, but I do. Well, I try to at least, but her affair, her desire to move across the Atlantic with a man ten years younger than me was a shock, not to mention a major blow to my ego. But truth be told, I didn't have time or a chance to even process that, because I was so busy trying to minimize the damage to the girls."

"I'm sorry. That had to have been—"

"Brutal? Soul-shattering? Take your pick." Another disbelieving laugh. "I had failed. In my marriage. To my girls. I was terrified I had ruined them. It took me a while to realize that I can't be responsible for other people's actions. I can only work on me. I can only be the best at that."

"You're way more mature than I am." I snort. "I'd be immature and lay that blame at her feet like there is no tomorrow."

Just like my parents always blamed their misfortunes on me. Their drinking problems. Their inability to hold down jobs. Their hatred of me.

It's no wonder I took the first bus out of there with my pointe shoes in hand and never looked back. After struggling for a year, I thought finding Kaleo was a godsend. A person who looked at me and loved instead of looking at me and hating or blaming.

He stood backstage after one of my performances and refused to leave until I spoke to him. His good looks and charm won me over immediately. His personality and dedication cemented his hold on my heart in the following months. I'd never been loved the way he loved me. Adored and cherished. The exact opposite of my parents . . . or so I thought.

I have a right to be bitter, to lay the blame at Kaleo's feet, for everything that happened—just like Crew does with Brittney.

And yet he opts for the higher road.

"More mature?" Crew repeats and snorts. "Hardly, Tenny. I definitely did blame Brittney. I still do. But I've also learned that it's not my fault she did what she did just as it's not your fault he did what he did, whatever that is, to you."

"I know," I murmur.

"But do you?"

Crew's question sits with me long after our walk, our dinner with the girls, and as I burn the midnight oil editing a book about a High Fae Prince and his chosen princess who fights her attraction to him for a large portion of the book.

Do I know that what Kaleo did wasn't my fault?

Do I understand that while I loved him—maybe parts of me still do—that I was being controlled within an inch of my life so he could save his own image and forge his own protection?

Do I get that this whole process—creating a new life for myself and fearing his wrath—has its own emotional trauma that has resulted in me becoming introverted? Has made me keep my guard up and fear living because I'm afraid that those I become close to might get hurt in the shock waves if he were to find me?

But do you?

Such a good question.

And one I think I'm still trying to answer.

Chapter Twenty-Six

Crew

S HE TRIED TO HIDE IN THE BACK ROW TODAY.

She thought I didn't notice. Hell, she thought no one would. But it's pretty hard not to notice how she conveniently took off before the first shot was taken when I can't take my eyes off the woman.

Or get her out of my thoughts.

Or stop imagining the things I want to do to her. With her.

But she did.

And now I can't stop myself from wondering why.

Even more so after our discussion tonight.

The light has been on in her room for some time. Normally she comes out for something to drink or those sour gummy things she likes to eat while working and that I have made sure we have a stockpile of.

But she was quiet tonight. On the walk home. At dinner. As she excused herself to finish up some work.

She was quiet and withdrawn when she had never been before.

She's hiding.

That much is clear.

She's hiding, and it kills me that she isn't opening up to me, but who the hell am I to her, right?

We're sleeping together. We're still in that newness phase where every waking thought is wanting more of her, but with that said, there have been no promises of more. No hints at a future together. I'll be gone at summer's end, and she'll still be here, so why do I think she owes it to me to tell me more? Why do I want to know so badly?

Because you want to help her, that's why.

Your savior complex is showing again, Crew.

Is that why I took her on the walk today? Is that why I let her know I understood there was more there than a simple panic attack and a fear someone had broken into her house?

I wanted her to know she's been seen.

But what happens when I leave Redemption Falls? I won't be here to watch out for her. To protect her. *To save her.* What then?

Vivian asked me to come help her when she was in trouble. She *needed* me to come help. There's a huge difference between jumping in and trying to help when you're not asked. *And Tenny hasn't asked.*

The thought has me hesitating with my knuckles an inch from her door and ready to knock.

Maybe seeing her right now isn't the best thing for either of us. Maybe I need to put myself in check while she needs some time to process?

I take a step back, the floorboards creaking beneath my weight as I move toward the girls' rooms. I stand between their two doors and watch them sleep. Addy is snuggled with her stuffed elephant that she swears she's too old for and doesn't sleep with. Paige has some kind of sleep mask on that presumably makes her feel like she's five years older and cool.

What would you do if whatever happened to Tenny happened to one of them?

I shiver at the thought, knowing I'd be spending the rest of my days in a six-by-ten-sized cell, unapologetic for righting the wrongs I'd no doubt committed.

The funny thing is?

As I head back to my room and eventually drift off to sleep, my blood boils. All I can think about is doing the same thing to whoever hurt Tenny.

Chapter Twenty-Seven

Crew

"So?"

Adele looks down and finishes jotting some notes in her notebook as I stare expectantly at the computer screen and watch her.

"So?" Her smile is placating when she looks up, her dark brown eyes meeting mine behind the red frames of her glasses. "How often are the nightmares?"

I think of the one that woke me up in a cold sweat last night. The darkness I was immersed in. The muzzle flash. Justin's scream, a sound I hope I never hear again all around me so I didn't know where he was or how to help him. The laughter on the other side of the door as we lay there bleeding. The smell of gunpowder mingled with the metallic smell of blood.

"Not as often as they used to be. Not as little as I'd like them to be." It's a non-answer, answer, but she's used to those from me by now. I never know what's going to keep her from clearing me and what will help, so I've opted to be as vague as possible at all times.

"I'll take that as a *frequently* then," she says matter of fact and makes some more notes. It's her sigh when she looks up as she clasps her hands in front of her that I don't like. "As you know, there is no schedule on when one recovers from a traumatic event such as the one you experienced, Crew. Each person has their own timeline. That does not make one person weaker than another because each person processes things differently. You went through something traumatic. You were trapped for quite a long time after the unspeakable happened to you and your partner."

"What are you getting at, Doc? That I'm going to be messed up forever? That these headaches and nightmares will never go away? That you're never going to clear me to go back to work? I've done everything you've asked of me even when I thought it was bullshit. Exposure therapy, cognitive therapy, that stress inoculation shit, medication . . ." It takes everything I have to sound calm when I'm raging inside. "I mean, can you at least give me something to go off here to know if I'm getting my life back?"

"It seems to me you have your life back."

"What's that supposed to mean?" I snap.

"You said your girls are thriving. You've made a ton of headway on your uncle's property. That you've been seeing a woman who makes you laugh. It sounds to me like you have your life back—at least compared to what it was when we first started meeting."

I open my mouth and close it, unsure what to say. "That's not fair."

"Why? You being healthy isn't the goal here? You being happy should be underrated? Yes, the job is important to you, Crew. But when we started, that was how you rated your happiness and contentment with life. Now it seems you've found a different metric, and I think it's extremely important you realize that. Being a cop is and will always be a part of you, but it seems like it's no longer the measure of who you are as a person."

I nod, her words hitting me harder than I ever imagined. How many mornings did I come off shift and my time off was dictated by what happened on shift? How many days was my time spent with the girls overshadowed and ruined because I couldn't put the job to sleep?

Fuck.

Just fuck.

"While we're on the subject of happiness and metrics, have you talked to Justin yet? Really talked to him other than *superficial bullshit* as you call it?"

"What does that have to do with any of this?"

"Perhaps once you clear the air with him, the guilt you feel will abate and that will become another metric to look at."

"You talk to him too. What does he say?" Even I can hear the defensive nature of my tone.

"You know I can't divulge that information to you, Crew. But I can say that maybe that conversation will help you get over that final hurdle. It might be awkward and uncomfortable. The comradery you had over the years might feel off—but that's okay. It's expected for a while. But once you actually talk, hear his version of things, and compare it to yours, perhaps it will help fill in the blank spots you seem to have."

I'm about to argue that I don't have blank spots, but that's bullshit, and she knows it.

"Maybe that's what is holding you back."

We end our teletherapy call, and I sit and stare at the blank screen for some time, mulling over her words. My head often feels more messed up after our department-mandated sessions than it does before them. Too many thoughts. Too many suggestions. Too many doubts.

This house is too quiet with the girls gone. Tenny volunteered to take them to dance and art since the time conflicted with my "business meeting" as I told her. I'm so used to the noise—the girls chattering, Tenny murmuring to her manuscript as if it will convince the words on her screen to change, the soft hum of music or TV that always seems to be on here—that when it's this quiet, it's almost deafening.

I shove up out of my chair, needing something, anything, to do to quiet my head. To feel useful and purposeful.

I tackle the shutters. Now that they are freshly painted, I busy myself with hanging them. Each whirl of the screw gun, a memory from that night I try to work away. But even the physical exertion doesn't help. I'm still restless. Still worked up.

"Now it seems you've found a different metric, and I think it's extremely important you realize that. Being a cop is and will always be a part of you, but it seems like it's no longer the measure of who you are as a person."

Is Adele right?

I was a cop before I ever became a father. Have my priorities been that screwed up that I was so truly focused on my job that I never fully owned being a dad as my number one priority? Did I let the girls down? And if so, does that mean I was an absent husband too?

Fuck.

Just fuck.

But hasn't being away from the force pushed me to realize this with or without Adele's inserted opinion? My whole focus has been on getting well, on being a dad. I've fucking loved every damn minute of being with my girls, of being more present and in the moment with them. Am I further wrapped around their fingers? Without a doubt. Do I feel like I'm a huge part of their life instead of standing on the periphery like I used to be? Definitely.

It's funny how I never took the time to truly realize that before.

So maybe I knew what Adele was saying all along but needed to hear her say it to make me realize it.

"It sounds to me like you have your life back—at least compared to what it was when we first started meeting."

Funny how the definition of getting my *life back* has suddenly shifted. What exactly is it, though? It sure as hell includes the girls, but what about the force? What about Tenny and Redemption Falls?

What will it mean to truly have my life back?

That's the new question, isn't it, Crew?

Fuck me. Just when you think you figure one thing out, more questions need to be answered.

I have the sudden urge to do something that will put me closer to the world I now feel so left out of. To test that new definition I'm attempting to find the parameters to.

My cell rings and interrupts my thoughts.

"Dusty."

"What's the story, brother?" Dusty asks.

"I have what you asked for. It took me a little longer than normal, but I think you might be surprised that I think you're looking at the wrong guy."

"No shit?"

"No shit."

"The money trail leads to your suspect, but when you burrow down into the details, it seemed like it was too convenient. So I traced it backwards and found a few peculiar things." I go on to explain to him what I've been chasing most nights.

Chasing, that is, until the girls are fast asleep and Tenny slides into my bed.

It's then that I can forget the world outside.

It's then that everything seems a little easier.

It's then I can lose myself in a woman who feels like she is slowly becoming more than an infatuation and more like an addiction.

Chapter Twenty-Eight

Tennyson

SOMETHING'S OFF WITH CREW.

Maybe if I hadn't been living under his roof for the past two weeks, I wouldn't have caught it. But it's the subtle way he's sitting back tonight. Observing rather than participating. The murmured answers instead of lively responses that always has at least one of us laughing. The comments about whether dinner is going to be another disaster as we may or may not have had a few more of those over the past week.

But tonight he's reserved, pensive, preferring to be on the sidelines rather than in the middle of everything as per usual.

Does it have anything to do with his appointment today? The girls made a few comments in passing that allowed me to deduce it might have something to do with the department and getting cleared to go back to work.

And by his disengagement, I'm assuming he didn't get the answers he wanted.

Worried about him and wanting to help but uncertain how, I slide glances his way as the girls chatter on about all the new friends they've made here in Redemption Falls. From Pheebs (aka Phoebe) who has three big dogs and two horses and swears they can come over whenever they want, to Gretchen who is the cool one with five thousand followers on her influencer account. Then there is Fernie, whose mom is the school principal, so she has the inside scoop on every kid in town, followed by Dani, short for Danielle, whose parents own the movie theater and who says they can get in to watch a movie anytime they want so long as they text her first.

"Wow. It seems like you guys have made a ton of friends here," I say.

"So many," Paige says, drawing the words out. "It's like everyone wants to be our friend because we're twins, and they've never met twins before."

"I'm sure it has more to do with your sparkling personalities, good manners, and sense of humor," I say, surprised Crew hasn't jumped in to humble them as he normally would.

"That too." Addy giggles.

"I'm glad you're liking it here," I say.

"Loving it. I mean, they have a dance team at their school here. Can you believe that? We don't even have that in Chicago," Addy says, eyes wide and grin crooked.

"That's pretty awesome," I say.

"Were you ever on a dance team?" she asks.

"Most dance teams don't have ballerinas on them." I chuckle. "I wanted to be, though. I may have begged and pleaded and tried to negotiate to get the chance, but my mom was adamant that school came first, ballet came second—sometimes even the other way around—and everything else came third."

"Really? Dance came first?"

"Sometimes."

"Wow." Addy's eyes grow wide as she studies me, trying to figure out if I'm telling the truth or not.

"What is your mom like?" Paige asks, brow furrowed and curiosity owning her eyes.

Drunk. Pushy. Obnoxious. More obsessed with the bottle than she was me, and that's saying something considering she constantly wanted to live vicariously through me.

"My mom was complicated," I say. The pang hits, but it's a familiar one. One every child would feel having a parent not want them. One I'm sure the girls might feel every now and again. It never goes away though, and for these two, I hope with everything I have that all will be righted for them and their mom will see the error of her ways. "To be fair, we were like oil and water."

"What does that mean?"

What does it mean?

Nonstop fighting. Blame laid at my feet for my father drinking himself to death—simply because as a child, I needed to be provided for. Never being good enough, pretty enough, smart enough, when she was the one who was truly ugly inside.

I think her resentment hurt the most. When my studio gave me a part-time job to pay for the dance lessons she required I take, she was angry I wasn't bringing the money home to her instead.

It feels like forever ago and yesterday all at the same time. Especially when I look from Paige to Addy and see what a great job Crew is doing raising them.

My smile is soft. "Let's just say that we never really got along."

"Really? You're easy to get along with," Paige says, only serving to put more of my heart firmly in their hands.

"Does she come and visit you?" Addy asks and saves me from having to respond to her sister.

"No." She doesn't even know where I am, let alone that I'm still alive. The minute I left that town, I never looked back, and I don't believe she ever looked for me. But that was the case when I was with Kaleo too. It's not like my current situation plays into it or would matter to her anyways. "We've lost touch to be honest. She struggles with . . . *things*, and so it's better off that she focuses on herself more than anything."

Both girls nod softly and share a glance. I chastise myself for not thinking through my response more. Did my words make them think of their mom? Did it make them miss her and think she's better off focusing on herself than them?

I'm struggling with how to amend my response when Addy gracefully changes the subject for me.

"Dad is always saying we need to do things because *we* love them, not because we think he does or that it will make him happy." She twists her lips and looks down at where she's picking off her nail polish before looking back up and meeting my eyes. "Is she why you stopped dancing? Did you hate it because she made you do it?"

My smile is quick to cover the sudden bout of sadness her question brings. "No. I still loved it despite her."

Dancing was my escape. From a home life I'd rather not be at to my identity after marrying a man as dominating as Kaleo. When I glance over to Crew, his head is angled to the side as he watches me. I swear he can read my thoughts. That he can sense I'm censoring the truth for the girls. He nods for me to continue, and once again, he makes me feel heard without even saying a word.

"To be honest," I say, "I ended up having to quit because life got in the way. I had to move away from the studio where I taught—"

"Why?" Paige asks.

I hope my stuttered smile doesn't give my lies away or the utter devastation I felt during that time in my life. From what I saw with Kaleo, to the lies I had to tell to keep myself alive, to how I felt leaving the one thing I'd ever truly loved for me.

"I had to pay bills," I say and stick out my tongue. "Icky adult stuff that you guys won't have to worry about for a while."

"Do you ever dance now?" Addy asks. "Just for fun?"

"I haven't in a long time. No."

"You should," Addy says.

"Dad says everyone has to do something for fun to relieve stress," Paige says. "Back home, Dad and Uncle Justin used to golf. *A lot.* After they had a tough day, they'd go and play a round of *horrible golf* as they called it. But not anymore . . ." She glances at her dad and then grimaces as if she shouldn't have said something.

That, in and of itself, has my curiosity piqued.

"Golfing is your thing?" I ask Crew, not exactly picturing him as a golfer—a bit too calm for a man who lives in the chaos of other people's lives—but then again, maybe that's why he does it.

But the minute the words are out, he stands abruptly from the table and moves toward the sink. "At times," he says gruffly before turning the water on and effectively ending the conversation.

"Tell me about what you're working on in dance?" I ask Addy to try and alleviate the sudden awkwardness.

She proceeds to show me a few moves, and while I am paying attention to her, I'm also watching Crew. For a man who's normally so easygoing, there's definitely something eating at him.

He opts out of playing a game of Yahtzee with us when he's usually the one rounding everyone up. He tells us to go ahead when the girls ask if I'll go upstairs so they can practice hair styles on me.

And when the girls are finally in bed, books in their hands, and the promise of lights out in ten minutes, I head downstairs to find him.

He's sitting on the couch, a beer in one hand and his head resting against its back. Music is playing softly through the speakers and the lights are dimmed.

I find myself stopping on the last step to take him in.

With as much as I'm worried about him in this moment, the sight of him there staggers me. His broad shoulders. The curl of his hair, a little too long, in need of a trim. The flex of his bicep as it lays across the top of the couch and he lifts his arm to support his head.

My history tells me I should be wary of a man who's moody and drawn into himself. Isn't that what Kaleo was like those last few months before my world came crashing down? Using his quiet brooding and harnessing it like a weapon to keep me in line? Isn't that how I remember my dad acting before he went on a bender?

And yet somehow, I feel the exact opposite with Crew. Sure, he's been somber all evening, even a little distant, but I have no qualms about walking over to the couch and curling into him. In offering him silent comfort to help combat whatever is going on in his head.

How did this become so easy? Being here with him and the girls? The laughter that rings out more often than not and the level of comfort always present? The cottage down the road that's soon to be ready for me to move back into but that neither of us have mentioned once?

How was it a few weeks ago I didn't know Crew, Addy, and Paige existed, and now I simply can't imagine a world without them in it?

It's crazy to think of how alone I was but didn't even realize it myself until I came here. *Until him.*

What's even crazier is how little I think about Kaleo. It's almost as if being with Crew has proven to me that having a normal life is actually attainable. It's like he's shone a flashlight in the shadows that once lurked in the darkness to prove they were completely harmless.

"They in bed?" Crew asks, startling me. I didn't know he knew I was here.

"Yep. I told them they have ten minutes of reading before lights out," I say as I move across the room and sit down next to him, making sure I'm keeping a safe distance in case the girls decide to head downstairs.

"Wow. They negotiated for more reading time and you caved?" he teases, and for the first time all night, there's some levity to his tone.

"I'll never say no to books or to reading." I shrug. "Occupational hazard ... or more like occupational appreciation."

He shakes his head and grants me the smile that's been lacking all night. "They really do have you wrapped, don't they?"

"It's easy when they're such good kids."

"Hmpf," he murmurs before falling quiet again. We sit there for a few minutes, listening to the music and enjoying the simple yet important feeling of putting the kids to bed and knowing it's our time to be together. A concept I never understood until now.

"Do you ever want kids?" Crew asks out of the blue.

"Yes. At some point. When I meet the right person." I fumble for an answer in regards to something I thought I knew to be a certainty but has since been turned upside down and rethought. "Sometimes things don't turn out the way we planned in our mind. Why do you ask?"

"You're really good with the girls is all. One would think you might have done this before."

"I haven't had the chance yet. Besides, I'd never leave my kids behind. I'd rather die than . . ." My words trail off, my kneejerk reaction falling flat, as the thought hits me. His own wife did just that. *Left.* Walked away and left their girls behind. I'm sure she probably would have said the same thing too when they first met.

I think he gets my train of thought because he shakes his head ever so slightly and meets my eyes as if to say that's not what he meant. That's not what he was searching for when he asked the question. "I'd hate for you to not take the chance at having kids yourself someday because some asshole robbed you of that dream for one reason or another."

Our eyes hold in the dim light, the apology heavy in his before it slowly changes back into somberness. I don't know what to do or say or how to fix things I can't fix, but before I can decide, Crew reaches out and pulls me closer to him. *Against him.* I freeze momentarily because the girls are still awake, and they could come down the stairs at any moment.

"Crew. The girls—"

"No. Just . . . I just need this, okay?"

His words hit me with a resounding thud. His vulnerability humbling. "Of course." I snuggle in closer, curling my legs up under me, and resting my head on the crook of his arm and shoulder while resting a hand on his chest.

His heart beats softly, strongly, against my cheek while I can all but feel his mind mulling something over and over. I just wish those thoughts of his had words to go with them.

"I'm sorry you had to quit teaching, quit dancing. That must've been hard. Devastating."

I give a subtle nod, trying to figure out what to say. Were the girls right today about his meeting and his possible return to the force? Am I right to assume what is bugging him has to do with that?

Somehow, this man knows what to say to me at all times. He takes a back seat to tend to my needs when I don't even realize they are needs.

How selfish am I that I didn't stop to think he might need someone too? That the strength I see him exude every day is much like mine—masking a pain or fear beneath that you don't want anyone to know or see or understand?

"I'm sorry you haven't been cleared to return to work. That *must be* brutal."

His body tenses against mine, his sigh long and heavy before he finally responds. "It is. I guess. I don't even know anymore."

His tone guts me. The sadness and confusion woven in with a touch of lost little boy. I want to wrap my arms around him and hold him close, but I'm not sure if that's what he wants. Will he see it as me pitying him? As me thinking he's weak?

This is uncharted territory for me, and the last thing I want to do is make a wrong move. Say the wrong thing.

"Do you want to talk about it? Whatever's been on your mind tonight?" I ask and run my hand up and down his chest as if that's going to help anything.

"Not particularly," he says and then stands abruptly so that I almost fall over without him supporting me from behind. He holds a hand out to me and smiles. "Come on."

I look around the room and then back to him like he's crazy. "Come on? Where are we going?"

His answer comes in the form of grabbing my hand and pulling me off the couch.

"Crew?" His name starts out as a laugh and ends in a sigh as he pulls me against him, his lips finding mine in the softest, sweetest of kisses.

"It's not ballet, Tenny," he murmurs as his feet begin to move to the music, "but we can definitely make you dance again."

He takes my hand in his while he slides his other one so that his palm presses against my lower back, and we begin to move. The family room is now our dance floor. His lead is now what I follow. His compassion, when clearly he's hurting, deserving of the tears that well in my eyes.

"Don't cry," he whispers and presses a kiss to my lips before spinning me slowly out and then pulling me back in against him.

We dance around the small space. Him selflessly trying to bring me a piece of something that once made me happy while I accept it and helplessly know I can't return the favor.

I can't give him his work back.

His life back.

And just like that, I'm reminded that there is a world beyond Redemption Falls for Crew Madden. One that has danger and another house where all his things are probably folded in neat stacks.

One without me in it.

The thought hits me hard, and this time when the tears well, I don't fight them. I let them spill over as I'm reminded in one of the most romantic moments of my life that my time with him is almost half over.

That I need to soak up everything I can because before I know it, the summer will be over, and he'll be gone.

"Don't cry," he says and kisses the tear tracks on my cheeks as we move around the room.

"I can't do the same for you," I whisper, the tears falling a bit harder. "I can't help you get back to what you love."

"Shh. Don't." Another tender kiss. A lean back so that his hands can frame the sides of my face so I don't dismiss his next words. "You're giving me more than I ever expected."

When I meet his lips this time, I pour all the emotion rioting inside of me into it. Into him. Into this man who came so unexpectedly into my life and has made it so much better in so many ways. I didn't know if I'd ever trust a man again, if I'd ever feel so connected with someone. *If I'd ever love again.*

"What are you doing to me, Tennyson?" he whispers as we sway to the music.

I don't know, but I don't want it to end.

Chapter Twenty-Nine

Tennyson

SOMETHING WAKES ME.

I don't know what it is, but the hair stands up on the back of my neck as I slowly sit up in bed. Shadows from the branches outside dance across my walls and only add to that twisting in my gut.

Was it a dream? A nightmare? Or is there something more there?

Fear. *Welcome back, old friend.*

A strangled cry pierces through the silence. I'm up and off my bed in seconds.

Crew.

The girls.

Kaleo doesn't care about collateral damage when he has an endgame in mind.

He's found me.

I've brought this on them.

I fling open my door to hear another shout. Another choked cry of agony.

Crew.

It's coming from Crew's room.

I fling open the door, expecting to see the worst—Crew hurt and bleeding like the men on the yacht—only to find him wrestling with unknown demons in his sleep.

"Crew." I say his name. One time. Two times. A shove to his shoulders. His name again. "Wake up. It's just a nightmare."

He fights against me, but I know the minute awareness hits him because his body jolts and a slew of profanity falls from his lips. He shoves up out of his bed almost as if he has to move so his mind registers that the nightmare is over and that he's in his bedroom.

I watch him as he paces, his hair a mess, his body misted in sweat, his face pale as pale can be. He walks past the bedroom door, and for the first time, I notice Addy and Paige peeking their head in the doorway.

"Girls," I say softly as I move toward the door. "It was just a bad dream. He's okay."

"I'm okay," Crew says weakly behind me, but I've already ushered the girls out of the room.

My hands are on both of their shoulders as I steer them down the hallway towards their rooms. "He's okay," I reiterate, trying to think how scared they must be seeing and hearing the man they think as invincible, struggling. "It was just a nightmare."

"About that night?" Addy asks softly as she rubs her eyes.

I hope he's okay.

"Probably." My smile is fake, but I try to sell it. "But now he knows it wasn't real." I press a kiss to each of their heads, their concerned eyes breaking my heart. "Do you guys want me to tuck you back into bed?"

Nods are their answers, but instead of each sleeping in their own beds, they opt to climb into Paige's bed together. I press kisses to their foreheads and leave the hall light on per their request before making my way back to Crew.

He's standing at the bathroom sink, splashing water on his face, before bracing one hand on the counter as he wipes the water away with the other. He turns to look at me with bloodshot eyes and a still pale complexion.

I sit down on his bed, my back against the pillows and headboard, and wait patiently for him to take whatever time he needs. Seconds stretch to a few minutes before he walks back into the room and stands at the foot of the bed. His eyes search mine, but there is still a hollowness to them that I'd do anything to erase.

"It was about that night." He runs a hand over the scar on his abdomen. "This night."

"What about it, if you want to tell me?"

He starts to run a hand through his hair, hesitates for a second, as if making up his mind.

"You can trust me, you know." I murmur something similar to his own words back to him.

"A man doesn't like to admit he's weak, Tennyson." He smiles, but it doesn't reach his eyes. "We're vain like that."

"Almost dying isn't weak. Surviving seems quite the opposite actually."

"Aren't we the glass half full kind of girl."

"We are." I pat the spot on the bed beside me.

He stares at my hand, then at me, before crawling up the bed. He grabs a pillow, places it on my lap, and rests his head there. My hands go to his head automatically, my fingers threading through his hair as he loses himself to his thought.

He's trusting me. He just let me see the vulnerable side of him, and he's still *choosing* to trust me.

How can he think that's weak? Opening up to someone after they've seen you at your lowest is the definition of strength in my book.

"Justin, my best friend and partner of eight years, and I went on a call. It was an apartment complex like a million others we'd been to. We were checking out a complaint that one of their neighbors had tried to lure their ten-year-old daughter into his apartment." He blows out a long, steadying breath. "The guy opened the door and invited us in like he had nothing to hide. After a few minutes of us asking questions, a baby cried in one of the bedrooms."

I lean over and press a kiss to his temple. A little show of support as he opens up to me.

"He went to check on his baby? The baby? Hell if we knew at the time. But he was taking too fucking long, and we started to realize there wasn't a single baby thing in the place. No baby monitor. No bottles near the sink. No toys or blankets. Nothing."

"Oh God," I murmur, imagining how he might have felt when the realization hit.

"Something was hinky, and we both knew it. Justin lifted his chin toward the closed bedroom door the guy had disappeared behind. We positioned ourselves to breach it—Justin with his hand on the knob and me with my gun raised for cover. And just as he was about to make entry, the fucking baby cried again. I pulled my finger off the trigger for a second—because there was a baby in there—and then all hell broke loose." He rolls onto his back and looks up at me from where his head is in my lap.

The pain etched in the lines of his face breaks my heart. I'm afraid to hear what happened next. "I can't even imagine," I murmur and feel lame in doing so, but I want him to know—as he does me—that I hear him. That I'm listening.

"I remember bits and pieces of what happened after that. The boom of gunfire. The door splintering. Justin's body jerking as each bullet hit him.

Emptying my clip in return as I dove for cover . . . then realizing I'd been hit myself." He moves his hand to cover the jagged scar on his lower abdomen. "Justin's ragged breathing. The smell of the gunpowder. My own pain as I faded in and out. Christ, all I could think about was that I couldn't leave the girls. That I hadn't told them I loved them that morning." He scrubs a hand over his face and closes his eyes for a few moments, I'm assuming to collect himself.

I can't imagine how agonizing it had to have been for him. Trapped, terrified and bleeding out, listening to his friend dying, and worrying about his girls. My heart hurts for him and the memories that clearly haunt him.

"How did you eventually get out of there?" I ask.

"SWAT breached at some point. By then, I was pretty much out of it." He moves his hand up to where his tattoo covers another bullet wound. "I was shot in the crossfire during that . . . but don't remember much of that really."

"Jesus, Crew. What happened to Justin? He made it, right? And the baby? The guy?"

"The baby wasn't his. Hell, the kid wasn't even in his apartment—just a neighbor's we could hear through his open window. He used it as a means to arm himself." He shrugs. "As for the guy? He didn't make it. I hit him a couple of times, but SWAT finished him off."

"And Justin?" I ask softly, feeling callous that I don't react to the loss of the man's life, but at the same time, look at who he hurt.

Crew shifts suddenly onto his side so all I can see is his profile now. I get the feeling he doesn't want me meeting his eyes and looking too closely for some reason.

"He made it." I can barely hear him when he speaks. "A T10 spinal injury. Paralyzed from the waist down."

I suck in a breath when I hear the words. When I realize Crew's not only dealing with his own injuries and their aftermath, but also dealing with confronting the longstanding ones to his partner. His best friend.

Uncertain what to say, I settle on the one thing I can't stop thinking about. "You're a hero, Crew. You saved his life. If you hadn't returned fire then—"

"No. You don't get it." His tone is a mixture of frustration and anger as his body tenses before emitting a measured exhale, almost as if he's trying to control his reaction. "I'm no fucking hero, Tenny. Far from it. My hesitation cost Justin the use of his legs. Cost him the chance at a normal life. At the possibility of kids. I mean . . ."

And there it is. It isn't the damage the bullets caused as it tore through his body or the nightmares that haunt him that weigh the heaviest on him. It's the unfounded guilt that his split-second hesitation is what sentenced Justin to life in a wheelchair. *That he is responsible.*

"Crew." I lean forward and press a kiss to the top of his head, closing my eyes with my lips there and just breathing him in.

"Every time I talk to the goddamn therapist, I end up back here. In a bed, covered in sweat, reliving every fucking moment of it," he says softly. Anger would be easier to take, but the quiet resignation in his voice is gut-wrenching. "You'd think if she's going to stir all that shit up, I'd at least get something out of it. I'd at least be cleared to go back . . . maybe then . . . maybe then it would just help push it all away, and I can forget about it."

And therein lies his somber mood earlier tonight. *I'd at least be cleared to go back . . .*

I lean back against the pillows again and highly doubt he'll ever forget about it. How could he?

"Does Justin have the same nightmares?"

His snort is unexpected. "Don't you start in on me too," he says, thoroughly confusing me. "I'll talk to Justin about it when I'm goddamn good and ready."

Rather than ask what he means or make assumptions I have no business making, I opt to remain quiet, to run my fingers through his hair, and let him lead when he's ready again.

"Coming here to Redemption Falls was supposed to be a reset for us. A simplification of life that we couldn't get at home with reminders everywhere of this and of Britt. We needed a break so that I could focus on getting my head right, on the girls getting to just be kids without all this worry. And the plan was when we head back at summer's end, all will be fixed and we can resume life as it used to be."

"But do you want it to resume as it used to be?"

"That's the million-dollar question, isn't it?"

Chapter Thirty

Crew

STARE AT TENNY THROUGH THE DIM LIGHT, DESPERATE TO FORGET.

Eager to get lost in something—someone—other than my thoughts.

Needing to so I can erase the empty hollowness the nightmare always leaves me feeling.

I reach up and cup the back of her neck, urging her down toward me until our mouths meet. Until our tongues touch and our sighs meld.

I need her. I don't want to need anyone but fuck if I don't need *her* right now. And she's just proven that it's okay to want that.

She listened when I needed to talk. She comforted me when I needed solace. She was quiet when I needed to hear my own thoughts.

She was here for me when I can't remember the last time I've let someone other than my family or Justin simply be here for me.

I can't even remember the last time Brittney had been this giving, this selfless, this warm.

And so when I shift positions, when I sit against the headboard and guide Tenny to straddle my lap, I don't hide from the emotions that have owned me since the night of the shooting. I don't push them down and pretend they don't exist.

I let her see them.

I let her see me.

And while it scares the ever-loving shit out of me, what other choice do I have? I can't ask her to open up to me, to be vulnerable with me, when I can't be the same with her.

So with her eyes on mine, I draw in a breath and put words to what I'm feeling.

"I need you, Tenny." I bring my hands to her face and press a kiss to her lips before resting my forehead against hers. "I fucking need you right now."

"Then have me." She leans back and meets my eyes. "Take what you need."

Our lips meet as we move efficiently and without fanfare. Her tank top comes off over her head. Both of our shorts get discarded. And then I hold my cock as she sinks ever so slowly down onto it—her eyes on mine.

A wave of dizziness threatens to assault me from the all-consuming sensation. Tenny's pussy gripping my cock is otherworldly and just what I need to help me forget.

To make me remember what it is to feel again.

She doesn't look away as she begins to rock back and forth on me. She doesn't hesitate as my hands find her hips, my fingers gripping the flesh there, and control the pace. Instead, she holds my gaze so I can see what I do to her. So I can watch the desire turn to pleasure and the pleasure then turn to greed as she whispers words of encouragement.

Right there.

God, yes.

My name in a drawn-out, hushed moan.

She feels incredible.

Hell, she *is* incredible. The taste of her kiss. The feel of her pussy tightening around me. The scent of soap and sex on her skin. The sight of her before me slowly coming undone.

The only thing better than the feel of her is the taste of her.

That's a drug in and of itself.

I try to shift her off me with thoughts of her pink pussy and my wet tongue pleasuring it, but she clamps her thighs over mine.

"No," she murmurs. "This is about you tonight. For you. Let me give you what you need. Let me make you forget." She grinds her hips over me. "*Need me, Crew.*" Her eyes are still on mine but fall somewhat closed with pleasure as she cups her own breasts and rubs her nipples between her thumbs and fingers.

It's a slow build. A sensuous climb.

Of shuddered breaths followed by panted gasps.

It's hands grasping and thighs clenching.

It's need mixed with greed and want mingled with temptation.

It's her coaxing and me taking.

"Come for me," she commands as her hips piston a little faster and her fingernails dig into my biceps as my hands guide her hips. "Crew."

My name has never sounded better in that part moan, part demand of hers. My head begins to dizzy as the white-hot ache spreads from my balls to my lower abdomen to fucking everywhere.

I come, hammering my hips up to hers. Hard and ragged and desperate. I empty myself with a feral groan before sinking my teeth into her shoulder and then licking the nip away.

Our fingers link as she settles all the way down on top of me and her lips find mine again. Her kiss is tender. As gentle as the sex we just had was, it still felt raw. It still felt desperate.

"I'm here, Crew," she murmurs against my lips, giving me words I didn't know I needed to hear. "I'm here."

Chapter Thirty-One

Tennyson

STAY.

Those were his words as I tried to untangle myself from him to-night and sneak back to my room like I have been doing the nights we've come together.

Gray eyes met mine, telling me he meant it. Expressing to me that he wasn't ready to let go yet.

Telling me that he still needed me.

The man sure knows how to make a woman feel valued, that's for sure. Even on a night when it's clear he had to deal with his own personal demons, it still felt like he tried to put me first.

I don't know how, but it did.

I glance down at the top of his head and press a kiss to where it rests on my chest. His leg is hooked over my thigh, and his arm is tucked around my abdomen, pulling me against the curve of him.

I can't imagine wanting to be anywhere else right now.

Maybe that's why I can't sleep. Maybe that's why I find solace in hearing his breathing even out and feeling his muscles fall lax.

The events of tonight replay in my head. His sullen mood. Us dancing downstairs. Falling asleep on the couch in his arms only to wake up in my own bed where he must have carried me to. The abject terror thinking that I brought danger upon him and the girls.

The realization that I actually *am*.

Yes, his nightmare, his ordeal, his guilt, are horrific in so many ways, but I'm grateful for him finally confiding in me. In needing me. In letting me give him something he needs since I'm always the one who seems to be drawing strength from him.

But even with all that, there's one thought I struggle to drown out: I can't knowingly put these three into harm's way—especially when I know I'm falling for them.

All three of them.

And being with me will do exactly that.

Chapter Thirty-Two

Tennyson / Tessa

Four Years Earlier

"S O MANY QUESTIONS, KU'UIPO." KALEO NARROWS HIS EYES AND studies me. "Do I need to worry you're going to try to overthrow me and take control of my businesses yourself?" He winks at me from across the desk as I take him in—the unbuttoned collar, the bow tie hanging around his neck, the glass of Scotch he's swirling around in his hand. Any other day I would have stared at him like this and marveled how of all the people in the world, he picked me to love. I would have thought how damn lucky I was. I would have been turned on. But now I stare at him and only see a monster. One I've researched and questioned and asked about over the past few weeks. One I have to pretend to love and desire when all he does is repulse me.

"Never. No." My smile is quick. Believable. I take a sip of my wine and lift my feet up to rest on his lap like I usually do. "Just curious is all."

He makes a noncommittal sound as he sips his drink. Those eyes of his unrelenting as he does. "You surprise me."

"Why do you make it sound like that's a bad thing?"

He twists his lips. "It isn't."

He's fishing for something, and that something has me fighting the need to fidget and move about.

"I'm not going to lie. I would have rather you told me than find out the way that I did."

"That was an . . . *unfortunate* mistake on my part. You were supposed to be asleep." He shrugs with a nonchalance that is like digging a fingernail into a fresh wound. The goddamn drink Carlo brought me. *I was supposed to be asleep.* He tried to ensure it with whatever he'd put in it. But my revelation goes unnoticed as I struggle to keep my expression stoic. "But it's for the better now that you know the truth."

A truth I never asked to be a part of.

"Weren't you afraid that I'd freak out? That I'd run?" I struggle to deliver my statements with conviction. I know who he is now. The violence he doesn't bat an eye at. The trigger he'll pull without proof.

"You love me. That means you'll accept every part of me, even the parts you don't like." He pushes my feet apart and pulls on my calves so that my chair rolls toward him. My legs are on either side of his waist now, his face inches from mine when he speaks. "You're mine, Tessa. I don't let things go very easily that are mine." There is an edge to his voice. A warning.

I smile to cover the panic reverberating through me as his fingers dig into my upper thighs. It's not painful, but it's a hint, *a reminder*, of what he is capable of.

I don't hide the fear in my eyes this time. I let him see it. I let him know I hear his warning.

"Kaleo . . . I don't even know where to—"

"There's a reason I let you keep teaching at the school. It made us appear normal. It helped squash suspicion."

"You used me." I know he sees the hurt in my eyes, but his low, even chuckle tells me he doesn't care.

"Just like you used me, Ku'uipo, to get the things you never had. Love. Security. Wealth. Status."

"I did not. How can you—"

His lips come crashing down on mine. Even his kisses taste different now, tinged with the tang of evil. He leans back and runs a thumb over my bottom lip as he frames my face. "I never expected you to want to be a part of this life. It's sexy as fuck that you do. I get hard even thinking about it." Another brush of lips. "And for the record, I don't care that you used me. I never cared because our love—this love—is like no other. Even with the truth out there, you still love me. You'll never be able to stop."

You'll never be able to stop.

Isn't that the struggle I'm fighting? Loving the warm and funny man I thought I'd married while trying to bring down the despicable and cold drug lord?

Copies of documents. Schedules of shipments. Access points to certain properties. Warehouse layouts. Isn't that what's being asked of me to give in return for complete immunity against persecution?

Asked to be found and copied and uploaded in a house under the many watchful eyes of all his people?

Sure, it's my house, but I'm no longer blind to the fact that these people who surround us on a daily basis—housekeeper, guards, personal assistants—know what it is my husband does for a living. Know how the money is earned that makes up their paycheck.

Are they suspicious of my sudden need to find a *receipt* for my new Birkin bag that *might be* in Kaleo's office? Have they noticed how jittery I am? How I'm always asking questions—the main one being *when's my husband expected home*? Has anyone in the staff quarters heard my alarm go off at two in the morning so I can sneak downstairs and go into his office unnoticed?

My nerves are shot.

My paranoia is at an all-time high.

I can't sleep. I'm not eating. I fear everything and anything is going to reveal what I'm doing.

But I make sure I keep smiling in front of the staff.

And to my husband, I love him just the same.

I'll be surprised if I don't have a nervous breakdown by the time this is all over.

And I'll gladly accept it if I'm able to pull this all off and still live.

Kaleo was right that night on the yacht. There is an informant in his ranks. And that informant has provided the DEA with more information than I could ever know.

But there are some things missing.

And I'm being asked to supply them in exchange for my freedom and a new life.

Chapter Thirty-Three

Crew

"SO, PHEEBS'S MOM IS ON HER WAY TO PICK US UP."

I glance over to Paige, my putty knife mid-scrape on the patio railing. "What are you talking about? For what?"

She shrugs. Clearly she has an agenda. "We're going to spend the night there."

I chuckle. "Did you forget that you're eleven, and you still have to ask to do things?"

She puts her hand on her hip and juts it out. "We're not babies, Dad. We have social lives."

"Uh-huh." I stand, cross my arms over my chest, and give her the stare down. "Give it to me straight, Paigey. What's really going on?"

"Nothing. I'm serious." She huffs out a breath that is more than a warning that the teen years are going to be anything but easy.

"Then I guess you're not going."

Three.

Two.

One.

She stomps her foot and huffs again right on cue. "That's not fair."

"Neither is you not telling me the truth."

She doesn't back down from my stare for a good thirty seconds. "We just figured that you and Tenny needed some non-kid time—"

I bark out a laugh. "Non-kid time?"

"Yeah, so you can talk about 401ks and the weather and ... I don't know, so you can finally get the guts to kiss her and stuff."

I nearly choke at her words, fighting back my grin. "What makes you think I want to *kiss her and stuff*?" Lord, help me.

"Well . . . I don't know." She shrugs, and her cheeks turn red. "She's really pretty and funny and can cook way better than you. We think you should like her."

"We?"

"Yep. We." She gives a resolute nod. "So we asked Pheebs if we could spend the night so maybe you could take Tenny on a date and finally make her your girlfriend or something."

"*Or something.*"

"Exactly." She glances over to where her sister has just walked out onto the verandah.

Addy eyes the two of us, and before she can run back in the house and avoid this conversation, I say, "Uh-uh. Get your butt out here."

"It was Paige's idea."

Wow. She sure threw Paige under the bus fast. That's unusual.

"It was *our* idea."

"Girls." I sigh and take a step toward them. "Thank you for thinking of me. For wanting to give me some adult time, but—"

"We saw you kiss," Addy blurts out. "The other night. You were dancing, and *you* kissed her."

"Um. Okay." Well . . . *shit*. I fumble over what to say. For how to explain. For—

"So see? We're going to Pheebs's house so you can take her on a date or buy her flowers or something. She's a girl. Girls like that kind of stuff," Paige says so matter of fact that I'm left a little stunned.

So much for keeping things under wraps.

"We're okay with it, Dad," Addy says.

"Totally okay with it," Paige repeats.

"Thanks for the approval," I say and tip the bill of my ballcap at them in an attempt to try and cover up the shock over their comments and the simultaneous guilt over hiding it all from them and pseudo getting caught.

"Did someone forget to invite me to the meeting?" Tenny asks as she comes out the door looking from the girls to me and then back.

Both girls start giggling as they tell Tenny about their spontaneous plans for a sleepover. I watch the three of them together. The ease between them, the way they read each other, and I realize that even if the girls had never found out about Tenny and me, they're still attached to her regardless.

There was no way I was *or am* going to avoid that. Hell, I should have realized that the night of my nightmare. How she handled the girls with such a natural ease and how they allowed her to comfort them.

It was ridiculous for me to think they wouldn't attach themselves to her when I'm attached to her myself.

When I'm worried about how bad it's going to sting too.

"She's here," Paige shouts excitedly and grabs her bag about the same time as a dust plume kicks up farther down our driveway as Phoebe's mom arrives.

We spend the next few minutes chatting with Phoebe's mom and getting the girls in the car. Tenny and I both stand at the foot of the steps, and as they pull away, she waves her hand in front of her face to swat the dust away.

"It's horrible, isn't it?" I ask. "The damn dust gets into the house regardless of how much I keep it closed up." I glance back to the dust that's still settling. "If I owned this place, if I lived here permanently, that would be the first thing I'd do."

"What's that?" Tenny asks me as she takes a seat on the top step and uses her hand to shield her eyes to look up at me.

"Asphalt the road."

"That would definitely help cut down on the cleaning. Why do you think Ian hasn't done it? Is it the cost?"

"My uncle's not hurting for money," I say, thinking of the text he sent me the other day. The one where he's sitting on his forty-foot fishing boat that's docked outside of his sizeable house in Palm Beach. He may be slowly losing his mental faculties, but he sure isn't spending like it. "But in his defense, why go to the expense when he doesn't plan on keeping the place."

"Maybe whoever buys the place will."

"Maybe," I say and hate the feeling of knowing someone else might be living here. Might be spending time with her.

What's it to you, Crew? It's not like you're going to be here. It's not like she's going to sit here and wait for you on the off chance you bring the girls back here to visit.

So why does looking at her and realizing our time is limited feel like a weight has been dropped into my stomach?

"What's that?" I ask, so lost in my thoughts—of her—that I don't hear her.

"I said hopefully the new owners will be decent and abide by the contract and lease that Ian drew up for me. He might not have been the best at getting handywork done, but he swore he'd take care of me so that I could keep my place, and he did. Speaking of places, do you have any idea when the cottage will be livable again?"

I hook her around the waist and pull her onto my lap as I sit beside her. "Why? Are you trying to get rid of me?"

There's a quick flash of a smile that doesn't sit well with me. Especially when the last thing I want is for her to be back in that cottage. It's more than the built-in sex and the company . . . I like Tenny. Like *really* like her.

"No. Not at all. I just figured I'd give you and the girls your space back. You're all probably sick of me."

I stare at her, trying to get a read on her and her sudden caginess. I'm missing something, and I can't quite put my finger on it. It's been since my nightmare last week. Hasn't it? Tenny's been a bit more reserved. Seems to be pulling back a bit. Or am I just projecting because I'm insecure over her seeing me like that?

Then again, is something there, and I'm just so blissfully ignorant that I've missed it—just like I missed it with Britt?

"Talk to me, Tenny."

"There's nothing to talk about." She gets up, picks up my putty knife, moves to the railing, and begins to scrape the paint there with no skill whatsoever.

Definitely something going on.

"So you won't talk, and you're clearly trying to avoid me because you actually picked up a tool to use it." She stops mid scrape and looks up at me with a look that says I'm being ridiculous . . . but that look alone tells me I'm not. This is definitely not the afternoon I had planned ten minutes ago when the girls climbed into Phoebe's car. "So . . . what's really going on here? Are we about to have our first fight?" I clap my hands together and rub. "You never really know someone until you have that first knockdown drag out. So come at me. Tell me what you hate."

"Crew." My name is an exasperated sigh as her hands drop down to her sides.

"What? Do I chew too loud and it drives you crazy? Do I talk obnoxiously loud on the phone? It drives the girls crazy that I pace when I'm on it, so I'm sure you think that too. Or is it my cooking? Do my stellar culinary skills make you so jealous that you can't even be in the same room?" I rise from my seat and move toward her, that stony façade of hers slowly cracking as the corners of her mouth upturn just slightly. "*I know.* You're envious that I know every single lyric to every Taylor Swift song on the face of the earth. I mean, that takes some serious talent. But what can I say?" I blow on my knuckles and then shine them on my shoulder. "When you've got it, you've got it, and I'd hate me for it too."

"You're being ridiculous," she says as I put my hands on both of her hips, and she looks up at me from beneath those thick lashes.

This woman is just . . . Jesus, she does things to me with just her smile.

"Not ridiculous if it's true. I mean, I haven't even gotten to the part where I leave my shoes on the stairs, and for that—I mean, those are serious offenses you should be furious at me for."

She just shakes her head with that expression on her face that makes me want to kiss her and never let her go.

Or rather, I'll let her go so long as I can do other things to her that involve a bed, a wall, the kitchen counter . . . I mean, the possibilities are endless.

"So . . . are you going to talk to me, or are you going to be mad at me and make me keep guessing what our first official fight is going to be about?"

She lowers her eyes again and focuses on where her fingers play idly with the hole on my favorite, old, dark blue T-shirt.

"I can't keep doing this to you, Crew," she says softly.

No, no, no. "Doing what?"

"Using you."

I bark out a laugh. Here I thought she was ending things, and this is the problem? That she's using me?

Then let me be used. Especially when it's by her.

But I don't exactly think she'll appreciate me saying that. "Hey," I say in an attempt to get her to look at me. When she doesn't, I hook my fingers through the belt loops on the sides of her jeans and tug. "Is that what this is? You using me?"

"Mm-hm."

My smile is brighter than the fucking sun as I bite back more laughter. "You know what? You're absolutely right. How dare you? I mean it's more than clear that I'm getting absolutely nothing out of whatever this is here. No friendship." I kiss the side of her neck. "No pleasure." I kiss her cheek.

"No release." This time I brush my lips to hers and fight the urge to take the kiss even deeper. "No *anything*."

She laughs against my lips. "That's not what I—" She sighs. "Never mind."

"Never mind? Oh come on. We can do so much better than that. You can't end a fight on a *never mind*." I shake her hips. "Where is the throwing shit and yelling at each other until you can't remember what you're yelling at each other for? I mean . . . we're clearly lacking in our fighting skills."

"You don't fight fair," she says, but a smile creeps onto her lips.

"Ha. I don't like to fight at all. So are you going to tell me what it is you're trying to say, or do I need to go get my shoes off the stairs for you to throw at my head?"

I don't get the laugh I'm working for. Instead, she continues to play nervously with the hole in my shirt when all I want her to do is meet my eyes. But it hits me that maybe she's not used to fighting how I fight—which is not fighting at all. Maybe she's used to cruel words, maybe even indiscriminate fists. Jesus.

The thought staggers me and makes me question if I need to double down on my humor or back off altogether.

But before I can figure it out, Tenny clears her throat and speaks. "I . . . there can't be more than this. I can't *give you* more than this."

"I need more than that," I say softly as I lower myself to my knees on the step in front of the top one she's sitting on. "Talk to me."

"You're leaving at the end of summer. I'm . . . staying here. Damaged. Introverted. And there can't be more than that."

"Huh."

"What does that sound mean?"

"It means you're supposing I want there to be more. Pretty bold of you if you ask me."

Tenny's eyes flash up to be met with my grin.

"I'm serious," she says.

"Okay. Be serious. But what if I say this is a quid pro quo?"

"You lost me."

"What if I'm using you too, Tenny?"

She sputters out the words, "For what?"

"Ouch." I hiss. "Is the sex that bad you have to ask?" I laugh and press a kiss to her lips with a resounding smacking sound.

"No," she says in frustration. "That's not what I—"

"What if this—*you*—what if I'm using you to help me forget?"

"Forget what?"

"The things I can't seem to do right at home. The things I can't seem to overcome in here." I point to my head. "To realize Britt can't define me. To simply know what it is to feel alive again." I hold her chin between my thumb and forefinger. "You have my permission to use me, Tennyson, because I assure you, I'm no worse for the wear because of it. In fact, I think I'm doing pretty damn good in spite of it. So, if you're trying to break up with me, you're going to have to try a little harder."

"You're exasperating."

"Thank you. I try hard to be." This time when I kiss her, I give in to the temptation and delve my tongue between her lips. Maybe to reassure her we're good. Maybe more so to reassure me.

"We have to think about the girls," she starts the minute the kiss ends. "The summer will be over before we know it, and . . . it's probably better if I go back to the cottage. So they don't get too attached."

And there she goes winning my heart by putting my girls front and center again. "Tenny—"

"I mean, the last thing I want is for this to get messy for them."

I lean back and meet her troubled gaze. There is something more here, but I don't know what it is, and she isn't telling me.

"Guess what?"

"What?"

"The girls saw us kiss."

She freezes momentarily. "What do you mean they saw us kiss?"

"That's what you were interrupting on the porch. They arranged this whole sleepover tonight because they said you deserve more than a kiss in a living room. They say I should buy you flowers and take you on a date. That girls love that. Is that what you like, Tennyson?"

She eyes me warily, thoughts fleeting through her eyes—ones that look like doubt and reasons why we shouldn't do whatever it is that we're doing—but she doesn't put words to them. That tells me I've won the battle for now.

Let's hope it isn't a Pyrrhic victory.

"This is the best part of our fight."

"What is?"

"The kiss and make up part," I murmur and capture her lips again.

"It is?"

"Most definitely." I slide my hands under her shirt and along the soft skin of her back as a soft sigh falls from her lips. "And then I let you use me again."

"Is that so?"

"Trust me. I know what I'm doing." She laughs, and I love the sound of it. "And then after you're done punishing me with your great body and incredible sex, I'll take you out for the date you deserve."

"I think you have the order backwards there, Madden."

"Who says there has to be an order?" I shrug, this time trailing my fingertips over her abdomen. "Maybe sometimes I like dessert before the main course."

I capture her laugh with my kiss. Then my hands begin to roam. Over her hips. Beneath her shirt to the bare skin of her back. Over and then past the waistband of her yoga pants to the apex of her thighs.

My groan is automatic when I feel how slick and ready she already is for me. When I see how aroused she is by our kiss alone. When I hear her mewl and see her spread her legs apart more for me. Welcoming me. Wanting me.

Decision made.

I'm eating dessert first.

She yelps when I lean forward and close my mouth over her clit through the fabric of her pants. My warm breath heats the fabric as I draw in the scent of her arousal.

Definitely dessert first.

Chapter Thirty-Four

Tennyson

I LEAN AGAINST THE BEDROOM DOOR WITH MY EYES CLOSED AND EVERY part of my heart full—yet aching at the same time. Somewhere downstairs, the girls chatter on to Crew about their sleepover. Their giggles and his exclamations float upstairs where I excused myself to get some work done.

But I don't need to work.

I simply need a minute. To think. To breathe. To lie to myself and say I did everything possible last night to slow things down with Crew. To move back to my cottage. To protect him and the girls from the possible danger that could come to them—the danger that haunts my nightmares where Kaleo finds me and hurts them out of vengeance.

I tried.

I did.

But then Crew was the incredible human being he is.

He could have been a prick. He could have taken the first out to have this scattered, guarded woman gone from his house, but instead, he made me laugh with his declaration of our first official non-fight fight.

Then there was the official non-makeup makeup that was . . . it is why I'm standing here with my eyes closed, my head against the door, just trying to take every single memory we made last night and commit them to memory.

Crew made everything about our unanticipated night together perfect. The drive to the top of Freemont Hill, where we sat and watched the lightning bugs flicker to life while eating a picnic-sized charcuterie board complete with a rather nice zinfandel. Then venturing three towns over to Summerset Steak House where the only thing we ordered was one of every dessert on the menu. We went on to have an impromptu judging contest over each of the eight desserts. Then with stomachs full, cheeks sore from laughing, hearts full, and heads a bit loopy from another bottle of wine once we got back home, we did a little skinny-dipping in the pool. Or rather we did only *after* turning the security cameras off, followed by sex where for the first time in a long time, we didn't have to worry about being quiet.

Or where we actually caved to our whims and had said sex.

The way he made everything about the past sixteen hours carefree and uncomplicated, romantic and understated, made me love him more when I already love him as it is . . .

Love?

The word staggers me. The thought more so. The feeling that warms my entire body when I repeat it in my head triumphs both.

Love.

We never said anything about love. I never told myself I was allowed to love anyone again, let alone a man as incredible as him. *Because love takes trust . . . and I never thought I'd trust another man again either.*

But here I am, falling for Crew. Correction, already fallen for Crew. I don't know why my revelation strikes me by surprise. Aren't the classic symptoms of love waking up thinking about someone, wanting to be with that someone all day, and then going to bed dreaming about them?

Because outside of work, of helping Bobbi Jo and her merry band of helpers, of giggling with the twins and teaching them the proper way to torment their father . . . that's pretty much been the past six weeks.

And it can't be.

It can't happen.

But here we are.

Here I am.

What the hell am I supposed to do about it now?

Because I'm still convinced there is no place I could ever hide from Kaleo Makani indefinitely.

Chapter Thirty-Five

Tennyson / Tessa

Four Years Earlier

K ALEO.

Oh shit.

He's not supposed to be home. He's not supposed to be anywhere near here.

My fingers freeze, poised over his keyboard, as documents slowly upload to a secure cloud I was given to use. At no time in my life did I ever peg the transition from being a classically trained ballerina to a computer hacker as being on my bingo card.

But here I am.

And I'm definitely not cut out for it because at the unexpected sound of Kaleo's voice, my hands are trembling so bad I keep hitting the wrong keys.

C'mon. C'mon. C'mon.

"It's fucking bullshit is what it is." But that's his voice saying those words in the kitchen. That's his anger echoing down the hallways.

I close the drive, not caring what did or didn't transfer because not getting caught is my biggest worry right now.

Images of the three men on the boat flash through my mind. My husband's callousness. His cruelty. His complete and utter indifference.

I shut the lid of the laptop as quietly as possible, almost as if Kaleo would be able to hear its quiet click in the kitchen, which is in the complete other wing of the house.

And yet I'm still terrified he will.

Paranoia has taken over my life in the three weeks since I received *that* phone call. And it increases with each and every phone call I receive on the burner cell phone that is currently stored inside one of my many designer handbags. Handbags that are amassed in my own private closet with my designer shoes and dresses.

I know he'll never find it, but that doesn't mean that every time Kaleo looks at me too long, every time he asks who I'm texting on my personal cell phone, or where I'm going when I leave the house with his driver, I worry that he knows. I fear that he suspects.

I worry that I'll be next.

"Fuck," he bellows, followed by the slam of something on the marble counter just as I walk into the kitchen. I bite back a yelp as his cell goes flying into the wall beside me.

But Kaleo is so lost in his rage that he doesn't notice me standing there as he paces across our spacious kitchen. The views of San Francisco Bay and its turbulent water beyond the window feel like they serve as a warning. I meet Rangi's eyes from where he stands opposite of me. The muscle pulses in his jaw, but his acknowledgement of me is a subtle, cautious shake of his head.

"Something's going on, Rangi. How do they fucking know our every move? Who are they getting their goddamn information from?" Kaleo keeps moving, his hands gesticulating as he rants but his mind clearly focused. "First the raid on the San Francisco warehouse. Now a bust at the port. What's it going to be next? Huh?"

"I don't know, sir."

"I thought we took care of the fucking informants."

"Maybe they were telling the truth. Maybe they weren't agents," Rangi says softly, afraid to poke the bear more than he already has been.

"Then who is it?" Kaleo shouts as he approaches his second-in-command. "Is it you?" In a heartbeat, Kaleo has Rangi pinned against the wall, his forearm pressing violently against his throat. "You know everything there is to know. Huh? Is. It. You?" He grates the question out.

Rangi's eyes widen, and his face begins to turn red. But he doesn't react or argue when we all know he could take on Kaleo one-on-one and win handily.

Instead, he just stares at his boss as he tries to strangle the life out of him.

Seconds feel like an eternity while I stand helpless and Kaleo continues to add pressure to his best friend's windpipe. And then just as quickly as the switch had flipped on, it's flicked back off, and Kaleo releases Rangi.

His laughter mixed with Rangi's ragged breathing fills the kitchen. Kaleo slaps a hand against his friend's chest like he didn't just try to kill him. "Not you, Bra. Never you." He cuffs the side of his head and meets his forehead to his top lieutenant's for a moment before stepping back.

It's only then that I swear Kaleo actually sees me.

His eyes lock onto mine, searching them almost as if wondering the same thing about me.

You're being paranoid again, Tess.

But I hold his stare, and it takes everything I have not to flinch despite the chills running through me when he speaks.

"But if I ever find out who is, there will be no place they can hide. Not even the ends of the earth will protect them from the things I will do to them. From the ways I will make them pay."

Chapter Thirty-Six

Crew

THE RAILING HAS BEEN SCRAPED, SANDED, AND PAINTED.

The gutters have been cleaned and de-leaved.

The baseboards in the den have been replaced and repainted.

The decaying boards on the outbuilding have been replaced, and the inside is cleaned as best as possibly can be until I get the consent to do more with it from Uncle Ian. It's his, after all, regardless of how much I feel like it's become ours.

The list of things to finish is getting pared down and checked off. And maybe it's easier to focus on it and possibly running into town to the hardware store than accomplishing the one thing I need to do most.

The one thing I gave myself a deadline to accomplish by today.

With a deep breath, I walk out to the verandah, take a seat on the top step, pick up my cell, and hit send.

"Well, well, well." Justin's gravelly voice fills the line and initiates a fresh wave of guilt laced with panic to surge through me. "If it isn't Mr. Busy himself."

"How's it going, brother?" I ask.

"Same ol', same ol'. Just figuring out my new normal." He chuckles. "I mean who knew having less use of your body meant you had to do a lot more shit to it? You'd think it would mean you'd have less."

I don't react to his attempt at humor. Can't. All I hear are the gunshots. All I remember is his ragged breathing.

"And Sheila? She good?" I ask, completely ignoring his comment.

"Yep. She got that promotion at work she was up for, but they're letting her work from home for the time being."

"Tell her congrats."

"What about you out there in no-man's land playing handyman?"

"It's all good. You should try it sometime." *Fuck. I can't believe I just said that.* "I didn't mean . . . I mean the country. The no-man's land."

"Don't worry about it. The girls? They're good? They seem like it when they text me."

They text him? They can talk to him, but I can't?

You're a real piece of shit, Madden.

"Yeah." I clear my throat, hating this forced awkwardness with a man I used to be able to tell anything to without giving it a thought. "The time away has done them some good. It's like everything is slowed down here. Like it's okay to actually act their age instead of skipping five years ahead like they were back home."

"Then all that worrying was over nothing. Good job, Dad. You made the right decision."

I run a hand through my hair and struggle with what to say next. With how to guide this conversation to where I need it to go but don't want it to go.

"The Cubbies, man." *Good fucking job, Crew. Way to demonstrate what an incompetent ass you are by focusing on his beloved Cubs instead of him as a person. Instead of what tore us both, mind and body, apart.* "I swore this was going to be our year."

"Better luck next year, I guess."

"At least we have hockey to look forward to. I hear they're thinking of signing LeCroix—"

"Crew?" I open my mouth to respond, but he beats me to it. "Are we going to stop with all this small talk bullshit? This is me you're talking to, for fuck's sake."

I hang my head for a beat and nod to no one. "I don't know what to say. I'm at a complete fucking loss. It's my fault—"

"I can't do this without you, man."

His broken words, his confession, are like a knife to the heart. A reminder that I've abandoned my best friend when I'm already reminded almost every second of every day.

"I hesitated, Justin. The baby cried, and I waited instead of firing. If I'd fired, you wouldn't have been . . . you wouldn't be . . . *fuck.*" I squeeze my eyes shut to fight the tears that well up in frustration. "I don't trust myself anymore. I don't know how to be the person I used to be."

Silence weighs heavily on the line.

Talk to me, Justin.

Isn't that what I begged for that day in the apartment? For him to talk to me? For him to prove we're both still alive? For him to give me a lifeline?

It seems I'm asking for the same thing now too.

He clears his throat. "I don't blame you, Crew. You know that, right? We were both there. We both got fucked up. I'm not like this because of you. I'm like this because of that crazy bastard who made a conscious decision to open fire on two policemen doing their job. I don't know how you remember things, but we both hesitated. We both needed to make sure we didn't kill an innocent baby. We played by the rules. He didn't . . . and yeah, it fucking sucks. But I don't blame you."

Bullshit. His absolution is hard to hear. It's even harder to believe when I have the chance to move about freely and walk my daughters down the aisle, when he won't ever have that opportunity.

"Don't say that," I say, barely audible.

"There are some days I wish I'd died. You know that? There are others where I cry and scream and feel sorry for myself. Those are the days I have to pack it all the fuck away so that Sheila doesn't worry I'm going to do something stupid. Those are the days I have to tell myself to snap out of it and remind myself that I'm so fucking grateful to be alive. That I get to grow old with Sheila."

"I'm sorry. I didn't know. I've been a shitty friend. The guilt—*fuck*, the guilt has para—" *Paralyzed me.* "It's eaten a hole through me. It's fucked me up. And how dare I feel that way when I'm here. When I'm walking. When I'm—"

"If I had to go back in that room again, I'd still want you by my side," he says, voice even, resolute.

"Don't." My voice breaks.

"What is it we used to wax on about? The Force Crew?"

"Yeah. We talked about a lot of our pipe dreams. So what? What does that have to do with anything right now?"

"I think we should do it. You and me."

"What do you mean *we should do it?*"

"Just what it sounds like. Let's start it."

"We said we'd do it when we retired."

"If this whole ordeal proved one thing to me, it's that you never know what happens next. You never know how much time you have. Why wait? I mean, let's face it, technically I am retired."

"But . . ."

"Take your medical retirement, Crew. Let's do it. Give me something to look forward to. A piece of the old mixed with some of the new. We could both use the change of scenery."

"Justin. Man." His suggestion throws me. All the times he used to tell me I was full of shit. That catering and pandering to pretentious celebrities, politicians, or moguls' spoiled heirs was beneath me. Beneath us. And yet now? Now he's asking me to do it. Asking me to give him the lifeline he needs.

"You know exactly what I'm talking about," he says quietly, almost as if he's as embarrassed by it as I am. "You're fighting the same goddamn battle in your head that I am. The jerking awake at night. The jumping at loud sounds. The wondering if it was all fucking worth it. The department shrink telling me that it just takes time, when I feel like it's more along the lines of a life sentence. Yeah, I'm dealing with all the same shit too, partner."

"I didn't know."

"Of course you didn't because you were too scared to call me. To talk to me. And I get that too, but it's *me*, man. I'm still the same surly fucker I was before. I haven't changed. *Well* . . . that's a lie, but you know what I mean." He chuckles, and I'm in awe with how easily he's handling all this when I'm still struggling with it.

It's because he doesn't have a choice.

"You and me, Crew. But not because you pity me. And *fuck you*, if you do. Do it because you need something more. Just like I want to do it because I refuse to be strapped to this chair and give up everything I used to be. *I need more.*"

"You're serious."

"As a fucking heart attack."

"Wow. Um . . . I need to—"

"Look. Don't answer me. Think about it. That's all I ask."

"I will."

"And enjoy Tenny."

"Wait. *What?*" How does he know about Tenny?

His laugh reverberates through the connection. "What can I say? The girls spill all your secrets when they text me. And since you haven't said shit because you're afraid you're going to get razzed, I know it must be serious."

"Jesus," I mutter but secretly smile that while I was an asshole friend to him, my girls weren't. At least I know where I've failed, they've been better than me.

"Don't worry, though. The razzing is still coming. And, brother?"

"Yeah?"

"Don't wait so fucking long to call me next time, you asshole."

I chuckle. "I won't."

"Prove it."

He hangs up, his laugh the last thing I hear. I lie back and stare at the ceiling as I try to process Justin's words. His offer.

"Take your medical retirement, Crew. Let's do it. Give me something to look forward to. A piece of the old mixed with some of the new.

You and me, Crew. But not because you pity me. And fuck you, if you do. Do it because you need something more. Just like I want to do it because I refuse to be stuck to this chair and give up everything I used to be. I need more."

"I need more too."

What is it that I need more of?

Am I ready for a step like this?

Can I—*can we*—really do this?

How the fuck does this figure in with my new metric of happiness?

Chapter Thirty-Seven

Tennyson

I GAVE MYSELF ONE DAY.

One day of reprieve where I told myself I could fully enjoy the moment and be present.

One day to help the girls celebrate their twelfth birthday without letting Kaleo—and the paralyzing worry and anxiety he brings with him—ruin the day.

One day to just be Crew and Tenny, the dad and his girlfriend celebrating the girls' birthday instead of damaged Crew and paranoid Tenny, fearful of the danger her past may bring to them.

It hasn't been easy. I've been trying so hard to distance myself, bit by bit, interaction by interaction, to save them from any and all hurt being associated with me may cause.

But I admit it. I got swept up in the girls' enthusiasm for their birthday and the sheer joy of helping do something special for two girls who truly deserve it . . . that I made a deal with myself: allow myself one day of reprieve so that I don't let the girls down, and selfishly so that I can *just be*.

Because they make it so easy to *just be* when it comes to them. Crew and Addy and Paige all make me feel like I belong here, like I fit in seamlessly with them—that fighting their pull is just that—a fight. A constant battle to remind myself why I'm pulling away. Because they mean more to me than I ever could have imagined they would when the girls showed up on my doorstep with Hani that first night.

One day.

That's all I'm giving myself. Easy to think and harder to do when Crew is walking toward me with that grin on his lips and mischief firing in his eyes.

"What?" I ask as he collapses into the chair beside me with a loud, dramatic sigh.

"They're going to be the death of me."

"Ah, it can't be that bad." I chuckle and pat his arm. "If you think the girls are exhausting now, just wait a couple of years."

"How would you know?"

I lean over and grin at his male theatrics. "Because I used to be one."

"Oh yeah. I guess you would know." He returns the grin.

I look out over the backyard. Colorful balloons and their long strings are tied in clusters all around the backyard. The pizza boxes are empty and stacked on one table. The cupcake station still stands untouched—waiting for candles, wishes, and a birthday song, but the candy tower beside it has been demolished. And when I say demolished, I mean canisters empty and all kinds of sticky, gooey pieces have been stomped into the ground from the mini food fight the girls initiated. The food fight that Crew deemed the Sugar War when he jumped in to join them without batting an eye at the mess being made. The presents are stacked in the shade on the porch.

And the pool is a splash-fest of activity as ten girls, high on sugar, are actually playing with each other—Marco Polo, tag, water volleyball—instead of being curled up staring at their phones.

It's official. With that thought, I've just cemented my status as an old person. Time to break out the AARP card about twenty years too soon.

"What's that smile on your face for?" Crew asks.

Just *one* day.

"I'm just thinking how much energy they all have and how it makes me feel old."

"Far from old." He hooks an arm around my waist, pulls me onto his lap, and presses a kiss to my lips.

And the fact that he does, and we can, is still so new to me after sneaking around for so long. I'm more than certain if I look toward the pool right now, the sudden feeling on my back would be from two identical pairs of eyes, complete with goofy smiles.

"You did good, Madden. The party. The music. The . . . everything. The girls seem to be having a blast."

"You may be used to all this organizing and planning and hosting now that you're thick as thieves with Bobbi Jo and the planning committee, but I'm not. It's exhausting and—"

"You know us, thick as thieves." I roll my eyes and laugh. "I think I should be offended by that comment."

"Considering your phone rings several times a day from her needing you for God knows what."

"Are you jealous, Crew Madden?"

"Desperately." He squeezes me. "I'm afraid you're going to run away with her and leave me here to manage all these girls tonight by myself."

"You're the one who agreed to let the girls have a sleepover. A sleepover after they've eaten sugar *all* day, no less."

"Don't remind me," he groans. "I admit. I fully fell for the bait and switch. How was I to know when they asked if Phoebe could sleep over that they were really asking for all eight of them?" I hold his hand out and pretend to wrap a bow around his finger. "Whatever."

"You love it, and you know it."

His expression softens as he looks from me to his girls. I can feel the love radiating off him for Addy and Paige. And then he sighs when he takes in the disaster of streamers and candy and wet towels thrown everywhere.

"See?" he asks when he turns to me. "Aren't you glad your place isn't ready yet?" I falter at his question. At the one thing I've been waiting on to help me separate myself from them. *Just one day, Tenny.* Think about that tomorrow. Obsess about it tomorrow. For today, just enjoy every second.

"If it were, then you'd sadly miss out on all this fun and exciting picking up we're going to have to do when this is all over with."

"No. I think you're the one who's glad because having my place ready would give me a place to conveniently slip away to so I could avoid it."

"You wouldn't dare leave me to fend for myself with this many girls."

"Better play your cards right, or I just might."

"Name your price. Anything. *Everything,*" he teases and throws his hands up in surrender.

I narrow my eyes and stare at him, a smile crawling across my lips. "How about it's enough for me to know you owe me."

"I owe you, huh?" I nod. "Like what kind of favors are we talking about here?"

"I'm sure I'll think of something."

"Like bedroom favors? I mean those I can most definitely do."

I hold his stare, and between the playful tone in his voice and the knowledge that he can fulfill those types of favors—and fulfill them quite well—I

shift off his lap and onto the seat beside him before I give in to the temptation of everything he is and kiss him.

"What's that look for?" he asks. "You're thinking of all those favors, aren't
you?" His chuckle, low and rumbling, is a seduction in and of itself.

"I have a confession to make."

He stops the beer halfway to his lips. "Go on."

"I saw you. I mean I saw you before that first night we met. I came to introduce myself to the new landlord ... well, since I'm telling the truth, I came
to complain about my pipes. And I saw you. Working in the yard. Lifting railroad ties. Looking like a hero straight from one of the romance novels I edit."

His grin widens. "You did?"

"I did." My cheeks flush. "And I was quite enjoying the show until one
of the girls ran up."

"Ah, the thirst trap spell was broken."

I swat at him. "Thirst trap? Really?"

"What can I say?" He shrugs. "When you've got it, you've got it."

"Oh, please."

His laugh rings out and draws some glances our way. "Wow. So, first
you ask for favors *and* then you admit you were a Peeping Tom." He nods
proudly. "I'm down with that."

"You're incorrigible."

"Maybe, but you know you love it. And why exactly are you telling me
this now?"

*Because I can't tell you other truths, so I feel the need to tell you the ones
that I can.*

"I just thought you should know," I say softly and then realize being sad
will only make him question me more, so I smile and shrug. "It's only fair that
you know I was ogling you way before you were me."

"Ogling?"

"That's what I said."

"What about ... other things? Fantasizing, maybe." He glances around
to make sure no one is near before lowering his voice to that panty-melting
tenor of his. "Getting off in the shower, perhaps?"

"Wouldn't you like to know?" I quirk an eyebrow, but I believe the deep-
ening red on my cheeks might give me away by the looks of his Cheshire
cat grin.

"Tell me what you did. What you were thinking of," he murmurs in that gravelly tenor of his.

"I pretended my fingers were your tongue. Sliding over me. Into me. *Owning me.*"

"You're goddamn right," he says.

I smile. How can I not?

"It's time for me to go help Bobbi Jo now."

Crew's hand is on my bicep, pulling me faster than I can think. "Oh, Tenny," he whispers in my ear. "You're not going anywhere. You don't get to say shit like that to a man like me without me making you re-enact it so I can watch."

I moan ever-so-softly, playing him with perfection. "Just know that you were good."

His lips capture mine in a hungry kiss that says he doesn't care who's watching or what rumors it just started. When he leans back, his cocky smirk is back in full force. "Let's go so I can show you just how good I can be."

Chapter Thirty-Eight

Crew

"I THINK I'M DEAF."

Tenny's throaty laugh floats over the warm, summer night air as she sinks down beside me on the slope of grass near the back of the property. It sounds so good to hear.

Today has felt more like normal between us. Like it had been before ... She's been more engaged, more tactile, more relaxed.

See? It was nothing. You were just insecure that she saw you after your nightmare and thought differently of you.

It was all in your head. Like the problems seem to be more often than not as of late.

"The decibel level *is* pretty high in there," she says with a glance back toward the house and its lit-up windows.

"Pretty high?" I chuckle and lift my eyebrows thinking of how many times I've winced in the past thirty minutes before escaping out here for a quick respite. "I'm trying to drink responsibly since I'm the one in charge in there, but every screech and scream and squeal makes me want to break out a bottle of brandy so I can celebrate that I survived each one."

"So that's why you're out here?"

"Yep." I take a sip of my beer, wishing it were said brandy.

"I thought maybe it had to do with what Justin asked you. You really haven't had much time to think about it."

But she's wrong because that's all I've done. In fact, I can't get it off my mind.

The pros.

The cons.

The what-ifs.

And pretty much every other thing in between.

"I've been thinking about it, but not today. Today's about the girls, and I want to be present for every single second of it. With Brittney bailing on them and thinking a two-minute phone call was more than enough, with my mom and little sister unable to come because of her hip surgery, and with Vivian being on location in England, I feel like I need to make up for everyone and everything."

"You're doing a great job. The smiles on their faces and the laughter that has rung out all day long shows it."

"Thanks. It never feels like enough, you know? Besides, I know at some point they won't want to throw parties where their dad is present, so I need to soak it up while I can."

"Very true." She presses a kiss to the side of my shoulder. "Well, like I said before, I'm here if you want to talk it all out."

I hadn't realized how much Brittney and I didn't speak about our lives, about anything above and beyond our day-to-day, until I told Tenny about my conversation with Justin.

It felt good to talk to someone, even if all she did was sit there, hold my hand, and listen.

Having Tenny do that revealed a stark reminder of how isolated I'd become in the aftermath of Brittney leaving and being shot. It reinforced that back then, Justin was the one I confided in more than anyone, and how after the incident, I lost my sounding board when I pulled away from him.

I didn't realize how much I'd been flying solo until I talked to Tenny. It felt good too. *Vital.* The fact that I opened up showed me how much I trust her. And this time with her, this piece of quiet we carved out right now, in the midst of the chaos going on around us, is even more important.

"There's something about watching the sunset that's relaxing to me."

"Agreed. When I first moved here . . . when I was figuring *stuff* out, I used to sit and watch them every night. Just me and Hani and a glass of wine. The way I look at it, no matter how shitty the day was, the sunset was proof that even a bad day could end in beauty."

"Says the book editor who always has a way with her words," I murmur, loving when she rests her head on my shoulder. There's something about the simple action that moves me. Maybe it's the ease with which she does it after being with someone who did *who knows what* to her.

I'm glad I can give that to her.

"I wonder what they wished for?" she murmurs quietly, almost as if we're afraid to disrupt the show Mother Nature is putting on with the pinks and the oranges owning the horizon.

"The girls?"

"Yeah. When they blew out their candles. I used to wish for the most ridiculous things. A pony for two years straight. Pointe shoes another. For Scott Lundy to kiss me after school. For Becky Decker to move away since she's who Scott Lundy liked."

I burst out laughing and press a kiss to her head. "I'm glad to see you had your priorities."

"Those *were* priorities back then. I mean securing first kisses were *very* important."

"Let's just hope that's not what the girls wished for," I say and then fall quiet because I know exactly what they wished for.

I walked into the kitchen to grab more plates and overheard them whispering feverishly. Typically, I would have passed right by, but this time I stopped because I wanted to make sure their party was going okay and that there was no drama happening that I was missing.

"Okay. So you wish for us to move here permanently so we don't have to leave Tenny or our friends, and I'll wish for Tenny to move to Chicago with us," Paige says quietly.

"Perfect. We'll have both of our bases covered—that we get to keep her—regardless of what happens."

The funny thing about overhearing what they said was that my gut reaction was to tell them that I've wished for the same thing too.

And that shocked me.

Our life is in Chicago. Leaving there isn't something I saw for us any time soon.

But I want the girls to be happy. And God knows I want more of Tenny. She makes me happy. She makes the girls happier. I mean . . . *shit*.

I need to feel this—us—out.

To see if we're real.

To see if I can trust my judgment this time around when clearly I made a huge error when it came to Britt.

But when we sit here like this in completely comfortable silence, when we had a day like today where we flawlessly worked together as a team, and when I look at her and imagine not just tomorrows but forevers, I know we could make a life together.

But Tenny's not leaving here. Not even when she knows that one might get lost better in a bigger city.

That much I know.

What about me? Is being a police officer so much of my identity, is it so ingrained in me that I can't part with it? Or is it something I thought defined me but have since realized there's so much more to me? A better, present father. An understanding, patient lover. A loyal, reliable friend.

Maybe coming here—simplifying things—gave me the clarity I was hoping for.

Which *do* I want more? The one thing that's been true, been steady, my whole life? Or the one who just walked into it, turned it upside down, and made me want more?

"You're awfully quiet," Tenny says.

More shrieks followed by laughter float out the window to where we are as I wrap my arm around her shoulders and pull her in close to me. "I'm just thinking about later."

"Later?"

"Yes, later when the door on my bedroom is locked, and ten girls are downstairs and passed out in a sugar coma, dead asleep to the world."

"What about it?"

I chuckle. "It'll be time to discuss those favors I owe you . . ."

Chapter Thirty-Nine

Tennyson / Tessa

Three Years Earlier

KALEO MEETS MY GAZE FROM ACROSS THE COURTROOM. HIS DARK eyes are almost black as they hold mine, his expression cold as steel.

He knows.

My mouth grows dry as the judge begins to address the court before she reads his sentence. As we wait to hear the punishment that is handed down. As we learn that his fate is sealed.

But he knows. Because the prosecutor slipped up when he entered a note into evidence. A note in my handwriting.

Handwriting that by the look on Kaleo's face, he and his team caught.

Yes. I'm the reason you're here, Kaleo. You decieved me in the worst of ways. This is your punishment. One you deserve wholeheartedly.

I lift my chin a little higher despite every part of me trembling inside and my pulse thundering in my ears. I refuse to back down. I refuse to let him know I'm terrified of him and the reach I'm sure he'll still have.

I did this.

I put a murdering drug lord in prison.

I'm proud that I did, but that doesn't mean I'm not worried about what my future will hold. It was one thing to agree to cooperate to gain immunity and know I was getting a new life. It's a whole other thing once it's about to happen, and you wonder if anyone will remember you when you cease to exist.

"And with that," the judge states, "I remand you, Kaleo Makani, to the Federal Bureau of Prisons for a term of—"

"Remember what I said, Tess," Kaleo calls out, cutting the judge off.

The judge bangs her gavel several times. "Mr. Shapiro, please control your client, or I'll have him removed from the court."

But even as Kaleo's defense lawyer leans over and whispers in his ear, Kaleo's eyes don't veer from mine. "Remember what I said," he mouths again.

In that moment, I know the smirk he gives me will forever haunt me. *He knows.*

I stand and give him one last look before walking out of the courtroom. If only walking away from him would erase the images burned in my head from that night. *If only I could never think of him again.*

Each step away from the courthouse doors is a goodbye.

To the life I once dreamt of having.

To the nightmare it then became.

To leaving the one true thing that never let me down. Teaching my students. Feeling like I made a difference.

To my friends.

To all that is familiar.

When I get in the car across the street, I'm going to be handed an all-new identity. Tessa Makani will no longer exist.

He knows.

Tessa is about to die in a fiery crash to prevent Kaleo from coming after her because even through the jailhouse walls, the DEA fears he'll still be calling the shots.

That's why this is happening so fast.

That's why I don't even get time to get my things.

Someone will be watching.

Someone has since the day he was taken into custody.

I approach the black sedan in the secured, underground parking lot, its windows tinted so dark you can't see in them. The low hum of the engine is the only sound besides the thunder of my heartbeat.

With a deep breath, I follow the instructions I was given and climb into the back seat as if everything is normal. As if this isn't goodbye to all I've ever known.

"Are you ready?" the driver asks without turning around.

He doesn't wait for my answer. Instead, he pulls deeper into the underground parking structure instead of heading toward the exit. I look around to see him drive through a set of K-rails complete with armed guards and pull up next to another black SUV with tinted windows.

I've been briefed on what will happen next. I'll climb into the new car while the one I'm currently in will leave with a full security detail ahead and behind it. It'll be a decoy for those who are most definitely waiting for me.

For someone like Rangi, no doubt.

And then this new car will take me out a different exit and hopefully do so without anyone knowing I'm in it.

The doubt seeps in. It seems too easy, too cliché to anyone who has ever watched a police drama. If Kaleo's team is smart enough to evade the authorities for as long as they did, it's hard for me to believe they wouldn't figure out what is happening right now.

"Miss?" the driver prompts.

I take a deep breath. It's now or never.

"Thank you," I murmur as I slide out of the town car and a female agent with a similar build and hair color takes my place.

I climb into the SUV, and just as I'm shutting the door, the opposing one opens. The strangled scream I hear is my own as Rangi stands there and looks at me.

He's here for me.

He'd do anything for Kaleo.

Anything.

"Hello, Tessa."

I slowly reach my hand for the door handle, my mind spinning, trying to process. How? What happened? Did he hurt the other agents trying to protect me?

He slides in the seat beside me and hits the back of the front seat two times to tell the driver to take off.

"Relax," he says. "The plan's still in place."

"What plan? How—"

"Who did you think the inside man was? The one who slipped you the phone? The one who protected you even when you didn't know you were in danger?" He reaches his hand out. "Special Agent Tom Halston. Nice to meet you."

I stare at him. A man my husband trusted more than anyone else. Talk about karma. The two people Kaleo trusted the most are the ones who betrayed him. I thought Rangi would be the one to try and kill me.

And now I'm meant to trust him?

Talk about being fucked up.

But he's here, and the agents I can now see milling around the outside of the SUV are alive and well.

I sure as hell didn't see this one coming, but that doesn't mean I don't double-check Agent Halston's hands to make sure he's not holding a weapon in one of them.

He's not.

My shock seeps into awareness.

"I don't understand," I barely whisper as I shake his hand.

"Look at those clear skies, will you?" he says as we exit the garage. "It's a good day for me to take revenge on you for betraying my best friend—or so the story will go."

"Are we ready, sir?" the radio at his waist chirps.

Agent Halston looks at me and grins. "No time like the present to be run off the road and killed in a fiery crash, is there?"

Chapter Forty

Tennyson

"Now that your first official Redemption Falls Founder's Day is underway, is it all you thought it would be?" I ask Crew as I slide a glance his way and chuckle.

"I think that I'll be in trouble no matter how I answer that."

"Hey, it's no skin off my back. All I did was sell signs for sponsorships."

"And those signs are bright and colorful. Let's not forget informative and sexy as hell while we're at it."

"You're really laying it on thick, aren't you?"

"Only for you, my love." He mock bows, and I roll my eyes.

"You're used to the grandeur and grandiose of Chicago. I'm sure this seems incredibly juvenile to you in comparison." I wave to Tanya who's across the street sharing cotton candy with a grinning little boy I assume is her grandson.

Crew tugs on my hand and pulls me against him so that we're chest to chest, and I'm forced to look up at him. "It's not juvenile." A soft kiss to my lips. "It's perfect. It's representative of every single reason I wanted to move the girls here for the summer. The community feel. Everyone knowing everyone. Letting the girls go hang out in the carnival section, knowing they're going to be safe because once again, everyone knows everyone." He slides his hands around my waist, puts his hands in my back pockets, and kisses me again. "And it gives me a perfectly good reason to kiss you in the middle of the town square."

This time when he kisses me, the world falls away for a few seconds, and I allow myself to get lost in him.

I've been doing that a lot more than I want to lately. Getting lost in Crew. Allowing myself to.

While I gave myself *just one day* at the girls' birthday party, that one day has turned into one week and then that one week turned into another week.

Being with Crew makes it too easy to forget every reason I shouldn't get lost in him. The irony is the way he makes me feel—adored, wanted, loved, *safe*—should make me want to protect him more. Should make me keep him at arm's length simply to keep him safe.

But admittedly, I'm being selfish. Completely and utterly selfish, and no matter how much I try to justify why I shouldn't be, I can't help it. *Crew is just that good.*

It's only when we start to stroll again that I notice several people are sliding glances our way. This is the first time the *town* has officially seen us together as a couple.

We just proved the rumors to be true.

"I guess the cat's out of the bag," Crew whispers.

"What cat is that?"

His chuckle rumbles. "I could say so many damn things in response, but I'll be a good boy and refrain."

I lean up and whisper in his ear. "Please. *Don't.* I rather enjoy that dirty mouth of yours."

"Don't tempt me to take you behind the school gym and have my way with you, West."

"Now that's a proposition you don't hear every day."

He stops and looks at me with a devilish grin, and I can only imagine what he's thinking.

It's probably along the same lines as what I am: *I can't get enough of you.* I should though, because we're together more often than we're not. It's been almost three months, the lust should have faded, but it's still stronger than ever.

"Dad." Addy runs up with a funnel cake in one hand and a stuffed animal Crew won her earlier in the other. "You're not going to believe it. We did a flash mob. All us kids. We did it, and it actually worked." Her words tumble out in an ongoing sentence. "And guess what? They let me lead it, and it turned out sooooo good."

Crew glances at me, a tad bit lost. "Flash mob?"

"A spontaneous dance that's choreographed," I say. "They're all over social media. One person starts dancing and then another joins in and, before you know it, a big group of people are—"

"Oh. Yes. How could I have forgotten what they're called?" He puts the heel of his hand to his forehead as if he's an idiot, earning the laugh and eye roll from Addy that he was working for.

"Did someone record it?" I ask.

"For our channel?" Her eyes widen, and I take the shocked look in them as a telltale sign that she didn't get it recorded. "Oh my God. We have to do it again. Right now before everyone leaves—"

"I want to do it." We both whip our heads over to Crew and his earnest expression. "What? You don't think I can do it?"

"Dad." She snorts. "You *don't* dance."

He looks from her to me and then back. "There's a first time for everything." He holds his hand out to her. "Lead the way."

And for the next fifteen minutes, I stand aside and watch the girls try to teach their dad how to dance. There are a lot of frustrated sighs, even more giggles, and about as many heads in their hands as rolled eyes.

And as much as I want to join in and be a part of this with them, I'm having more fun watching Crew be the attentive, silly, incredible dad he is.

I mean, I don't know how anyone can say single dads aren't sexy. Because this one? He is over-the-top incredible in every sense of the word.

And I'm the lucky one he's chosen to be with.

The girls begin to cue everyone back up to their places, and while he waits, Crew meets my eyes.

Every woman should have a man who looks at her like he looks at me. Like even when he's in the midst of being in the moment with his own daughters, I feel like I'm the only one in the world he sees.

And nothing could be further from the truth . . . but it's how he makes you feel.

I smile softly at him. Loving Crew Madden is one of the easiest things I've ever had the pleasure of doing.

It's the self-preservation that's much more difficult. The keeping it to myself and trying to pretend that casual is all we are.

The constant reminders that Crew and the girls are leaving in just a few weeks.

There hasn't been a day that's passed that I don't have to repeat it to myself.

It's a telling sign that I've let him think that I believe his excuses as to why the cottage isn't complete. Even more so that I haven't called him on it by moving my things back there when he wasn't around.

But I don't want to leave this family I've grown to love. A love I've felt in silence to protect myself from the devastation I'll feel when he leaves. A pain that will hurt like hell but that will reaffirm that this was real. That this really happened.

So I sit here and watch Crew and his uncoordinated dance moves, hear his rich laughter, revel in the glances he slides my way, and try to soak up each and every minute I have left with him.

Hopefully the memories will help ease the sting.

But I'm not sure if anything ever will.

Chapter Forty-One

Crew

THE NIGHT IS WARM. THE LIGHTS STRUNG UP ALL OVER TOWN CAST a soft glow that one might say is romantic. The song is slow and bluesy. And the woman dancing in my arms owns me.

So much so that when the fireworks go off overhead, I have more fun watching her react to them than watching them myself.

The girls walked to the lake that borders the festival with Phoebe and her parents so they could watch the fireworks there—supposedly it's a better show because of the reflections off the water.

But I don't need a better show.

I have it right here.

Tenny turns and looks at me with narrowed eyes. "What?"

Nothing.

Everything.

So much that I haven't said and desperately want to. But I don't quite know how to say it because it was a shock to me as well.

I've fallen for her.

I love her.

But haven't I felt that way for some time? Haven't I questioned and doubted and told myself I was full of shit because I'm not exactly the expert person on picking who to love?

And yet here we are.

A girl who's never going to leave here, whose secrets remain untold. And a boy who doesn't know how to feel any other way for a woman who seemingly jumpstarted his heart again.

Maybe it's the finality of the night. Founder's Day. The celebration of the end of summer. Of getting one day closer to packing up and leaving for home. For Chicago.

But is it still home to me?

Or is this house here, the one I've put time in, the one I've heard my girls giggle and huff in, the one I've sat many nights on the porch with Tenny's head on my shoulder watching the sunset . . . the one that feels more like home?

"You want to tell me what you're thinking about?" Tenny whispers in my ear as color explodes overhead.

"You."

"Me?" She smiles, and before she can say another word, I slant my lips over hers.

I don't care who's around or who's watching or that we're in the middle of a goddamn fireworks show. I take the kiss I want. The kiss I need. The one that tells her everything my words have lacked.

And when the kiss is done, when the moment should have passed but only feels so much more powerful, I rest my forehead against hers. "I love you, Tenny. I didn't think I had it in me to love again, but I do. *And I have.*"

Her hands tense on my shoulders. Her breath hitches as she shakes her head back and forth, physically rejecting what I've said while her eyes tell me she knows. That she loves me too.

"Don't say that, Crew. Please." She presses a kiss to my lips that is in such contradiction to her words my chest aches. "I can't give you what you need. What you deserve."

I take her hands in mine and squeeze gently so that she looks back at me again.

The fear is there. It swims with love, and I don't know how to conquer that. I don't know how to right wrongs that someone else caused other than to be patient.

Even if it fucking kills me.

"You're telling me you don't feel the same? All it takes is a simple shake of the head to tell me otherwise."

"I told you before that I don't want to lie to you . . . so I'm not going to answer that."

She didn't shake her head. She might not be able to say the words, but she sure as shit didn't shake her head.

A smile tugs on the corners of my mouth as relief—and even more love—flows through me at her non-answer answer. Just like our official first non-fight fight.

I'll take that.

The question is . . . what in the fuck am I going to do with it?

Chapter Forty-Two

Tennyson

WHEN THE HOUSE IS ASLEEP, I STAND AT CREW'S DOORWAY AND watch him sleep, his words from earlier tonight on constant replay through my mind.

"I love you, Tenny. I didn't think I had it in me to love again, but I do. And I have."

The expression on his face. The look in his eyes. The words on his lips. All three own me. Own my heart. And kill me silently knowing I can't tell him I feel the same.

I do.

God, do I.

But if I were to voice the words, if I were to tell him how I really feel—that I've fallen just as hard for him—then it would only make what I have to do that much harder on a man who's already been abandoned once.

What's crueler? To tell him I love him, a man who didn't think he had it in him to love again, and then to push him away? Or to love him silently, never saying the words, so it's easier on him when we part ways?

One option will kill me.

The other would kill him.

I wipe the tear that has welled and slipped down my cheek. My heart swelling and breaking simultaneously as I enter the room and slide into bed with Crew.

My lips find his in the darkness. My heart beats against his in silent protest to the words I can't speak but that it feels.

Crew startles but slips into the kiss, his hands moving to frame my face, to guide my head back and meet my eyes through the dim light.

Our breaths feather against each other's as his eyes search mine as best as they can in the dim light.

I'm not sure if I'm glad he can or can't see what my eyes say. The words my lips won't.

I love you too.

I think I have for some time.

I don't know if he finds the answers he needs, but when I lean forward to claim his lips again, to pour my emotions into him, he lets me.

He matches me kiss for kiss. Touch for touch. Sigh for sigh. Need for need.

He kisses away the lone tear that slips down my cheek without saying a word, but rather accepting the numerous reasons it might be there.

There is no finesse in our meeting. No need to direct or guide. It's just two bodies coming together. Two people who know what each other needs, what each other wants, and knowing how to give it to them.

Unwavering needs mix with unapologetic wants. Urgency escalates with each touch we share in the early morning hours. Open-mouthed kisses placed on my neck. My hand pressed against his heart. His bare hands skimming down the skin of my back. My lips to the scar on his shoulder.

I open for him without prompting. He pushes into my wet heat with a feral groan of pleasure from the intimacy of that first connection. He stills when he settles all the way into me, pausing for a beat to capture my lips with his. To tease and taunt with a tender kiss.

And then he begins to move. We're slow strokes and soft murmurs. We're grinding hips and hushed pleas for more. We're tense muscles and satisfied sighs.

I pour everything I can into our joining. I touch him every chance I get. I hold his eyes the entire time. I meet him match for sensuous match. Anything and everything I can do short of saying the three little words that are burning in my throat and bursting from my chest.

I come first. Silent but powerfully as my body sinks into the intense gentleness of my climax, made more intense by my refusal to look away. I let Crew see every emotion flicker through my eyes and over my expression. The pleasure. The adoration. The gratitude. The vulnerability.

The love.

He moves slow and steady, but it's not much longer until he crashes over the edge. But his eyes don't waver as his body soars. He affords me the same courtesy I did him. He lets me see everything I do for him. How I make him feel. How I complete him.

And when he sinks down on top of me—his body half on me, his face nuzzled under my neck, his hand over my own heart—all I can hope is that he now knows.

How I feel.

Why I can't say the words.

Why this will never be able to work.

And selfishly, I hope he'll still love me in spite of it.

Because of it.

For it.

"We'll figure it out, Tenny," he murmurs, the heat of his breath against my neck reminding me this is real. That he knows it too. "We'll figure it out."

Chapter Forty-Three

Crew

"GIRLS?" I call up the stairs. "FAMILY MEETING TIME."

Three.

Two.

One.

The groans come down the stairs as if on cue. The *seriouslys* come shortly after.

"*Seriously*. Now, get your butts down here," I say just as two unhappy tweens tromp down the stairs with eyes already rolling and sighs heavy.

"We're in the middle of filming a makeup tutorial," Addy says, looking up for the first time and greeting me with a face covered in rainbow colors. "Clearly we're not done."

"Clearly," I say, forgoing asking what in the world they are trying to paint on her face because at this point, I have no clue. It's way easier to just smile and nod than to accidentally say the wrong thing and cause tears to burst out without knowing why. "Looks great. Take a seat."

"Shouldn't Tenny be here?" Paige asks.

"Why?"

"Well, she's part of our family, right? Shouldn't she be part of our family meeting?"

Paige's words put a hitch in my step as I move to sit in the chair opposite the girls. And just like that, the girls have accepted Tenny into our family as if it's a no-brainer. Whereas I'm overthinking and struggling with every minute detail of it.

What I'd give to be a kid again so I could just go with the flow and allow change to happen without fighting it.

"Well, true," I finally say, "but this is about us, and so I wanted it to be just the three of us."

"Don't tell us we're leaving yet," Paige says matter of fact.

"What do you mean?" I ask.

"We don't want to leave yet," she says. "We're having so much fun with our friends and with Tenny . . . and you're so . . ."

"I'm so, what?"

"You smile more here," Paige says, averting her eyes to her sister.

"Or maybe we don't want to leave at all," Addy adds and effectively knocks me on my ass.

"What?" I ask.

They both shrug in unison. "We like it here, Dad."

"But you only know summer here. You don't know what the school is like or what—"

"We know enough," Paige says.

"Plus, there's no Ginny." Addy winces for show.

"Girls . . ." It's a half-hearted sigh because isn't this partially what I wanted to hear? But now that I'm hearing it, I'm silently freaking out.

"What did you want to talk to us about? What's the big family meeting over?" Addy asks.

I shake my head and chuckle. "Honestly? I wanted to see what you guys thought of Redemption. If you liked it or if it made you miss back home, is all. Just a temperature check."

"Temperature check?" Paige looks at her sister and giggles. "That's the weirdest phrase *ever*."

"I guess it is," I mutter.

"We like it here, Dad. There are no George Vinson's to be gross in class. We can go outside and hang out until dark when at home we can't do that. You let us have more independence here. And we have a lot more friends here too," Addy says.

"And there's Tenny." Paige's eyes hold mine, and I swear to God she's waiting for a reaction from me.

I meet her stare and nod. "There is."

"And we're pretty sure she's a big part of why we're all smiling more so . . ."

"So?" I ask.

"So, it wouldn't bug us if Uncle Ian called and asked you to work more on the house so that we had to stay longer," Paige says.

"Okay. Well . . ." I run my hands down the tops of my thighs, more than blown out of the water at how this conversation just went. I expected groans and protests. Drawn out *dads* and huffed breaths. No way in hell did I expect them to tell me it's okay to stay here in Redemption Falls. To move here.

They were supposed to be the ones grounding me. The ones holding me back from taking this ridiculous leap of faith that I'm being completely tempted by. The voice of reason.

Instead, they fanned the flames.

"Earth to Dad?" Paige is waving her hands in front of my face.

"Yes. Sorry. I was thinking."

"Hopefully about what good thing you're going to cook for dinner, right?" Addy asks.

"Smart aleck."

"Always." She stands and takes a bow, looking almost like a clown with the vibrant eyeshadow and half-blue, half-red lips. "Can we go now?"

"Yes," I say.

Long after they've run upstairs and started filming again, I stay where I am, running the conversation over and over through my mind. Making a mental pros and cons list. Thinking about the repercussions of staying. Of going. Of everything in between.

My sighs fall heavy.

My head is still confused.

And when Tenny opens the front door, a few shopping bags in hand and a soft smile spreading on her lips when she sees me, I finally have my answer.

It may not have come as easily as the girls', but they were right. Tenny needed to be here.

Because all it took was one look from her for me to know the answer.

And honestly, I'm pretty sure it's been looking at me right in the face this whole time.

Chapter Forty-Four

Crew

"**C**REW?" ADELE ASKS. "WE DON'T HAVE AN APPOINTMENT scheduled until next week. I got your message. Is everything okay?"

I close my eyes for a beat and smile, feeling like a thousand tons have been lifted from my chest with my decision.

"Everything is great. I just wanted you to know, you were right."

"About?"

I chuckle because I sure as hell won't miss the ever-constant question to answer a statement. "About my new metrics for how I measure my happiness."

"How so?"

There's another one.

"Being on the force was my profession. It isn't who I am. It doesn't define me."

"And?"

"And I'm so much more than that. I thought the shootout, this delay in getting back, the goddamn shit in my head, was the worst thing that has ever happened to me. I was wrong. I think it just might be the best."

"Okay. Um . . ."

"It made me sit back and look at life through a different lens. A different perspective. It also made me make a change of scenery. I thought I was doing it for my girls, for their mental health, but it ended up being exactly what I needed too."

Silence hangs on the line for a few moments. "I don't quite know what to say, Crew, other than I'm so pleased for you. You sound truly . . . happy."

"I am." I run a hand through my hair and look out the upstairs window with perfect timing to see Tenny with her arms around each one of my girls' shoulders. Talking to them. Laughing with them. I smile as she gets behind the wheel of her car to head to the store.

I'm fine with non-answer answers.

I'm perfectly content with her being my non-girlfriend girlfriend.

The plan someday is to make her my non-wife, wife.

But baby steps.

That much I know.

"So you can cancel my appointments that are already booked. I don't need clearance to come back to the force because I'm not coming back. This is the time for new beginnings, Doc, and I'm about to start mine."

I give a mental fist pump, my mind more than scattered as we finish our conversation. And when we do, I take a few minutes to let the adrenaline and panic that rushes through me subside.

I just did that.

I really just did.

I pick up my cell again and dial.

"I was wondering how long it was going to take you."

My grin is automatic.

The sound of his voice alone tells me I'm doing the right thing.

The only thing.

The thing that's best for me.

Chapter Forty-Five

Tennyson

WE HAVEN'T ADDRESSED THE ELEPHANT IN THE ROOM.
What happens when Crew heads back to Chicago? To his real life. To everything that's not me.

When we fell into whatever this is between us, I was certain he understood that anything more than fun was off-limits for me. That I can't feel how he feels. But the "We'll figure it out," he said after we made love on Founder's Day still hangs in the smothered air around us.

And it does nothing to abate everything rioting around inside of me nor the discord over knowing there is nothing that can really be figured out.

The complex game of betrayal my own heart is playing on me is strong. To feel the love you have but deny yourself of it all at the same time.

I don't want him to go back to Chicago. God, I don't think my heart can take that.

But in the same breath, if he goes back, then this life of mine, this past of mine, can't put him and the girls in danger.

On the flip and more than ironic side, isn't being with Crew the reason I feel that having a real life, a life full of love and laughter with someone else, is possible?

I hate to dream but live to dream for it.

For waking up with the girls giggling downstairs, squabbling over what's for breakfast while Crew hands me a cup of coffee and grants me that quiet smile of his.

Normalcy.

Simplicity.

Stolen kisses in pantries.

Slow dances on living room floors.

Sunsets in comfortable silence.

Tangled sheets and soft sighs.

Unconditional love.

A life everyone deserves but that I never thought I'd get to have again.

Is it too much that I want to be selfish for once? That I deserve the chance to be?

I love him.

Plain.

Simple.

I love him, and I need him to know.

Quite the revelation when I'm standing in the snack aisle at Target. But I don't care. I throw my head back and laugh. I'm in love. He loves me.

We'll figure this out.

Isn't that how love works?

Forget the chips. I need to get home.

I leave my basket in the chip and cracker aisle and start heading through the store, distracted in thought and filled with a hope I haven't felt in the longest time.

Crew.

Addy.

Paige.

They're my hope.

I dig in my purse for my phone as I pass the electronics section, and when I look up, I stop dead in my tracks.

Rangi.

Agent Halston.

His face is mirrored on every single television for sale that lines the walls.

I stand there dumbfounded as I read the subtitles on the screen. Words like *brutal murder, hunted down, revenge killing,* scream at me from their two-dimensional world. *No. No, this can't be happening. Fuck. He found Rangi . . . Tom.*

To other shoppers, I must look like a deer caught in the headlights. Scared. Transfixed. Waiting for the worst to come.

And then the time that felt like it was in slow motion suddenly feels like it's slamming into me in fast forward.

I run out of the store, my phone unsteady in my trembling hands as I search for more. A horn blasts, making me jump. I'm so preoccupied I almost walked in front of a car. I don't stop, though. I keep going until I slide behind the wheel of my Jeep and lock the doors.

Long Waited Revenge Ends in Brutal Murder

What could be a plot right out of a popular crime novel came to life late yesterday afternoon in the quiet suburbs outside of Baltimore, Maryland. The characters could seemingly be pulled from its pages. An imprisoned drug lord whose long arm had seemingly reached beyond the walls and his second-in-command who has supposedly carried his orders out for years.

Yesterday morning, these two things resulted in a brutal set of murders. Rangi Haloa, the second-in-command in the Makani drug organization, was murdered along with his wife and infant son inside their modest home. Sources say the scene was unspeakable due to signs of unimaginable torture.

Sources believe that Haloa's boss, the currently incarcerated, Kaleo Makani, ordered the hit on his long-running lieutenant for what some perceive to be Haloa's attempt to take more control of the distributing empire.

Haloa was no stranger to federal investigators for his role in a considerable list of unproven accusations against him. Among the top ones is the suspected murder of Makani's own wife, Tessa Makani, in retribution for her help in building the federal case against her husband.

When asked to confirm or deny what our sources have divulged, police have stated no comment. There is no further press conference planned until a break is made in the investigation.

I read the article again and again as if the words will miraculously give me more information. But it doesn't. And neither does any other article I find in my frantic search.

They all say Kaleo's second-in-command is dead.

But I know different.

He wasn't just an associate. He was an FBI agent. A traitor in Kaleo's eyes.

Did Kaleo find out somehow or was what the article said true? Rangi was killed simply for trying to gain control?

And if it was true, what did Kaleo's hitman find out through torture? What secrets did Agent Halston spill to try and save the life of his wife and child?

My hands tremble as I start the Jeep. As the images from the articles replay in my head—sheet-covered stretchers, a house crawling with law enforcement, a female agent with her head bowed and tears streaming down her face.

My heart races as I pull out from the parking lot. As I look in my rearview mirror to make sure no one is following me.

If he can assassinate an FBI agent—a man who is most likely protected in all aspects considering his double life—then what says he won't get to me? *Won't find me? And why haven't I heard from Peter? Do I call him? Do I wait for him to call me?*

What. Do. I. Do?

By the time I get back to the cottage, I've worked myself into a frenzy.

I have to leave.

I can't stay here. I can't put Crew and the girls at risk. It would be selfish of me to do that to them.

Chapter Forty-Six

Crew

I T CAN'T BE.

She can't be.

But . . . but she always looked familiar to me. Familiar in a way I couldn't place but then eventually let go.

I stare at the picture in my hand. The one that fell out of the apothecary cabinet when I tried to move it so the flooring company could finish the flooring. How could I have known when I moved the cabinet that the drawer was going to slide open and this was going to come out, softly flutter to the ground, and more than rock my suddenly settled world?

How could I have known the woman I'm in love with is the same woman standing beside Kaleo Makani? A man I know from my time in narcotics. A man who is the furthest thing from a good human being?

But it's her.

The hair is darker now, her slight curves a little fuller too, but it's Tennyson. I'd stake my life on it.

It only takes a few seconds for me to pull up on my phone article after article about Tessa Makani's death. About the recent murders in Maryland.

The fiery crash after being chased off the road by an unknown vehicle.

The over-the-top funeral that her widower somehow managed to arrange from his prison cell.

Not Tennyson West's. Fucking hell. *It's the missing piece. The piece I haven't been able to put my finger on.*

Pieces begin to fall into place.

The panic attacks. The perfect record that was too squeaky clean. Tenny not wanting to tell me lies. Tenny hiding from newspaper pictures.

Her confession that she can't give me what I need.

I don't deal in assumptions, but I'd bet the farm that Tenny's presence here was more of a placement by the Federal Witness Protection Program than by her own choice. Her fear. Her skittishness when we first met. The freak-out over thinking someone had been in her house.

If Makani can have his second-in-command killed from prison, if he doesn't believe she's really dead . . . then she could be his possible next target. She could be forever on his radar.

Fuck.

Fucking hell.

Just as I wrap my head around the thought as best as I can, Tenny's Jeep flies up the driveway toward the house, leaving an agitated plume of dust in its wake.

I stare at the photo again before tucking it into my back pocket and heading up to the house.

What am I going to say? I don't have a fucking clue. I'm just glad the girls aren't home so we can have this talk without interruption.

And that thought—what do I even say—becomes more prevalent when I walk in the house to find Tenny in her room, frantically stuffing her things in trash bags.

What the fuck is going on here?

How does she know that I know already?

But she's so frenzied that she doesn't even notice I'm there until she goes to grab her computer and sees me in her periphery.

"Crew!" She jumps back almost as if she's afraid of me, guilt-laced surprise swimming in her eyes.

"Where're you going in such a hurry?" I lean my shoulder against the doorjamb and tilt my head to the side.

"Um . . . back to the cottage. I think it's time. I mean—"

"Don't bullshit me, Tenny. Least of all don't do that. This"—I point to the trash bags—"isn't someone going back to the cottage, especially not how you were just doing it."

"You're right. It's not." She shakes her head, and I can see how hard it is for her to swallow over her lies. "I'm leaving. I got an opportunity in Atlanta. With a publishing house."

I chew on my cheek. "No, you don't."

"What do you mean?"

"Just what I said. No, you don't." I take a step toward her. "You can stop running now, Ten. It must be exhausting."

Chapter Forty-Seven

Tennyson

"WHAT MUST BE EXHAUSTING?" I ASK, VOICE SHAKY, PULSE pounding.

"This. You. Always hiding."

I almost don't hear him because all I see are three stretchers leaving Rangi's house. All I can think of is the three people here who I don't want that to be.

I have to get out of here.

I have to leave before I bring that to them.

And to think an hour ago I was on cloud nine and now this . . .

"I'm not hiding," I say and offer a strained smile I know he doesn't believe. "I told you before, and I'll tell you again, I can't give you what you need, Crew."

I begin to shove more of my stuff in the black trash bag. Each item I add is like a dagger to my heart. But I keep my head down, afraid he'll see right through me.

And then his feet come into view, and I'm forced to look at him when his fingers push my chin up. "You don't get to use that excuse anymore."

"What excuse?" I barely whisper.

"The one about how you won't let yourself get attached to anyone because you can't let them fall in love with you."

"It's true."

"It's only true if you tell the whole truth. And you're not. You're not saying the second part. The part about how you fear loving somebody means you're also putting them in danger."

What is he talking about? My heart that was already racing heads into double time. "Crew? What—"

"Don't. I know, Tenny. *I know*."

My racing heart suddenly comes to a dead stop. It feels like all the blood in my body pools at my feet as my head spins and my eyes blink—as if any of those things will help me process what I think he's saying.

"You know *what?*"

"Tessa."

It's one word, but it's all I need to hear. "You can't know." The words are barely audible.

He digs my photo from his back pocket and hands it to me. "This fell out when I was moving the cabinet for the flooring company. I know who that is." He points to Kaleo. "And I know this person died in a horrific crash that authorities think her husband was behind."

I shake my head back and forth. Over and over.

My breath is short.

My body feels hot.

"I know the what and the why and the how and the danger that comes with it all. The danger that you lived through. But you know what, Tenny? I still choose you. Even with all your secrets bared on the table, I choose you."

"You can't, though. What if—"

"If I haven't earned your trust by now, I never will. But I know I have. And just as important, I know I can protect you if need be."

Three stretchers. Torture. That smirk Kaleo gave me in court.

"I won't put you and the girls in that position. I refuse to. You don't deserve that burden—"

"Don't tell me what I can and can't do, Tennyson. Stop giving yourself excuses to run away instead of living. Stop living in what-ifs when frankly, he has many more pressing things to worry about—living day-to-day in a cell with enemies at every corner while he thinks you're dead and gone. Stop giving him power over you."

"You don't understand."

"I do fucking understand. And I'm sick of you using it and him as the justification to why you can't love me when the real reason is you're fucking scared to. *Well, guess what?* I am too. I'm fucking terrified. The last person I loved blindsided me when she left. Devastated my girls and took their happiness, their definition of family, and their sense of self with her on the way out the door. But you know what? You're worth swallowing every ounce of that goddamn fear I feel when I look at you. When I think about you. When

I touch you. You are worth it. So let me make the decision on whether I want to be with you or not. I've had enough people making decisions in my life, and this time, I'm making my own."

His words hit my ears but don't register.

I can't let them register.

Loving me could be a death sentence.

When I don't say a word, Crew steps forward and kisses me with the fire of a thousand suns. Almost as if every thought, emotion, and feeling we've left unsaid is poured into it. As if he's trying to sear his taste into my brain so that I won't have a choice but to think of him.

"Think about that while you're packing your bags and scurrying away because you're too much of a coward to love me back."

"I just need time," I lie. Time won't erase Kaleo's reach. And if I leave for a while, then by the time I get back, they'll be gone.

In Chicago.

Away from me.

Safe.

"Don't leave. I know you care about us. And I know it will break both of our hearts if you run. I love you, Ten. The girls love you. *We love you.*" He steps forward and presses a kiss to my forehead before settling his head on my neck. "I love you. That's my spiel. That's what I have to offer. Me. *Us.* Something special we never expected nor wanted to happen but did. Something I never thought I wanted again *until you.*" He takes a step back, every emotion I've craved for so long reflected back at me in the depths of his eyes. "I can't force you to stay. You've had enough parameters and people telling you what to do for so fucking long that this decision needs to be one hundred percent yours. You have to *want to.* You have to want this."

He takes a few steps back, and I worry that this right here will be my lasting image of him. Handsome but worried. Perfect but damaged. Mine but unattainable.

I start to speak but the emotion rioting through me is overwhelming. How do I explain to him that this is for him? For his girls? That me walking away is my ultimate demonstration of love for them? Instead, I don't say a word. I let the lone tear that slides down my cheek and the subtlest shake of my head do all the talking for me.

He closes his eyes for a beat when he sees my answer. "It's your decision," he says one final time. His face is pained, and his eyes are swimming with regret ... *and love.* "I'll let you have time so you can make it." He steps through the door and looks at me one last time. "Trust fall."

Those words.

Their meaning.

Trust that I'll catch you when and if you need to fall.

I bite back the sob that threatens when he shuts the door.

I fight the urge to chase after him when his truck's engine rumbles to life.

And then I sink onto the bed as the loneliness hits and the deafening silence begins to eat at me whole.

Within minutes, I trace his tire tracks with my own as I make my way down the driveway, tears streaming down my face.

Trust fall.

It's me who's catching him now.

It's me who's saving him.

Chapter Forty-Eight

Crew

Two Weeks Later

MY SHOULDERS BURN LIKE A MOTHERFUCKER AS I HANG DRYWALL in the outbuilding. It's hard but fulfilling work.

Everything is these days as I try to keep busy. As I try to exhaust my body physically, so I don't have the chance to think before I collapse into bed each night.

"Looking good, Dad," Paige says as she stands in the doorway, hands on her hips, and nods her head in approval.

"It's getting there." But I drop my screw gun and step back to look at the small space that I'm slowly transforming. When I look back to Paige, I catch her glancing down the driveway toward the cottage. "What's on your mind, kid?"

"How can you be so sure she's coming back?" she asks me softly.

"Because I am." I step outside with her and risk a glance there myself. It's been a tough few weeks with the girls asking why Tenny had to take off for a bit. It's been even tougher realizing just how much I miss her.

But the changes here are keeping us busy. We're figuring out new routines. We're getting ready for the start of the school year.

Deep down, I know she'll be back. After she left, I read all I could about the breaking story about Kaleo's second-in-command. His and his family's brutal murder . . . and Tenny's reaction made even more sense to me.

I don't have to like it, but it made sense to me.

I just wish she'd talked to me first. That she'd pick up the phone when I make my daily call and talk to me. I'd have explained a dozen different ways why what happened to him is not the same as her situation. That for all intents and purposes the *old her* doesn't exist so why would she be tracked down? Why would she be hunted?

But she won't pick up.

I can't talk to her.

It's a frustrating fucking radio silence.

And yet, like I just told Paigey, I know she's coming back.

It doesn't hurt that she direct deposited three months of rent into Ian's—soon-to-be *my*—rental account.

That might have helped solidify my opinion.

And it also pushed me to get the shit done that I needed to get done so it's ready when she comes back home to me.

Chapter Forty-Nine

Tennyson

Three Weeks Later

I'M HOMESICK.

For my own bed. For my own things. For all I've learned to call home over the past couple years.

And of course, I'm missing Crew and the girls. Their laughter. His quiet presence beside me. The waking up and going to bed, knowing he's near.

But I'll take the suffering so long as they're safe.

I'll own the guilt knowing how badly I've hurt them because by hurting them, their decision to head back to Chicago was easier. Back to their old life, back to before me.

The pang never dulls.

But this is for the best.

I have to keep telling myself that so I can put one foot in front of the other instead of running back to be with them.

And part of that keeping one foot in front of the other is moving every few days to a new place to explore, a new place to fall in love with.

New Hamish is the town of choice today with its farmers market that runs almost a mile long through its historical district.

The brochures didn't disappoint. The bright flowers and savory scent of food are enough to dull my loneliness for now.

When I go back to my hotel later tonight, that's a different story.

I turn from a stall of oversized sunflowers when a stranger bumps firmly into my shoulder.

"Hey," I yelp in reaction, spinning around to glare at the jerk.

I'm met with a pair of eyes I know on a face that's changed some. The hair is a bit lighter, the nose cosmetically altered, and there's a goatee when there never used to be one.

But it doesn't matter.

I'd know that face anywhere because he's the man who saved me.

The man I thought was dead beneath a sheet on a stretcher.

We stand in the middle of the walkway with people passing all around us, but I can't take my eyes off him. Off Agent Tom Halston. He gives me the subtlest of nods and the slightest of smiles as one would a stranger. And before I can speak or act or even process who I'm seeing, Agent Halston turns on his heel and disappears back into the crowd he must have come from.

I want to run after him. To shout questions to answers he can't probably give. To tell him how glad I am he's alive.

But I don't.

Can't.

And when I get to my car minutes later and go to reach for my keys, I find an envelope there when there wasn't one before. My fingers can't open it fast enough.

T-

It was time for my demise. You can only push your luck for so long, and I feared mine was running out. Yes, we publicly blamed it on him just as your death was blamed on me. All loose ends were tied up.

Please know you're still safe. You always have been. K never doubted your fate once. He trusted that I took care of it, and that trust never wavered.

Have a nice life.

You deserve it so very much.

-R

Tears blur my vision as I read and reread the note. As every part of me sinks into the knowledge of something I never thought I would feel again.

I'm safe.

How did he know that's what I needed to hear?

Maybe because just like he knew how to take care of me before, he's still taking care of me now.

One day you'll wake up and suddenly realize that you really are Tennyson West.

Is this that day Peter told me would happen? That I'd finally feel more like Tennyson than Tessa?

I want that future, that reality, and I can finally feel that it's a possibility.

I'm ready to be Tennyson West. To let go of the fear that has ruled me and to step into this new life of mine wholeheartedly.

It's time to go home.

Chapter Fifty

Tennyson

I SLOW THE JEEP TO A STOP AS I COME TO THE DRIVE.

The driveway that used to be dirt but that is now paved in fresh asphalt.

"What the . . ."

I drove all night to get back home. The plan was to get here, to drop off Hani with the pet sitter, and then to beg and grovel with Crew over the phone until he agrees to let me fly out to Chicago and make it up to him.

To figure out how we can make this work.

Because that's all I want right now is to make it work.

But the driveway is paved.

I turn onto it and drive super slow as if I'm going to damage the fresh asphalt. But instead of pulling into the cottage, curiosity has me driving past it.

Each foot feels like a mile.

To the big oak tree.

I'm almost afraid to look. Almost hopeful what this paved road might mean.

I startle when a truck turns the bend in the drive, right in front of me. But it's not Crew's truck. It's not his tattooed arm resting on the open window.

It's not Crew.

My heart sinks into my stomach.

He's gone.

The house was sold.

Crew's back in Chicago. The girls are back—

"Ma'am," the man says out of his rolled-down window as he pulls up to a stop beside me. If he had a hat on, I swear he'd tip it at me. But I don't want to see him here on Crew's driveway. I don't want to talk to him in a truck that Crew should be in. I don't want to see his arm hanging out of his window with a hint of tattoos beneath his shirt because it reminds me too much of my first glimpses of a man I ran away from.

"Are you the new owner?"

He chuckles, and its deep tenor rumbles louder than the engine of his truck. "Owner? No. I work here. Name's Rhys. Rhys Palmer."

"You work here?" I ask, his name already lost to me as I try to understand. To believe. To hope.

He hooks a thumb over his shoulder toward the house I can't see. "Yep. Hired last week. Came in to finish up my paperwork. Now I need to find a place to live in this . . ." He looks around, his expression all but saying he's not used to small towns. Not in the least. "*Place.*"

"Oh." It's all I manage to say.

"Are you here for an interview? He seems like a pretty cool guy. Like he'll be a decent boss. Plus, he knows his shit." He nods while my head spins over what he's talking about. "Good luck. Maybe I'll see you around."

Position?

But before I can respond, he eases off the brake and drives past me, allowing me to do the same.

If I owned this place, if I lived here permanently, that would be the first thing I'd do.

Pave the driveway.

Look up, Tenny.

Dare to hope.

And when I do, it's my own strangled cry that fills the cab. Crew's truck is in the driveway.

He's still here.

I speed the rest of the way, honking my horn like a mad woman before pulling to an abrupt stop right behind it.

Before I can get out of the truck, Crew is jogging around the side of the house. His feet falter when he sees me.

And then I note the expression on his face. The tension in his posture. The pulse of his jaw.

Oh God. Am I too late?

And then he's running.

"Tenny," he cries, that hope I was holding on to flooding his voice as he pulls me against his chest and holds on for dear life. "You came back to me."

I cling to him with hands and heart, more than grateful that Agent Halston sought me out to let me know—I'm safe.

I'm safe, and Crew is still here.

Thank God, he still wants me.

Thank God, he held out hope for me.

"You stayed," I say, the words muffled against his chest.

"I did." He presses a kiss to the top of my head before leaning back and meeting my eyes. There are tears of happiness swimming in his. "We did. I'm buying it from Ian. *For us.*" He points to the outbuilding that now looks like a completely new building. Especially with a new sign above the door that says The Force Crew. "For good."

"You—*what?*" I look at the sign and then back at Crew, realizing what it means. Justin Force. Crew Madden. *The Force Crew.* He's making his pipe dream become a reality. But more importantly, he's staying *here.* "I'm so proud of you," I murmur and stand on my tiptoes to press my lips against his.

"I'm terrified, but I have to take a chance. I have to try to make this work. To make us work. It's what I want."

"Trust fall," I whisper against his lips.

Let me support you.

Let me catch you if you fall.

Let me love you even though you're scared.

I don't have to say the words because by the hitch of his breath and the tears swimming in his eyes, *he already knows.*

"I know," he says, resting his forehead against mine and sniffing back his emotion.

"I'm not going anywhere. My place is here. With you. With the girls. I love us. I love what we have and what we're going to build together."

When Crew leans back and meets my eyes, I've never felt more loved. I've never felt safer. I've never felt more complete than I do right here, in his arms.

"Welcome home, Tennyson West."

My future is here with him.

It's always been him.

Epilogue

Crew

One Year Later

"**T**HE GIRLS ARE WAITING FOR YOU."

I look up from my desk to see Tenny standing there. She's in a soft yellow sundress with the sunlight at her back streaming through it. Her hair is pulled up but pieces are falling all around her face, highlighted like a halo. And her smile is there—like it always seems to be these days—shining bright just like the diamond that sits on her left ring finger.

Jesus.

How the fuck did I get this lucky?

How the hell did I go from broken and defeated to the happiest fucking guy on the planet?

It's because of her.

That's why.

Plain.

Simple.

Her.

"I know. I'm just finishing up reading Rhys's notes. The poor guy's up to his neck in diva-ness while trying to protect said diva from all the threats that come with her last name."

"I warned you she was going to be trouble."

"Don't I know it. The two are like oil and water. Rhys can handle her though. He's a take-no-bullshit kind of guy."

"Yeah, because hardened asshole goes great paired with a combative, pretentious socialite."

I chuckle. "Since Daddy's paying the bills, all we care about is what he thinks of us. Not her."

"Tell that to Rhys. Poor guy has to be gritting his teeth so hard they might break."

I don't have to look up to know Tenny has moved behind me. I can smell her perfume before her hands rest on my shoulders and, just like every other time she's near me, I only seem to want more.

"He's been through a hell of a lot worse than protecting a spoiled brat. Besides, I happen to know for a fact that his employer provides great dental insurance."

"He does now, does he?" she murmurs.

"He does."

The thought still fills me with pride. How far The Force Crew has come in the last year. From the cluelessness of those first days as we figured out what was needed to become an official business to today. We have ten employees on our staff, a stellar reputation that has netted us more requests for protection than we can meet, and a profit margin that is shockingly good for a company in its infancy.

"Come on. Put it to rest," she says as I make a few more notes on my pad. "You don't want to keep your girls waiting now, do you?" She presses a kiss to my head, prompting me to drop my pen, turn my chair, and tug her down so she's sitting on my lap.

My lips find hers instantly—like they always do—and smother her laugh. I take the moment of solitude without the girls or our company near to enjoy my wife. To sink into all this woman is and everything she's given me—shown me I deserve to have.

"What's that for?" she murmurs when the kiss ends, fingernails playing with the hair at the base of my neck.

"Just because."

"Just because, huh?"

"Yep." Another tender kiss. "Just because I love you. Just because you're incredible. Just because you've made me happier than I ever thought possible. Just because until you, I never thought any of this was possible for me."

"Ditto." She smiles against my lips.

"And right on cue." I chuckle when a chorus of girls rings out and into the open windows of my office—the old outbuilding on the property.

She rises and holds out her hand to me. "Let's go. The girls are busy showing Justin and Sheila their latest jumps into the pool. They might need a break and some adult libations to enhance their enjoyment."

I bark out a laugh as we move across the yard, hand in hand. The girls have been so excited to see their uncle Justin and aunt Sheila again that they've been overwhelming them with dance routines, pool jump competitions, makeup tutorial watching, and everything in between.

Even when you're used to them, it's a lot . . . and since my partner is only here for the week, they've been inundated.

"Bravo," I say and clap as Addy perfects a jackknife off the diving rock.

"Come on, Addster. Show your old man the one I taught you to do," Justin says, his grin wide. He looks good with some sun on his face. The time here has done him well.

It's done me well too.

Besides, I give him a year before I get the call that they're moving to Redemption Falls. Six months, maybe.

"Whoa!" I shout out when Addy jumps and spins into the pool, a mass of arms and legs and complete grace. "That was awesome. A perfect ten for sure."

I look from a grinning Addy to Paige and then back to my best friend and his wife . . . and then to my wife.

"What's wrong?" Tenny asks.

"Nothing."

She nudges me. "Spill it, Madden. You have that look in your eyes."

"Just thinking about the difference eighteen months can make. For you. For me. For Justin. I mean . . . there were days I didn't think I wanted to live, and now . . . now I can't wait to live every single day."

Tenny gets that soft smile on her face she reserves just for me and links her fingers with mine. "Crazy huh? But I don't think I'd want it any other way. It makes all this that much sweeter because of what we went through to get here."

"I love you," I whisper and press my lips to hers.

"I'll love you even more if you get the grill going," Tenny says. "Your four girls are starving for hamburgers."

"Yes, ma'am," I say with a mock salute as Justin wheels over to the poolside and lifts himself into the sling we had installed so he can swim with the girls.

"Here, let me help," Sheila says and stands.

"Don't you dare lift a finger," Tenny says. Sheila works around the clock to give Justin what he needs, so when they visit us, we like to make sure to give her the help and break she deserves. "You're here to relax and let us take care of you for a bit."

"Tenny, you know I don't—"

"Let us spoil you," I say. "And we won't take no for an answer."

"I know what you can do," Tenny says. "You can drink another glass of wine."

Sheila laughs, and it sounds so good to hear. "Now that? That I can do."

I half-heartedly listen to Sheila and Tenny chat about nothing before heading over to the pool to watch the girls shriek and laugh while they play with Justin in the pool.

Tenny brings out the tray of patties and sets them down beside me.

It's only when I go to put the burgers on the grill—when I count them out to make sure I make enough—that something Tenny said hits my ears again.

Your four girls are starving.

My four girls?

But . . .

When I look up, Tenny is standing, back leaning against the patio pillar, eyes on me, and a look in her eyes I know I'll never forget.

"What do you mean my four girls are starving?" I ask as I take a few steps toward her.

"Just what I said," she says coyly.

"But Sheila's a vegetarian."

"I'm more than aware." She chuckles.

"Then . . ."

"Then . . ." she repeats as tears well in her eyes, and she rests a hand on her belly.

I freeze, my synapses trying to fire while my heart already does. "Tenny?"

"Crew?" she says, imitating my tone.

"What are you telling me?"

"Exactly what you think I'm telling you," she whispers seconds before I swoop her up into my arms, shout out a whoop, and spin her around.

Pregnant?

She's pregnant?

I'm going to be a daddy again?

"Ten. *What,* I mean *how,* I mean—"

"I'm pretty sure you know how it happened." She laughs against my lips before leaning back and meeting my eyes. "In fact, you're very good at that."

Her teasing goes by the wayside as I stare at her dumbfounded. "You're serious."

"I am in fact serious." She gets that shy smile on her lips that owns me. "Good thing that employer of yours offers top tier medical."

"Good thing." I can't stop smiling.

I don't think I could if I wanted to.

I get a chance to do this with her. *Together.*

"I never thought I could have a life like this. A love so real. A family so beautiful. A happiness that fills my heart. *Not until you, Crew Madden.*"

Want more Tennyson and Crew? Go here for a bonus scene:
https://geni.us/aDKV

Are you looking for another small town romance and book boyfriend to warm your metaphorical bed? Why not get acquainted these other K. Bromberg's heroes:

Cockpit: (Single dad, first responder, pilot, small town) The last person Medevac pilot and single dad, Grayson Malone, wants to see on his doorstep is Sidney Thorton. She's not high on his list of high school classmates he ever wished to see again, and now she's telling him he's in the running for the title of Hot Dad with her magazine. Can he win the contest for his son and keep her at an arms' length while doing so?

Then You Happened: (small town, enemies to lovers, Yellowstone inspired, forced proximity) Widow Tatum Knox was the disaster Jack Sutton should have walked away from. For Tatum, it was hate at first site but desperation had her hiring him to manage her horse ranch. But long nights on a secluded ranch slowly turned into nights warming each other's beds. They say it's better to have loved and lost, then not to have loved at all. Does that hold true when the love is based on a lie to begin with?

Sweet Cheeks: (second chance, small town, destination romance, childhood sweethearts, brother's best friend). Hayes Whitley. Mega-movie star. The man who has captured the hearts of millions. But I gave him mine years ago. He was my first love. My first everything. Right until he up and left without so much as a simple goodbye. When he showed up out of the blue ten years later, I should have known to steer clear of him. I should have rejected his offer to take me to my ex's wedding to show my ex I was better off without him. I should have never let him kiss me.
But I didn't.

About the Author

New York Times Bestselling author K. Bromberg writes contemporary romance novels that contain a mixture of sweet, emotional, a whole lot of sexy, and a little bit of real. She likes to write strong heroines and damaged heroes, who we love to hate but can't help to love.

A mom of three, she plots her novels in between school runs, sports practices, and figuring out how to navigate parenting teenagers (*send more wine!*). More often than not, she does all of this with her laptop in tow, and her mind daydreaming of the current hero she is writing.

Since publishing her first book on a whim in 2013, Kristy has sold over two million copies of her books across twenty different countries and has landed on the New York Times, USA Today, and Wall Street Journal Bestsellers lists over thirty times. Her Driven trilogy (Driven, Fueled, and Crashed) has been adapted for film and is available on the streaming platform Passionflix, Amazon, and other streaming platforms.

You can find out more about Kristy, her books, or just chat with her on any of her social media accounts. The easiest way to stay up to date on new releases and upcoming novels is to sign up for her newsletter or follow her on Bookbub.

Made in the USA
Coppell, TX
22 February 2023

13296364R00188